HUMPTY DUMPTY

Tor Books by Damon Knight

CV
Humpty Dumpty
The Observers
A Reasonable World
Rule Golden / Double Meaning

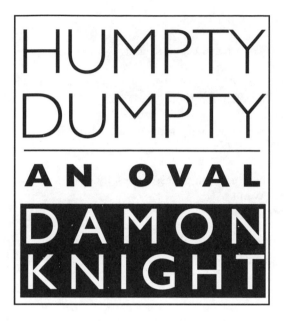

HUMPTY DUMPTY

AN OVAL

DAMON KNIGHT

A TOM DOHERTY ASSOCIATES BOOK
NEW YORK

HUMPTY DUMPTY

Copyright © 1996 by Damon Knight

This book is printed on acid-free paper.

A Tor Book
Published by Tom Doherty Associates, Inc.
175 Fifth Avenue
New York, NY 10010

Tor Books on the World Wide Web:
htpp://www.tor.com

Tor® is a registered trademark of Tom Doherty Associates, Inc.

Edited by Patrick Nielsen Hayden

Design by Basha Durand

Library of Congress Cataloging-in-Publication Data

Knight, Damon Francis, date
    Humpty Dumpty: an oval / by Damon Knight. —1st ed.
       p.   cm.
    "A Tom Doherty Associates book."
    ISBN 0–312–86223–7 (alk. paper)
    I. Title.
    PS3561.N44H86   1996
    813'.54—dc20   96–18274

First edition: September 1996

Printed in the United States of America

0 9 8 7 6 5 4 3 2 1

For CHRIS and ROSANNE

My ears were made keen by always listening. Often, wherever I was, even at the top of the house, I waited motionless for the enormous clock to strike, lest the boom take me by surprise.

Robert Aickman, "The Fetch"

HUMPTY
DUMPTY

A *foreign place*

Mimmuzmaz. Kunruht: somebody was snoring. A rustle, a catch, a pause, then again: *Mimme. Nene. Droohoohoot,* off in the golden half-darkness. I could tell I had been here, lazily adrift in bed, a long lost time listening, but where was *here?* That was a very good question.

I moved my hilly arms and legs, patted myself in dumb show. Limbs all present, cock-and-ball story, and down inside I was still Wellington Stout as ever. But I found a thick bandage on my forehead, and my head hurt in a remote village way.

"Hullo!" I called. "Anyone?"

I listened. Now I heard voices whispering or muttering in the distance, old women's voices by the sound of them. And stifled old-lady laughter.

—*Poor man, why's he here at all?*

—*Why, don't you know, he was shotten in the hode.*

—*Do tell! Where was that, pray?*

—*In the lavateria, o' course, eatin' a plate o' calzoni.* (Giggles, or senile titterings.)

"Hallo?" I called again. A rustle, and the voices fell silent. After a moment a figure loomed, a woman in yellow.

"You are awake?" she said.

"Yes, I am. Is this a hospital?" I reached for her sleeve

to make sure it was real, but she drew back without moving.

"It is the Ospedale San Carlo Borromeo," she said, and thrust the cold catch of a thermometer into my mouth. "You have had an injury, but you are better now."

Italy, of course, and now it was coming back to me. Well, of course, I had touched down in Milan on the way to my stepdaughter's wedding in Rome; I remembered that all right. I had a date to hand off brother Tom's mysterious packet to Roger Somebody, and then . . . a solid London fog, but before I could ask another question she had gone, and the thermometer too. Pretty brisk, I thought.

It was a different room now, smaller and brighter, with daylight blaring through the windows. And the voices were coming in again, apparently from the cold telly over the foot of my bed.

—*Did you hear now what he done with that houri in the Underground?*

—*Ah, that's an old weave's tale.*

—*Tall it to us all the seam.*

—*Well, she came from the south, and rolled her Rs like; then his jool fell out his panics and she pricked it up lipo, lapo.*

—*It was her fall-openin' tubes, you know, the dirty slit. They mizzures them in metros and it's slup it up, slap it out. Daid or alive-o, it's all one to thim.*

Were they talking about me? "Nothing of the sort!" I called. "That's total rubbish!" On consideration, I wasn't sure what I was indignant about, as I hadn't understood half of what the old women said. But I admit I was feeling a breath of alarm. Abandoned in a foreign place, perhaps a loony bin, and nobody knew where I was or gave a damn. *You have been injured,* and what was that about *shotten in the hode?* "Nurse!" I called. I tried levering myself up; that was not a success. Instant hollowness inside, sharp pain in my left arm, bed skating back and forth.

"*Uncle Bill, guess what, Roberto and I are getting married in October.*" Her voice, clear as a tinkerbell over the wire.

"Are you sure?" I said, or remembered saying.

"*Oh, yes, it's all decided.*"

"But I mean, you've only known him a month? Who are his people?"

"*Oh, they're a very solid family. Bankers and lawyers. They wanted to know who my people were.*"

"They did, did they?"

"*Oh, yes, I had to sit through an inquisition in his grand-mother's parlor. It was awful.*"

A silence, full of things unsaid. "Are you going to live in Italy?"

"*Oh, yes. In Rome, but we'll be spending some time in France and Switzerland too. Will you come to the wedding?*"

"Try keeping me away."

"*All right. I love you, you know.*"

"I love you, Cis."

She rang off, I suppose, and for some reason I found myself lying with my eyes shut thinking of Potamos, Pennsylvania, where I hadn't been since my mother's funeral. On certain streets there were frame houses behind white picket fences, and I was a boy walking up the middle of one of those streets, all alone in the deep silence. The houses were dark, but the pales of the fences were cotton white in the crazy eye of the moon. Now I was climbing the hill where the black pines began to close in, and I knew something awful was waiting up there.

Then the bed fell plump under me, and I lay watching patterns squirm like serpents on the ceiling until a nurse came in. She was shorter and thicker than the other, just a blur although it was daylight, and I realized that was because my contacts had gone and I didn't have my glasses.

"Buon giorno," she said.

"Buon giorno. I want to see a doctor, please."

"Non capisco." She cranked my bed up, swung a tray-table over, handed me some pills in a plastic cup, then a glass of water with a bent straw in it. She waited while I swallowed the pills.

"Donde è il doctore?" I asked. She turned away. "Donde son il mia espectaculos?" Damn, she had gone. Italian not good enough for her, probably, but I was doing my best.

Another nurse came in, a slender little thing who didn't understand my Italian either. She brought me a duckie to piss in, then lathered me from a can of plastic cream and shaved me very nicely with a blue plastic razor. She combed my hair, too, looked me over critically and smiled. Then I must have gone away and come back again, because when I looked up, a brown young man in a white coat was seated beside me.

How are you feeling?

"How are you feeling, Mr. Stout?" he asked.

"Not very well, thanks. Why am I here?"

"You were shot. You don't remember that?"

"No. My head hurts."

"That's because you were shot in the head. But it was a very little bullet."

I touched my forehead where the lump of bandage was. "Who shot me?"

"I don't know. What is the last thing you remember?"

"I was just going out to dinner. How long will I be here?"

"Not long. We'll see."

I must have got a touch leaky at that point; the doctor handed me a paper handkerchief to wipe my eyes. That reminded me, and I asked him, "Where are my contacts?"

He looked up and spoke to a nurse. "She will bring them," he said. He got up.

"Doctor," I said, "before you go, what day is it?"

"It is Saturday." He went away, and the nurse with him.

Saturday. I had been here three days, and Cicely was already married.

The box of paper handkerchiefs was empty, but I found another one in the drawer of the bedside table. Under it was a newspaper, folded open to a headline: TUR- ISTA INGLESE ATTACCATO. After a moment I realized that

the story was about me, although they had got my nation-
ality wrong and misspelt my name. I translated it slowly to
myself, moving my lips in the hard parts.

> An English tourist was wounded in the head
> yesterday in an altercation at the Flavo
> Restaurant in the Via Postumia. The as-
> sailant, Emilio da Lionghi, a 27 year old em-
> ployee of the restaurant, fled into the street.
> The Englishman, Willingdon Stout, 64, is in
> serious condition at the Ospedale S. Carlo
> Borromeo.

Carlo Borromeo was a rich nobleman who might have
spent his life eating grapes and tupping gentle ladies if a
papal inadvertence had not made him a cardinal and a
saint. There was still a Borromeo Palace and a Piazza Borromeo in Milan. But who was Emilio da Lionghi? I had
never heard the name before. I remembered going to the
restaurant . . . no, not even that, I remembered leaving my
hotel. Before that, I remembered the phone call from Roger
Something. Roger had suggested the restaurant. I remembered getting into a taxi, or was I making that part up? "Ris-
torante Flavo, per favore." Had I said that, or only planned
to say it? The rest was a wall of white cotton; I leaned my
head against it but couldn't get in.

I turned to the first page of the newspaper to see what
the date was. A large headline caught my eye: PIANETA
MISTERIOSA SI AVVICINA. A mysterious planet?

The nurse came with another plastic cup; this one was

half full of clear fluid. I looked a question at her. She pointed to the cup and said, "Le lenti." Then I understood, and stirred the solution with my finger until I found one lens after another, and put them in my eyes. The improvement was wonderful; I could see every thread in the nurse's cap and every hair in her mustache. "Grazie," I said.

"Prego." She went away, pushing her bosom ahead of her like an icebreaker. A 42 D, if not more.

I looked around. I was in a peach-colored room big enough for my bed, two tables, a little red Italian television braced to the ceiling, and a Paris green armchair. There was a modest crucifix on the wall. A bottle hung from a chrome coatrack sort of thing, with a tube ending in a needle taped to the inside of my left elbow. The burnt-orange drapes were open; I could see clouds and the tops of trees, possibly Arctic maples or elms. I caught sight of a lemon telephone on the other table, not the bedside one. On the bedside table there was nothing but my box of paper handkerchiefs and a kidney-shaped little basin, suitable for vomiting into.

The phone rang then and I picked it up without thinking. "Stout here." I leaned back and put my feet up.

It was my brother in New York. He was ten years older than me, and he was wheezing: too many cigars and cigarettes. *"Welly, are you getting any rain in London?"* He was the only one who still called me Welly, because he knew I hated it.

"Cats and dogs, Tom," I said. "Did you ring me up for a weather report?"

"No, it's something else this time. I hear your step-

daughter's getting married in Rome. You going down for the wedding?"

"Yes, of course. How are you, Tom?"

"I'm fine, and Eunice is fine. Now look, Welly, I need a favor. Can you drop something off in Milan when you go?"

"Why not send it by FedEx?"

"It belongs to some friends of mine. It's too sensitive for regular channels, in fact it's so hush-hush that they can't use their own people. And you have to forget about it afterward."

"Oh, hell."

"Meaning you'll do it?"

"It's a damn nuisance, Tom. Wait while I look at my diary. My flight's on the thirteenth, is that any good to you?"

"The wedding's on the fifteenth, I thought."

"Right, but I wanted to get there a couple of days early. How do you know so much, Tom?"

"Oh, it isn't hard. I don't suppose you have a layover in Milan?"

"Afraid not."

"Well, see if you can get another flight. The guy in Milan will meet you in the airport or wherever you say. You hand him the parcel and bye-bye."

"Tom, that won't work. The only flight stopping at Milan has a thirty-minute layover. That's not long enough to go through customs. What if I just check your parcel and give somebody the ticket stub?"

"It's got to be carried by hand, Welly. Spend a day there, have some dinner, get a night's sleep."

"Tom, sorry, it's out of the question. If I go to Milan, I'm going to get shot in the head. Can't you understand that simple thing, for once in your life?" I rang off, and for a minute I lay feeling the sweet joy of having altered the past, turned a wrong decision inside out. It had been so wonderfully easy, too. Then I saw the bottle on the chrome stand. This was reality, then, and I was stuck to it like a bug in lemonade. And the voices were talking again.

—*He says she's married now, and him not there to lift her skirrits.*

—*High time too, the huzzy! Didn't her mother catch them in the cupboard the time he was gettin' her head handed to him?*

—*She thried to thwart him, but he buggered her with a broom.*

—*She's barren then?*

—*Only in the bums.*

—*She was censered, you know, be the viaticum. There's mony a schlap twixt the cope and the lap.*

—*O yes, the people sint in a little bull, but it's papa who pays.*

The nurse came in, the one who spoke English, and I said, "Nurse, can't you do something about those old women?"

"The women?"

"The cleaners, or whoever they are. They keep talking and muttering about me, and I can't stand it any longer."

She went away.

—*His pockets is full of fleabuses and conomdoms, and there's an airman badge in his ivory. They calls him a brisk Arab, the dirty bagger.*

—*O yes, he's a master baker, and boils up his rolls in the latrine-ay-oh.*

—He takes it after his auld grandam Anna Gramma. His fadder was a pissant, he was, and kept an urchard, but he swallowed a bitter green applesin.

—In Isaac's fall we skinned all. Till evensong, thy thumb belong, thy kingdom kong.

And so on; there was no end to it. Presently I found the remote control on the end of the flex hanging over the head of my bed, and switched on the television and looked at Italian soap opera. I didn't understand one word in nine, but it saved me listening to the old women's voices; they couldn't talk through the television when it was on.

The nurse came back and pulled the needle out of my arm, put a patch where the puncture had been, and wheeled the trolley out of the room. I didn't speak and neither did she.

Another nurse came with grape gelatin and Oxo, and then it was night again and the old women were muttering from the telly.

I switched on the television, although there was nothing on the screen but white noise. After a while I noticed that the dancing particles were coming together into a sort of face. Then it was morning.

The nice brown doctor sat down beside my bed. "Tell me about the voices you hear."

"They've stopped now, I think." I listened carefully. "Yes, they've gone. I haven't heard them since last night."

"We have changed your medicine," he said. "If you hear these voices again, or if you see anything strange, please tell the nurse."

"Strange how?"

"Oh—faces on the ceiling, for example."

"All right." My arms were covered in goose bumps.

"Have you seen something like that?"

"No, no, nothing at all."

"Good." He went away. I don't think he believed me.

My mother's family

My mother's family were Irish, Scots-Irish, and Scots, Irish predominating; they settled in Pennsylvania and Ohio and were farmers, preachers and schoolteachers until the end of the nineteenth century, when they diversified into politics, millwork and journalism. My father's people were mostly Germans; the name was Stauf until three generations ago. There are a couple of undistinguished artists on that side of the family tree; the rest are solid tradesmen, draymen and brewers.

My mother was seventeen when she married my father. He was a high school teacher in Potamos, a little town on the Delaware in southeastern Pennsylvania, and she was one of his students. My brother Tom was born that year, but he was already in college when I was eight, and I barely knew him until we were grown.

My father quit teaching, probably because the school didn't renew his contract, but he stayed and went into business in Potamos, where my mother's grandparents lived. They died before I was nine. They were tall and silent; I have a memory that one of them pinched me or hurt me in some way.

In 1945, when I was ten, my father and mother moved to a town named Seaview on the Oregon coast, where my father bought a hardware store. They were divorced three years later, and my mother took me back to Potamos. She married a classmate of hers named Don Fry in 1951, but didn't keep his name after he left her in the early sixties.

My parents were both great readers and Anglophiles; she named me Wellington after the hero of Waterloo, and he supplied my middle name, Nelson, for the hero of Trafalgar. Taking the two together, I should have been a mariner, but instead I went to the University of Oregon and entered the architecture program. The math and the all-nighters were too much for me, and I dropped out after two quarters to become an English major (the closest I ever came, says Tom, to being an English admiral).

When I got out of college, Tom offered me a job selling ladies' undergarments. To everyone's surprise, I discovered a sort of talent for it. In two years I was a district sales manager, and a year after that I became the assistant to the sales manager of the British division with headquarters in London. After that came thirty-nine busy and eventful years, in which I had never been ill a day apart from colds and flu. Now here I was, shot in the head, a helpless and possibly deranged prisoner in an Italian hospital. It was enough to make a strong man weep.

Bang in the middle

In the afternoon a nurse helped me out of bed and held my arm while I walked to the can and back. It was somewhat like wearing stilts made of noodles.

The doctor came and sat beside my bed. "Mr. Stout, you will be going soon. I hope we have made you comfortable."

"Oh, quite comfortable," I said.

"Before you go I will give you some tablets, just for a few days. Your own doctor at home will prescribe for you after that. He can send to this hospital for your records."

"Good."

"Mr. Stout, you know that the bullet is still in your brain. It is in a place where we might make some damage if we try to remove it, so it's better to leave it there. If it causes some trouble later, you may want to have surgery."

"Now you tell me," I said. One moment the bullet wasn't in my brain, presto, the next moment there it was, bang in the middle.

"It may not cause trouble for years, but you should be prepared."

"Is it likely to kill me, do you think?"

"It will certainly kill you, but the surgery might kill you too."

"Yes, I see. Thank you."

The doctor put his hands on his knees and leaned

back a little. He needed a haircut, and he looked older than he had before; perhaps he was not the same doctor. "Mr. Stout, you know I have recently left my wife."

"No, I didn't know that."

"Yes, it was impossible for us to live together. There are no children."

"That's something, anyway."

"She was a virgin when we were married."

"Oh, yes."

"I loved her sister, but she married someone else."

"How awful."

"Now she is unhappy, and I am unhappy. My wife is unhappy too."

"Ah."

"So." He stood up. "We all have our problems, Mr. Stout, isn't that so?"

"Indeed it is. I'm glad to have had this little chat, Doctor." We shook hands and he walked away.

Later one of the nurses came in smiling, with a newspaper in her hands. "A present for you," she said. It was the *International Daily Express.*

"Thank you, that was very kind." When she was gone, I glanced over the first page. I read under the headline NEW PLANET CONFIRMED:

A second Italian astronomer has confirmed the existence of the hitherto unknown planet which is approaching the earth. The planet, dubbed "Mongo" by the press, has not been officially named. Dr. Carlo Geppi, its discov-

erer, says that the elements of the new
planet's orbit have not yet been completely
worked out, and its sudden appearance is un-
explained. It is visible in the night sky in the
constellation Aries, near the present position
of Saturn and Jupiter.

A nurse brought in a brown man in a topcoat, smelling
heavily of tobacco. He sat down beside me, took out a
memorandum book and opened it. "Who shoot you?" he
asked.

"I don't know."

"Where you were sitting when shoot?"

The nurse said something in Italian. I answered again,
"I don't know."

"Remember nothing?" the man said.

"No."

The man exchanged a few words with the nurse,
shrugged, and put his book away. He got up and shook
hands with me. "Buon giorno," he said. Then he went, or
else I drifted off somewhere.

A little problem with the parcel

When I came back I saw another man beside my bed,
plump, about forty, pink and freckled, with ginger hair and
a bristling ginger mustache, pale blue eyes and almost invisible lashes, just the kind of man I most dislike. He was

wearing a brown corduroy jacket, candy-striped shirt and a really sick-making orange tie.

"You awake?" he said. "Remember me?"

"No, who are you?"

"We were having dinner the night you got shot. Roger Wort." He put out his hand; it was fleshy and moist, as I expected. "How are you feeling, anyway?"

"Rotten."

"That's good, that's good. Now the thing is, Welly, is we've got a little problem with that parcel."

"Call me Bill, if you don't mind."

"Oh. Right, right. Now the thing is, Bill, is that you didn't give me the parcel."

"I didn't?"

He hitched himself closer and stared at me with shifty, earnest eyes. "No. You said you thought it was in your pocket, but you must have left it in the hotel. So we were going to go back and get it after dinner, but in the meantime I gave you my business card and you gave me yours, and it could be that somebody thought that was the parcel, or rather that the information in the parcel was on the business card, you see what I'm driving at?"

"Yes, I follow, more or less." I noticed that my speech was slipping farther towards the British end of the scale; that always happened with Americans I didn't like.

"And so then you were shot, and your blood splattered all over me—"

"Sorry about that."

"Hey, no problem, but I had to throw away a good shirt. And anyway, then there was a lot of jumping around and yelling, and when it was all over, I mean that night when I looked for your business card, it wasn't there."

"It wasn't?"

"No, but maybe that didn't mean anything, see, because when we searched your room afterward—"

"You searched my room?"

"Well, I mean, I personally didn't search it, but somebody else searched it, and the parcel wasn't there. So this could mean the information was really in the parcel and they wanted us to think it was on the business card, see, or else it was really on the business card and they wanted us to think it was in the parcel."

"Very complex."

"You can say that again. Now guess what?"

"I can't possibly."

"The next day we found the parcel."

"No! Where?"

"In a garbage can a couple blocks away."

"Then the information must have been on the business card."

"No, because by the time we found it, the information in the parcel wasn't the information they wanted."

"Do you mean it wasn't the same parcel?"

"It may have been the same parcel, but in that case somebody must have switched the parcels before they gave it to you. Anyway, Bill, we need to connect all the dots right away, and that means getting you the heck out of here. Can you walk and everything?"

"I think so. What time is it?" The curtains were shut; the room had a closed nighttime feeling.

"Little after seven."

"A.m. or p.m.?"

"P.m." He got up and opened the door of the little wardrobe. "Here's your pants, here's your shoes—no socks or underwear, I'm afraid."

"No jacket? Where's my jacket?"

"I don't know." He came back to the bed, leaned over me with a grunt to get the control at the end of its flex, and pushed a button.

I said, "You're American, aren't you?"

"Right, from Madison, Wis. How could you tell?"

"Oh, I don't know. Been here long?"

"Seven years next March. It's a great country, but you have to know how to read behind the lines."

"Roger, who do you work for, if you don't mind my asking?"

"I'm Mallomar Pharmaceuticals' man in Milan, and I have a couple of sidelines, neckties and belts, but right now I'm just doing a favor for somebody. The thing is, is these are people who don't like being disappointed. They have a tendency to kill people who disappoint them, Bill. You see what I mean?"

Before I could answer, a nurse came in. Wort spoke to her in rapid Italian, and they had one of those long exchanges, complete with arm waving, that people have in foreign countries. When it was over and she had gone, he said to me, "She'll bring all the stuff that was in your pockets. They cut the shirt and jacket off of you, she says. Now look, I told her you need your credit cards and address book because you want to make some phone calls."

"I do want to make some phone calls."

"Yes, all right, but let's wait till we get to the hotel."

"Roger, they're going to discharge me in a day or so anyway."

"Don't you believe it. I have good information that they're flying in six experts from Switzerland tomorrow. They want to keep you as a specimen, Bill, put you in a jar. Here she comes."

The nurse handed me a plastic envelope and a pair of blunt red-handled scissors, then put a cup on my tray table and stuck a thermometer in my mouth.

"What are they giving you?" said Wort, looking into the cup. "Looks like Demerol, no problem."

I had cut open the envelope and made sure all my things were there—wallet, passport, appointment diary, pens, small change, and so on. The nurse read the thermometer, waited while I took the pills, and went away.

"Okay, let's get started." Wort threw my trousers and shoes onto the bed. "Put these on, I'll be back in a jiff."

I managed the trousers all right, but went all wivvery when I leaned over, and had to lie on the bed to get the shoes on. I was tying the laces when Wort came back. He went to the wardrobe, took out a gray terry dressing gown, and helped me on with it. Then he stood there in a listening attitude, actually with his hand to his ear. "Now what?" I asked.

"Wait a minute."

There was a muffled thump

There was a muffled thump in the distance, followed by voices raised in alarm. A nurse ran by the door, then a male attendant, both gabbling as they went.

"Now," said Wort. He took my arm and shuffled me out into the corridor past a nursing station, deserted. Down the other way there was still a clamor of voices.

"What did you do?" I asked.

"Just a little flash bomb." We got out into the peach-and-grey main corridor and Wort pushed the button for a lift. Several large men in white came out and brushed by without looking at us. We got in, the doors closed, and we went down.

In the lobby it was the same thing; people got onto our lift as soon as we got off, and nobody paid any attention to us. Roger pounced on a wheelchair in an alcove and got me into it, then pushed me about half a mile down the corridor to the entrance. We left the chair and walked out into a cool afternoon with a touch of rain in it, shocking after the closed atmosphere of the hospital.

Wort helped me into a taxi at the kerb. "I took the liberty of checking you out of that hotel," he said. "Just a precaution."

"Where's my luggage, then?"

"It's in the trunk, don't worry." As the taxi pulled away, he reached into his pocket for a cell phone and began talking so quietly that I couldn't understand him, although

I could hear that he was speaking English.

We drove along a main artery for ten minutes or so. Pale lightning blinked as we emerged into an avenue that took us in a long curve widdershins, and I saw that it must be one of the ring streets that followed the lines of the old fortifications. We turned past a hotel with a huge banner in front, WELCOME DENTISTS! Then we zigzagged several times and pitched up on a side street under a canopy that said GRAND HOTEL DUOMO. A doorman in a pumpkin yellow uniform was there to take my suitcase and garment bag as the driver unloaded them. Wort helped me out and manhandled me into the lobby, where a functionary in a charcoal suit was waiting. Behind him was a page with a wheelchair. He helped me into it, put the footrest up, and away we went to the lift.

Upstairs we trundled down the vast corridor and stopped at a maroon leatherette door. In we went, the pages and the functionary bowed and retired. The door closed behind them.

"Well, here we are. How's this, hey?" said Wort.

There were two king-size beds with pink quilted covers, and a shelf sort of thing along one wall with the television, phone and lamps on it. The dim lamps had red plastic shades. The walls were a kind of puce, the carpet snot-green. "Very nice."

Wort helped me to settle down on one of the beds with pillows behind me. He said, "Okay, it's getting late, so let's just run over the basics. Number one, if the parcel was switched sometime before you got it, or even if they stole it from your room and *then* switched it, there's nothing you personally can do about that."

"I'm happy to hear you say so."

"*But,* if it really was on the business card, then we've got an angle to work with. Luckily, there's supposed to be a radioactive tracer in it, and anybody who handled it can be identified. If they kept it too long, they'll turn up in a hospital with radiation poisoning."

That caught my attention. "Did I have it too long?"

"Well, that depends whether you had it at all, doesn't it? Don't worry; they didn't find anything like that in the hospital, did they? Of course it might not show that early."

"Reassuring."

"Right, but now the big question is, is did you give a card to anybody but me between the time you left London and the time you got to the restaurant? Take a minute and think."

"Roger, how could the information have got onto my business cards?"

"They could have printed up a batch of cards that looked just like yours, and you'd never know the difference. Who did you give cards to?"

I tried to remember. "The hotel receptionist, probably; I always do. Then, let's see, there was a woman on the airplane."

"Name?"

"I don't know. Rosemary Something, a Spanish name. It's on her card."

Wort was looking in the plastic envelope they had given me in hospital. He found my cardcase in the wallet, pulled out the card and looked at it. There was only the one; I make a practice of pulling the cards and filing them after every trip, or every few days when I'm in London.

"Rosemary Sanchez," he said. "Representing Diane Downey Fashions. Is she in the same business as you?"

"Not exactly. Negligees, peignoirs, sleepwear. We do have something in common, though; she's an American living in England."

"Did she tell you where she was going to be staying in Milan?"

"No, it didn't come up. It wasn't that kind of relationship."

"Anyway, she's here for the Trade Fair?"

"Yes, we talked about it."

"All right, good. What does she look like?"

"Heavyset, about five five, hundred and thirty pounds. Fiftyish, too much makeup. Very pleasant."

"All right, that gives me a place to start. Do you want me to order some dinner before I leave?"

"No, I'm not hungry, I'll just go to bed."

"Right, and I'll see you in the morning, thanks for everything." He was there one moment, gone the next, although I didn't see the door move.

My head reminded me of a time when Jenny used to hang flowerpots from the beams over the terrace, just where they would whang me a good one if I got up incautiously out of a chaise. It was a kind of pain that I particularly disliked, because it seemed to me that it ought to be avoidable, if people would only take the trouble to put their pots and doorways at a sensible height. In a tourist bus, my first time in Paris, I leaped blithely up the stairs to the upper level, under a doorway that turned out to be an inch too low. It felt as if someone had taken an ax to my head, and that was more or less how it felt now.

I got up and opened the drapes to see where I was. Directly in front of me, almost near enough to touch in the yellow light, was the Duomo with its thousand spires, like some alien artifact intricately carved from grey ice. Jim Baldwin had shown me over it when I first came to Milan— a nice Protestant cove, I wondered what had happened to him. The cathedral was all sharp peaks, no visible dome at all; an amazing thing to look at, and I had never seen it from this aspect before. A violet flicker of lightning fizzed in the sky behind it. I opened the casement window, leaned out in the cool evening and looked down. The piazza was empty and silent except for a cleaning machine that whispered slow figure eights on the pavement, trailing multiple wet brush tracks and whisking up a few scraps of litter.

I turned and looked at the red telephone on the shelf with a tourist pen beside it. I wanted to call Myra, but my limbs were so heavy that I could not force myself across the room to pick up the phone. Somewhere deep underground I felt a tickle of danger, yet all I could think of was lying sprawled between cool sheets.

I closed the window and the curtains, swallowed some aspirin, switched off the lights and got into bed. Thunder grumbled far away. Behind my closed eyelids, before I fell asleep, I watched an endless procession of little marching men in overalls.

Intimate undergarments

It's undergarments that we sell, or intimate apparel, or lingerie—pronounced *lenz*hree in Britain and France, lawnjer*ay* in America, God knows why. Never underwear. Underwear is cotton bloomers and flour sacks. Lingerie is the answer when upscale women ask you what you do for a living, but there's a certain stage with another type of woman when it's a plus to tell them, "I travel in women's underwear." If they laughed like they'd never heard the joke before, I'd get a little closer and say, "Don't you believe me? Do you want to see it?" Then with two drinks or three drinks in both of us, we'd go upstairs and the rest would follow naturally.

Caresse Crosby's husband shot himself to death in Paris in 1929 and made Ernest Hemingway sad. If he hadn't, she probably would not have gone home and invented the brassiere by tying two handkerchiefs together. Then the whole history of intimate apparel might have been different, and I might have gone into some other line of work, and then, of course, I wouldn't have been shot. Funny that that bullet ended up in my head seventy years later.

In a more sophisticated form, the brassiere came into general use in 1933. My father said he regretted that, but I don't. A frivolous brassiere in lace or dark net is a charming thing. Even when a woman wears a serious bra, the moment when she puts her hands on her shoulders to pull the straps down is enough to make a man hold his breath.

When you know all the ways a woman's breasts can be coerced into pleasing shapes, as I do, it makes you put a higher value on the ones that are shapely to begin with. There are big and little ones, firm and flabby ones, breasts like crab apples and breasts like volleyballs, but the rarest of all are the firm ones that have a double curve in profile, concave above the nipple and convex below.

When I first laid eyes on Myra, walking towards me across the lawn with her breasts nodding under the silk, I was like a bird-watcher who thinks he may have seen a thrush twit flittering through the shrubbery. I was right about that, although I was wrong about other things.

Herrick said, "A sweet disorder in the dress kindles in clothes a wantonness." He knew. And he said, "Whenas in silks my Julia goes, then, then (methinks) how sweetly flows that liquefaction of her clothes." I used to know all the love lyrics, and many's the time I've murmured them in the ears of hot little lingerie buyers. Women like that sort of poetry, it makes them cream in their knickers. Herrick knew that, too.

Liquefaction. You wouldn't think that would be a sexy word, but it is.

Myra's breasts were just as amazing as I imagined them to be when I first saw her, and she had other admirable qualities too, but there wasn't enough on her side or mine to make a marriage.

After the divorce, Myra went back to Virginia, where a few years later she met and married Paul Irving, a dipso-maniac lawyer. Her daughter Cicely was born in 1976, and nine years after that Myra went into a sanatorium to dry out. Her husband, who was just out of the sanatorium himself, shipped Cicely over to me—I was married to Janet then—and I loved her from the first moment I saw her, although she was no blood of mine. I had her company from the time she was nine until she was twelve, three and a half unforgettable years. In 1988 Cis's mother was straight enough to take her back, and I didn't set eyes on her again until she was in the flower of her girlhood, like the young Sunny von Bülow you see in photographs just before she was first married, that wasted promise, why did it all go wrong? She had been plump and childish; now she was slender and tanned in a white tennis costume not much different to the eye than a white bra and panties. Firm little B cups, rounded bottom, slender legs, sun-bleached hair. Uncle Bill, she called me, and that was what the relationship was, a child and her infatuated uncle. As she got older, there was an element of sexual teasing in it, just enough to add spice. It was pleasant to both of us, and she knew she was in no danger. Then, of course, Myra took her to Rome and she met this damned Italian.

I dreamed I was talking to Cicely on the phone; she was calling from Switzerland, and I realized that if I made myself small enough I could squeeze through the wire and be with her. I had never done it before, but it seemed quite easy, and I traveled like cold lightning for light-years along the wire, hearing her voice all the time. But when I came to the end I saw her speaking into the instrument, and she was a black toad in a cave.

My wedding present

When I was sure I was awake, I got up, hung my garment bag in the wardrobe and unpacked the suitcase methodically as I always do, putting shirts and underwear in the chest of drawers, shaving gear and toothbrush in the bathroom, medicines in the medicine cabinet; it saves time in the long run. I managed to shower and shave, although I kept seeing a face in the looking glass that wasn't mine. The bandage on my forehead had got soggy; I peeled it off and covered the spot with an Ace bandage without looking at it.

My wedding present to Cicely and Roberto was still in its pasteboard box. I didn't know when I'd give it them now. I took it out and set it on the long shelf across from the beds. It was a little *karakuri,* Japanese for "gadget," in the form of a woman coiffed and dressed like the servants in pillow books. Clockwork inside would make it roll across a table carrying a cup of tea. It was nineteenth-century, quite unusual, made of lacquered papier-mâché in red, black, white and blue. Its smiling head was on a spring. I had imagined that Cicely might keep it near her, and touch it when she was wondering whether or not to do something she really, truly wanted to do.

I didn't have a spare jacket, but I put on the black chino suit and black tie I had meant to wear at the wedding, and went up to the dining room for breakfast. It was just after eight, and the big vaulted room was almost empty.

In the cathedral hush, a silent waiter brought me coffee, a hard-boiled egg, toast cut in triangles, and a slice of melon. It was all very good, and I was hungry, but I didn't eat much. I turned the melon over and looked intently at the pattern of grey markings on the darker grey surface; it looked a bit like an exposed brain.

Downstairs in my room I opened the drapes and the window to let the cool air in. The Duomo was gray and dark, like a Martian battleship against the pearl grey sky. I picked up the phone, got the hotel telephonist and gave her the number of Roberto's parents in Rome. "Tell them I want to speak to Myra Irving," I said. "Call me when you get her."

"*Certainly, Mr. Stout.*"

I put the receiver down and sat down to wait. Ten minutes later the phone rang and I picked it up. "Yes?"

"*Your party in Rome does not answer, sir.*"

"All right, thank you." They were all in bed at this hour, probably. Or maybe they were seeing Myra off at the airport. Maybe she was already gone.

I rang off and went to the window. Foreshortened pigeons and people were stirring in the piazza; it would have been easy to drop something on them, but I went down in the lift instead.

An old woman, ugly as original sin, was standing in the piazza with baguettes sticking out of a paper bag, whatever they call them here. She said something to me as I got into a taxi. It's rare to see a really ugly person in Italy, or a fat one either; perhaps they keep them at home.

I leaned back into the cushions to watch the buildings

go by. I know Milan fairly well as a visitor; it's a modern city built over a medieval town, with three rings of fortifications circling the Duomo like a target. *Milano* means Midland, which I suppose makes it the opposite number of Coventry or Birmingham. I always find it a bit mournful and gray; when I see poor people there I feel sorry for them twice, because they're not only poor but Italian.

The driver let me out in front of the Fair, and then I remembered I hadn't had any money changed, because of course I was only planning to be in Milan overnight. I offered him a sinful amount in pounds, and he took it after quite a long lecture which I couldn't understand, and drove away.

The main entrance was beyond a huge semicircular courtyard covered by a canvas that whipped and boomed overhead; the canvas was dome-shaped, divided by an arched support in the middle, and when I looked up it was like being inside a white empty skull.

The pavilions were full of people wearing a good deal of scent, not all of it terribly fresh, and there was a surf sound of talk in a dozen languages, enough to make one dizzy. The lights under the distant ceiling were haloed with exhalations.

I went into the Knitwear & Undergarments pavilion and found the Weybright exhibit. It was our spring line, which was pretty much like our fall line; undies for daily wear can't really change, bar some technological breakthrough, but you have to make little finicking improvements twice a year anyhow. It causes endless trouble for the women, poor dears.

There was a sign on the Weybright booth, BACK IN 20 MINUTES, poor management I thought, but I left a note for Wort asking him to wait for me there. I cruised up and down the pavilion, greeting a few familiar faces; there was no sign of him or of Sanchez.

I passed the Ruhrinor exhibit and saw they were pushing their Lissom line, approved by the medical authorities here and in France but nowhere else so far. It was a revolutionary foundation that shaped the wearer to fit the garment; in medical lingo it caused lysing of the cells that were under pressure, thus the wearer grew slimmer until the pressure stopped. Customized cutout versions would allow you to exempt parts that were deemed to be small enough already, breasts for instance, and in principle the system would give everyone an ideal figure. There were rumors that several women had died of it. I had had a row with Louis Hostetler over Lissom; he wanted to pay it the flattery of imitation, and I didn't.

When I started in the business there were thousands of little independent shops selling sturdy, no-nonsense brassieres and panties for ordinary women to wear in their daily occupations. Now it's all department stores, chain stores and merchandising; the customer has to think she wants to look sexy, at least, or else feel déclassé and unpatriotic. Designers are taking more and more market share whatever we do; a thing like Lissom that worked properly would send us all to the museum of quaint old industries.

Once in our building in London I noticed that the nameplate beside the door of a sacked minion had been taken away, exposing the rather repellent plastic matrix underneath. I like knowing about the undersides of things, but it's always surprising to me that they are so ugly. You might think that any good craftsman would take pleasure in making a thing beautiful even if he knew it would seldom be seen. But it's the same with parts of bodies; the bits that are inside and not normally seen by anybody are ugly, as if the Creator thought he needn't bother. What's worse, the same thing tends to happen to the parts on the outside that we cover up. In the nineteenth century, everybody noticed how remarkably handsome the bodies of the bare-arsed South Sea natives were, but we didn't take the hint ourselves, and that's where the makers of undergarments come in.

The Vibralizer

After a while I went into the Footwear pavilion next door. Roger and Sanchez weren't there either. Every seat in the caff was filled, but I found a place to sit down for a moment in front of a display marked SPAETH. People on either side of me had their shoes off and were resting their feet on little yellow plastic boxes with slanted tops. A screen over the boxes lit up when I sat down.

IF YOU WOULD LIKE A FOOT RUB,
PLEASE PRESS THE BUTTON IN THE ARMREST.

After a moment it blinked and repeated the message in German, then in French and Japanese. When it came round to English again, I pressed the button.

TAKE OFF YOUR SHOES AND SOCKS, PLEASE,
AND REST YOUR FEET IN THE VIBRALIZER.

I did so. The oval depressions in the boxes were filled with soft vinyl tits, pleasantly cool against the soles of my feet.

PLEASE INSERT A CREDIT CARD
IN THE READER IN THE ARMREST.
THIS IS FOR INFORMATION ONLY; THERE IS NO CHARGE.

I saw that I had been had, but I was in for a penny, and I put my AmEx card in the reader. After a moment the screen blanked out and the vinyl tits began surging back and forth in a very pleasant way. When this had been going on for a few minutes, a man in a brown shadow-woven jacket and yellow shirt came out from behind the booth and approached me. "Mr. Stout?" He had very pale hair and skin; his eyebrows were almost invisible. His shoes were glove leather, pointed and glossy.

"Yes?"

"I'm Dale Hook. A pleasure to meet you, sir. You're with Weybright, I understand."

"Yes."

"An interesting line of work. Mr. Stout, our Vibralizer shows a diminished comfort level, especially in your right foot, and I wonder if we might help you with that."

"Well, I don't know. I do wear insole bars, but, I mean, they're perfectly satisfactory."

"Would you mind if I take a look?" He picked up the

shoe. "Ah, yes, I see. Very good workmanship. Where was this made, if I may ask?"

"It's a little firm called Collins and Watt, in Knights-bridge. I've been going to them for twenty years. They make any style."

"Of course they do, Mr. Stout, of course they do. But in general, how long have you been wearing insole bars?"

"Oh, all my life. It's a congenital problem—a short Achilles tendon."

"Yes, I see. Would it surprise you to hear, Mr. Stout, that modern technology has gone far beyond Messrs. Collins and Watt?"

"Well, I suppose. I mean, I don't try to keep up with shoes, it's not my métier."

He knelt gracefully on the floor and put his face closer to mine. His eyes were as pale as a kitten's. "Do you know what part of the body distinguishes man from the lower an-imals?" he said intensely.

I drew back as far as I could. "Well, the brain."

"The lower animals have brains. Think again."

"Okay, the hand. The opposable thumb."

"Certainly not. Beavers have opposable thumbs. Rac-coons and other animals have very clever hands. You really don't know?"

"Well, I suppose I don't."

"My friend, it is the *foot*. Haven't you ever noticed? Monkeys and apes have no feet, they have another pair of hands, on which they must try to walk. The human foot is unique. You talk about the opposable hand. What part of the body makes it possible for us to *use* the hand? It is the foot. Every secret of the human constitution is there, hidden by your stockings and molded by your shoes. What part of your daily wardrobe is the most important?"

"My shoes?"

"Exactly so!" Hook rose to his feet again and smiled down triumphantly. "Let me just take these shoes away for a minute, and I think I can give you some improvement." Before I could object, he was gone. I really had to admire his technique, but at the same time it was awkward to be trapped here without shoes; what if he never came back?

"*There* you are," said a voice. It was Wort, in a red sisal sports jacket and a bloody mary shirt with a saffron necktie. His shoes were brown loafers with leather tassels. He leaned over the man on my right and said, "Hey, would you mind?" He put a hand on the man's elbow and levered him up. The man stood there barefoot, looking bewildered, while Wort sat down and leaned towards me.

"Funny I should run into you here," he muttered.

"Why so?"

"The Spaeth people are in this up to their eyeballs."

"Do you mean they stole the whatever-it-is?"

"Maybe not, but I think we've got it narrowed down to them or the Dentists. Hey, we've wasted enough time, let's get out of here."

"I can't, they've got my shoes."

"Well, put your socks on, anyway."

The man on the other side was making a fuss. Wort turned to him and showed him a badge in a little folder. "Hey, guy, do you know you're obstructing a criminal investigation?" Without waiting for an answer, he turned towards me, but just then Hook came back with my shoes in his hand. He and Wort nodded to each other, not very cordially.

"Now then," said Hook. He knelt again and deftly shod me with the aid of a long-handled shoehorn. He laced up the shoes and stood back. "See if that isn't more comfortable."

I stood up and took a couple of experimental steps. "They do feel better." It might even have been true.

"Allow me to give you these brochures." Hook opened a brightly colored leaflet and showed me a cutaway view of a large foot. "You see here, the heel is a human invention, no other animal has it. This is what gives us the firm foundation to stand, to walk, to run. Now the arch, this again sets us apart from all lower animals, because they are flat-footed. This is the noblest architecture of the human body. And how important is it that the foot should be correctly supported and molded into its proper shape?"

Wort was muttering and pushing my elbow, but Hook was standing in the way and I couldn't get out.

"Very important?" I said.

"Correct! Do you know that by the time a child is five, its feet have often been deformed for life by bad shoes?"

"My, my."

"And how many doctor bills do we pay, how many aches and pains, how many headaches do we have, simply because we wear shoes that are stupidly designed, shoes that kill us?" Hook turned a page. "Now this is the Spaeth training shoe, or the diagnostic shoe as we prefer to call it. This patented system of sensors measures the stresses on your foot as you walk and stand, you see? And records them on this strip. Then at the end of the training period, the strip is removed and analyzed. Then your first real Spaeth shoes are custom built, to conform *and* correct your foot. But that is not the end. After six to eight months, you return for a new fitting. Again the stresses are analyzed and studied. Now a new pair of Spaeth shoes is custom built, for you only, and these you wear for a year. If your progress is satisfactory, you may receive your next pair immediately, or perhaps wait a little longer, say eighteen months. And so it goes on. Instead of getting worse, your feet are continually—"

"Excuse me." Wort put a hand on Hook's chest and pushed him back like a piece of furniture. We retreated together, and Wort led me down the mall at a brisk walk. "Did you find Sanchez?" he asked.

"No."

"Neither did I. I got your card back from the desk clerk, and that isn't it." We were walking by the caff. "Let's sit down a minute." He looked over the tables; every one was filled. "Your attention please!" he said loudly. All heads turned. "Is there a Mr. and Mrs. Jones here?"

A bald young man stood up. "I'm Jones."

Wort moved towards him, tugging me along. "First name?"

"Ian." Beside him, a young woman was looking up goggle-eyed.

"Mr. and Mrs. Jones, you're wanted in the Carabinieri station immediately. It's a matter of life and death."

"But we've just got our coffees," said Jones.

"We'll hold your places till you come back. Now hurry! Do you know where it is?"

"No," said the man sullenly.

"It's at the southwest end of the grounds, right at the end of the Viale Industria. Go on with you now."

The woman stood up and said something to Jones, and they drifted off uncertainly, glancing back as they went. Wort took one of the vacated seats and waved me to the other. He pulled one of the coffee cups nearer and took a sip. "I'm sorry you let yourself get mixed up with those Spaeth people," he said. "Have you got another pair of shoes?"

"Yes, in my room."

"All right. As soon as you get back, take those off and throw them away."

"Why, in heaven's name?"

"Ten to one they've put locator strips in them. They can track you anywhere on earth." He tore open a packet of sugar.

"But what's their purpose?"

He poured the sugar into his cup and opened another packet. "There are some things I can't tell you, and some I don't know myself yet. But do you think it's coincidence that these Spaeth people turned up just about the same time as the new planet?"

"I don't know, Roger. Do you mean—?"

"Hey, it's obvious, isn't it? Spaeth?"

"Well, if you lisp it is, I suppose."

"Don't laugh. That's what they expect you to do. They look human, don't they?"

"Well, that one did."

"Yes, I give them that. They're a crafty bunch of bastards. Never underestimate them, or the Dentists either."

"I won't, Roger."

"All right. End of sermon. Now have you thought of anybody else you might have given a card to, Bill?"

"No, I haven't. Just the receptionist and Sanchez."

He opened his mouth to speak, but caught himself and looked up suddenly. A few tables away, a man stood looking at us. He was fox-faced and brown-haired, dressed in a gabardine jacket and dark blue shirt. His shoes were blue cloth runners, matching the shirt. He made a sort of salute with two fingers, smiled, and walked away.

"Who was that?" I asked.

"That's my cousin Willie. I wouldn't trust him if I were you. I think he's mixed up with the Dental Underground."

"The *Dental* Underground?"

"Shh! Not so loud. You ought to be thankful your friends didn't chain the package to your wrist the way they used to. In the olden days they'd cut off a courier's hand and throw it in the canal."

"The dentists did?"

"Oh, sure. They're big boys, they play for keeps. I heard about a rogue dentist that had some way of regenerating teeth, using a tweaked gene that would prevent decay. Well, they found him floating in a canal, with his own teeth stuffed up his nose."

"Good heavens."

"So you see, Bill, this isn't just fun and games. Am I getting the message through?"

"You certainly are."

"Okay, now let's get serious. We'll track Sanchez down if she's still in Milan, but we've got to cover every other angle too, because if we don't I'm occupational cement, and so are you. There's one other possibility that I thought of after I talked to you. At the restaurant that night, I remember you handing something to the waiter. Could it have been a tip—a few lire?"

"No, I didn't have any Italian money."

"That's what I thought. So it could have been a business card, right?"

"I suppose it's possible. I don't usually give them to waiters."

"So if it's *possible*, we've got to check it out." He looked at his watch. "Almost one o'clock. They may be open for lunch." He took out his phone and punched in a code, listened, punched another code. "No, nothing till dinner," he said finally, "but that's okay, because it gives us more time to hunt for Sanchez. The Flavo Restaurant, okay? I'll meet you there at seven."

He disappeared into the crowd before I could ask him about the Demerols. I took a taxi back to the hotel, and the driver came in with me while I got some lire at reception to pay him.

As I stepped into the lift, something unexpected and frightening happened. The walls disappeared, and I was looking down a gloomy street. Near a wooden gate in a brown brick wall, something dark was seeping down. Two figures stood at the gate. One was small and looked like a young boy, the other was a tall figure in black. I felt they were about to pass through the gate, and that I ought to stop them.

All that went by in a flash, and when I put my foot down I was in the lift again. I took the next step, but then I was so shaken that I could hardly move. Finally I turned around and pushed the button. The doors closed, the lift went up. The door opened. I stepped out, afraid the same thing would happen again, but it didn't. I went to my room, swallowed some aspirin and lay down.

It took a thing like that to bring it home; I had been putting it off and dodging it all this time, but now I had to confront the real possibility that I was crazy. Was there any chance that I might harm someone? I was thinking of those people who spray post offices with bullets, or cram their wives into trunks, or gun down children on the playground. No one can explain why they do it, least of all themselves. If we could somehow give them imaginary guns and make them believe they were real guns, they'd be pathetic, wouldn't they, pressing the imaginary triggers and saying, "Bang, you're dead"? But they really do kill people with real guns, and that's horrible. It would be better to be dead than to be crazy in that way, but if I were crazy in a harmless way, I mean if I merely went around talking to people who weren't there, I could perhaps go on living and even enjoying my life to some extent. After all, imaginary people might be very interesting and entertaining. So it was important to determine if I was crazy, and if so which kind of crazy, but I couldn't think of any way to do it.

"Crazy" literally means cracked; pottery with a crack-led surface is called "crazed," and I felt sure now that my skull had been cracked in just that way, like a windscreen hit by a stone or a cocktail table by a heavy bottle. Perhaps it hadn't properly healed yet, and when it did I wouldn't be crazy anymore.

Meanwhile, what was best to do? I could go back to the hospital and turn myself in, and languish in loony bins probably for the rest of my life. I could go back to London and seek professional help of some kind, more discreetly, but perhaps with no better result in the end. And I couldn't even do that, just now, without leaving a black mark beside my name in the books of the international mafia or God knows what other all-powerful secret organization.

I saw now that I had only imagined I was in trouble before. I was thinking about the two canals that cross the lower part of the city, the ones Wort said the lopped hands of couriers used to be thrown into. A bit greasy-looking for my taste, even if they had been cleaned up since then, but if I could just get my hands on the Demerols Wort had promised me, then if I took enough of them first, probably I could just slide in and none the wiser. I closed my eyelids, and dreamed of being trapped in a small lift with a very large coloratura soprano who was having an anxiety attack.

Fuzzy with sleep, I thought I heard a knock at the door. I got up to open it; a little man in a grey windcheater was there. "Mr. Stout?" he said.

"Yes."

"I come in, please?" He slipped past me somehow and then broke into a torrent of Italian. I was able to make out that he was Emilio da Lionghi, that he had shot me, and that he was sorry.

I closed the door and sat down. No one paid you to do it? I asked.

Da Lionghi shook his head vehemently. No, no, no. It was an accident, a mistake. I was trying to shoot the manager, because he gave me the sack without a reason.

His eyes were moist with sincerity. He pulled a wad of bills from his pocket and thrust them at me. They were crumpled, faded, and unusually dirty.

No, no, I said, pushing them away.

Yes, yes, please. For the forgiveness.

On the bedside shelf, the little Japanese figurine remarked in a cricket voice, "If you don't take it, it means that you don't forgive him." Her head nodded cheerfully. "Then he may think you are going to kill him, and it will be better if he kills you first."

"Good," I said after a moment. "Put it there." I pointed to the shelf.

Da Lionghi opened his hand and dropped the bills. "Sorry," he said. "You forgive?"

"Yes, it's all right."

Da Lionghi ducked his head, turned and went to the door. He slipped through and was gone.

I stirred the wad with my finger. There seemed to be about five hundred thousand lire.

Dinner afterwards

My parents were not poor, but they were thrifty and did not waste money on trifles. We had a radio but no television and no record player. We went to the movies once a week, on Saturday, when the bill changed, and ate dinner afterwards at a Chinese diner in Port Jervis. My allowance until I was thirteen was a dollar a week.

My mother did not like to cook and had no aptitude for it. She could make a beef roast and stew a chicken, knew how to make macaroni and cheese, and once in a while she baked bread, coarse white bread with air bubbles in it that I still remember. She baked cakes for birthdays but at no other times; our desserts were ice cream, Jell-O, and fruit. We ate a good deal of Velveeta, Campbell's soup, Wonder bread and margarine. I remember their flavors with nostalgia, and I remember the candy I bought at Miss Lavery's little store: Hershey's with almonds, 3 Musketeers, Snickers, Baby Ruth, and the penny candies: licorice whips, both black and red (neither one really licorice), candy corn, flavored syrup in little wax bottles. The little dots of candy on white strips of paper didn't taste like much but looked like tremendous value because the paper gave them so much bulk and because having to pick them off one by one prolonged their useful life. What were the little red spicy ones called? I can't remember.

The Flavo was tucked away on a side street off the Via Novara; as far as I could recollect, I had never seen

the place before. It was crowded and brightly lit. There was
a deep narrow room downstairs, a cold buffet in a vitrine
on the left, and a sort of mezzanine above, where I saw a
man working at an oven with a long-handled wooden
shovel.

A waiter came towards me, in white shirt and black
bow tie. "Incontrò Mr. Wort," I said. "È qui?"

The waiter shook his head. "Your name?"

"Stout."

His eyebrows went up comically. He dropped his
menus, seized me by both arms and said, "Mr. Stout! Very
sorry! Too bad! Everything you want, everything on the
house."

Other waiters clustered around and led me to a table,
pulled out a chair, urged me into it. They uttered excla-
mations of regret and hospitality, fussed with the silverware,
produced menus. One of them came with a round brown
water glass which he deposited on its side with a flourish;
the glass rolled upright, weighted on the bottom like a children's toy, and another waiter filled it from a carafe.

A third waiter came with a pair of reading glasses
which I recognized as mine, although they had apparently
been stepped on. The frame was bent, one lens was starred
across and the other was missing altogether.

"Mr. Stout, you forgive?" asked the first waiter. "Not
our fault."

"I know it wasn't. Please don't mention it." I couldn't
see the menu at all well, and besides it was handwritten in
Italian. "What would you recommend?"

"Leave it to us. You like soup?"

"Soup, yes. Do you have a bean soup?"

"Of course! Many beans soup." He made a note on his pad. "Salmon? You like salmon?"

"I do, yes."

"Salmon, perfect!" He made a kissing motion with his fingers. "Some pasta?"

"No, no pasta."

"Okay." He rushed off, and another waiter came with a bottle and a wineglass. "Very special," he said, and poured dark wine. He waited for me to taste it, then turned and said something in a loud voice to the room at large. Suddenly all the diners were standing with wineglasses in their hands, and there was a roar of Italian good fellowship. I stood and saluted them in turn, and they clapped as if I were a film star.

I felt quite exhausted when I sat down again. It was blue dark outside now, and threads of silver rain were falling beyond the canopy. A man came in, brushing the water out of his hair; he looked vaguely familiar, but just then the waiter was insinuating a plate of brown soup in front of me. When I looked up, the man had sat down across the table. It wasn't Roger, although it looked a bit like him. Under his plastic mac he was wearing a gunmetal chino jacket, brown shirt and a bronze-and-yellow foulard. After a moment I realized he was the cousin, Willie, the one Roger had pointed out in the Milan Fair. I disliked him on sight, even though he was not plump nor ginger-haired like Roger; his hair was a sort of rabbit color.

"What are you doing here?" I asked him.

"Roger couldn't come," he said. "He's had a little accident, nothing serious. What are you having?" His accent was British but not English.

"Bean soup. What sort of accident?"

"I'll have that too." He turned and spoke to the hovering waiter at some length. The waiter smiled, bowed, and rushed away. Another waiter was filling his wineglass. Willie sipped and made an appreciative face. "They're doing you well here, I see."

"What sort of accident?" I repeated.

"Roger tripped over something and broke his kneecap. He'll be right as rain in a few days." He pronounced it *rine*. Australian, perhaps, but I didn't think so.

"Is he in hospital?"

"No, risting comfortably at home."

"Are you from New Zealand?" I asked.

"Yis. How did you know?"

"Just an instinct. I was hoping Roger would come; he's got my Demerols." I tried the soup; it was very good, and just what I wanted.

"For pain? Hold on, I can give you something." He reached into his pocket and offered me a brown bottle.

As I was about to take it, there was a flicker of light from behind us, and when I turned to look I saw that two waiters had collided. One was staggering, and it was the reflection of light from his tray that I had seen. The tray fell, and I was waiting for the clang, but instead there was another sort of flicker. When I turned around and reached for the bottle, it wasn't there; Willie was drawing his hand

back. He was wearing a pink-striped shirt and a red necktie, too, and in fact I saw now that it wasn't Willie, it was
Roger.

I felt a wave of vertigo and leaned my head into my
hand. When I looked up, Willie was there again, brown
shirt, yellow foulard and all. "What's the matter?" he asked.

"Just dizzy for a moment."

"Maybe you should call your doctor at the hospital.
What's his name?"

"I don't know."

"You don't know your doctor's name?"

"He didn't tell me."

"Well, did you have a doctor? What did he look like?"

"Young, sort of olive complexion, dark hair, handsome."

"Latin type?"

"I suppose so, Latin, yes."

"Like Rudolph Valentino?"

"No, more like Ezio Pinza. Or maybe a little like
Danny DeVito, only taller."

"All right, you're telling me he's from Calabria or
Sicily. That's where the Mafia is."

"What are you saying?"

"Listen. What did he tell you about the bullet?"

"It's still in there, I'm afraid."

"Do you believe that?"

"I suppose I do, why not?"

"Bill, did it ever occur to you that instead of just taking something out, he might have put something *in*?"

"Why would he do that?"

"And that he told you that story about the bullet to account for the shadow in the X rays?"

I was shaken. "But why?"

"And have you thought about the political aspect at all, Bill? Even for a moment?"

"I don't know what you mean. What political aspect?"

"Would it surprise you to know that a government minister was in this restaurant, sitting quite near you when you were shot?"

"I don't know if it would or not. What are you saying, that they aimed at him and hit me?"

"No, probably not, but they might have shot you just to show him they could do it. They have a word in Italian, *dietrologìa,* it means knowing how to look behind things. Never trust appearances in this country, Bill."

"I must say I don't know what you're getting at."

"Bill, I can help you. Trust me. Do you trust me?"

"No."

"I can help you anyway, and I'm the only one who can. Meet me tomorrow morning in the lobby of the Hotel Perrex."

"Why there?"

"You'll see. Will you do it?"

"I don't know."

"Here's my card," he said. He held it out, but I wouldn't take it, and he laid it on the table between us. "Be there," he said. He got up and left the restaurant.

The card read, WILLIAM F. WORT, and under that, *Investigations.*

I put it in my case, and that started me thinking about

Roger. If he had given me his card the night we had dinner, why didn't I have it now? I distinctly remembered that
there had been only the one card, Sanchez's, when Roger
opened the notecase in my hotel room. For that matter, if
we had had dinner on friendly terms, why had he begun by
calling me "Welly" and not "Bill"?

By the time I finished my dinner and left the restaurant, the rain had stopped; over the rooftops I saw three
brilliant stars in a diagonal line. The brightest was like a little polished medal. I couldn't remember ever seeing the
planets in a row like that, and I wondered if it had some as-
trological significance. Myra would know that sort of thing
if she were here.

I went back to the hotel, where I stopped at reception
and asked where the Hotel Perrex was. The receptionist
whipped out a map and a silver pencil. "It is just here, sir."
The pencil tip was pointing to a little square east of the
Duomo, the Largo Augusto. I thought I recognized the
place. "Is that where the dental convention is?" I asked.

"Dentists, yes. They are at the Hotel Perrex, not far."

Why dentists? I asked myself. I must have spoken
aloud, because the receptionist said, "I don't know, sir." He
was giving me a strange look. I made a mental note to tip
him nicely when I left.

When I got upstairs and undressed for the night, I
found the brown bottle in my pocket; I must have taken it
after all. The tablets inside were anonymous little white
things. I swallowed one, and fell into dreamless sleep.

It was after ten by my travel clock when I woke up; I
must have slept for almost twelve hours, but I didn't feel

refreshed. My head was stuffy, in fact, as if I had been up late. That reminded me of what Willie had said, about the surgeon putting something into my brain. I wondered if it could be big enough to make my head feel stuffy. I began imagining what I might feel like if the surgeon had concealed the missing card in there, and how big a hole he would have had to make in my skull in order to do it.

As I was sitting down to breakfast, a man appeared and came towards me. It was Roger, with a bandage across his nose. He sat down without speaking.

"How's your kneecap?" I asked.

"My kneecap is okay, that was just Willie's little joke. Now listen. I found Sanchez registered at the Jolly, but nobody there has seen her since yesterday. She's probably shacking up with somebody she met at the Trade Fair. I'll get her when she comes back to check out, but if anything goes wrong, you'll have to run her to ground in England, understand?"

"Yes."

"Okay, now one other thing. I know Willie's going to take you to the Dentists. That's okay. I want you to go, but when you go, take this with you." He passed a little black object across the table; it looked like a miniaturized Japanese radio.

"What's it for?"

"It will let us know where you are, and it will give you some protection. Don't tell them you've got it unless they ask."

"What if they do ask?"

"Tell them." He got up and walked out.

I looked at the thing. It was just big enough to fit in the palm of my hand; it had a dial and a number of colored transparencies, none of them lit at the moment. There were buttons or slides, but the whole thing was an even deeper matte black than such things usually are, black on black, the Nips' revenge for Hiroshima, and of course nothing was labeled or marked in any way. When I pressed here and there, all I got was a faint hiss and some static. I played with the thing in the lift, and had a little better luck—Frank Sinatra, singing "My Way," but I lost him halfway down.

It was a cool morning, with bright sun glowing through the overcast. The baguette lady was there again, this time with three stalks of bread leaning out of her paper bag. It had been two before; was that some kind of code?

I got into a taxi and drove to the Hotel Perrex in the Largo Augusto. The WELCOME DENTISTS! banner was still there, flapping in the wind. When I entered, the lobby seemed to be full of Americans and Germans, although there were some Asians and Indians too. Almost all were men, standing about in little groups. They all had name tags that said things like "Hi! I'm DOUG CANTOR from LAGUNA BEACH!" Although it was early morning, one or two of them appeared to be drunk.

In a moment a bell rang; the men began to drift by twos and threes towards the open doors of an auditorium, where I could see green chrome-rimmed seats and yellow curtains. I followed and stood near the doors, hoping for a sight of Willie.

On the distant stage three men in white dinner jackets appeared. They all had young-old faces and gray hair,

and wore large red polka-dot bow ties. When the audience
quieted, they put their arms on each other's shoulders and
began to sway. Music came from somewhere, a lively tune,
and they sang:

> *We are dentists three,*
> *We sing in har-mo-nee!*
> *We gift the world with healthy teeth,*
> *To left and right, above, beneath!*
> Teeth, teeth, teeth! *(Hurrah!)*
> Teeth, teeth! *(Hurrah!)*
> Teeth!

Each "Hurrah!" was joined by the audience, and at
the end there was wild applause.

A hand touched my elbow. I turned; it was Willie,
with a name tag on his plaid lapel. "Well, you're here," he
said. "Come on, they're waiting."

"Who's waiting?"

"The crowns. They don't like to wait."

"Willie, you just said 'in the morning.' What is this all
about?"

"I meant first thing in the morning, and it's *about* sav-
ing your *life*. Come on."

He led me at a trot down the lobby to a closed door
where a plump man in blue was standing. His name tag had
a yellow border; it said STAFF. He put his hand on the door
bar and said, "Just a minute. You're all right, but he can't
go in."

"He's with me," said Willie.

"That's nice, but he still hasn't got a tag, and he can't go in."

"How long have you been at this door?" Willie demanded.

"What's that to you?"

"Have you passed the Circle of Willis? Do you know who the Elevator is?"

The man's expression changed. "Yes."

"Have you heard of the Pelican?"

He began to tremble. "I'm sorry, sir. I didn't know— Excuse me."

He opened the door, and we went into a large lecture hall. Most of the seats were filled. At the podium, a gray-haired man was saying, "Once you have pulled all the teeth, there is nothing left to do except to fit *dentures.*" There were groans and murmurs in the audience.

We edged down the side aisle, attracting a few stares, towards a door at the very back. The gray-haired man was trumpeting, "A living tooth is a tooth that generates income. Never, never forget that. Drill, fill, cap, crown, but *save that tooth!*"

Thunderous applause, cheers, whistling, stamping of feet.

Willie opened the door and pushed me through. We were in a little room where three old men were sitting at a table. "Stout," said Willie. He turned again, and the door closed behind him. From the room outside came another burst of laughter and applause.

"Please sit down, Mr. Stout," said the tall, gray-haired man in the middle. "I know you have a lot of questions.

They will all be answered, but first we must ask you something. Have you met a representative of the Spaeth people?"

I sat down in the chair he indicated. "Yes, at the Milan Fair."

"His name?"

"Hook."

The gray-haired man drew in a hissing breath. "Did he put anything in your shoes?"

"Yes, but Roger told me not to wear them."

"And you followed his advice?"

"No, I meant to, but I forgot."

"Are you wearing those shoes now?"

"Well, in fact, I'm not sure. It was either this pair or the other one, but I don't know which."

"Mr. Stout, will you take off the shoes you are wearing now, please?"

I shrugged, took off the shoes and handed them over the table. He glanced at them and put them on the floor. When he straightened up, he had a pair of bedroom slippers in his hand. "Please see if these will fit, Mr. Stout."

I put them on; they were loose, but quite comfortable, and I said so.

"Good." He stood up. He was even taller and thinner than he had looked sitting down. "Will you come with me, please?"

He led me out a rear door into a service corridor, where we got into a lift. "Where are we going?" I asked.

"Mr. Stout, you are about to enter the stronghold of a very ancient order. Very few people, even among the dentists themselves, know of its existence. From this strong-hold, we fulfill the world's destinies."

"I thought you just filled teeth."

"That's very funny, Mr. Stout."

I thought so myself, but I said no more. The lift went down for what seemed a long way. The doors opened. We went along a dusty corridor to an iron door, which my guide opened, and we emerged onto a loading platform, empty and silent. The door clanged shut behind us. Beyond the platform there was a single track, and a coach on it, like a miniature Metro coach. It was dark inside, but when we came near it, the doors opened with a hiss.

"Go on," said my guide when I hesitated. I stepped in and he followed me. I sat down on one of the empty seats; my guide remained standing. I couldn't see anyone in the engine driver's compartment ahead. The doors closed; the dim lights from the platform began to flicker past the window frames, slowly and then faster; they suddenly winked out and there was nothing but the wide-spaced yellow lights of the tunnel that flew at us like falling stars.

"Do you know, Mr. Stout," said my guide after a moment, "that dentistry was practiced in the Egypt of the Pharaohs?"

"No, I didn't know that."

"Oh, yes. Our art is very ancient. May I tell you a secret? I myself am the living incarnation of a dental priest named Uer-Kherp-Hemtiu."

"Ah, I see, yes."

"But I knew nothing of the real Dentists until I was forty-five years of age, Mr. Stout. Then my accomplishments brought me to the attention of the Crowns. I was taken to an audience with the current incarnation of Uer-Kherp-Hemtiu, and he invaded me."

"That must have been shocking."

"No, not at all. And don't worry, Mr. Stout, nothing like that is likely to happen to you. I assure you that your visit to the Dentists will cause you no harm whatsoever, amen."

The coach decelerated; the lights of a platform appeared and coasted by. The coach stopped; the doors hissed open.

We got out onto the silent platform, and I followed my guide through another iron door into a passage, from which we emerged into a room full of shadows of mummy cases and sarcophagi. Then I knew where I was: it was the Egyptian museum in the dungeons of the Castello Sforzesco.

Evidently the museum was closed today; the room was cool, empty and dark except for the sconces on the walls. The painted eyes of one of the mummy cases seemed to follow us as we crossed the room to still another door; this one opened on a steep winding stairway that led down clockwise. When this door thudded behind us we were in darkness.

At first the steps were wooden, and there was a chill iron handrail. Later the handrail disappeared and the steps were stone, spiraling around a well from which arose a cold medieval breath. "Where are we going?" I asked. My voice echoed back; there was no reply.

After many years we came to the bottom, and my

guide, who was now wearing a miner's headlamp, led the way through a vast jumble that reminded me of a crushed chicken carcass. Walking ahead of me, he was constantly forcing bones apart with a creaking and popping sound; the bones were yellow at first, then grew white: books of bone, cornices, entablatures and volutes of bone, whiter than white, bluing white, bursting with whiteness.

Then we were in an obscure place. After a time a dim light slowly bloomed, or else my eyes became accustomed to it, and I saw that I was in a yellow-lit cavern where two men and a woman in long yellowish white gowns stood beside a yellow white table. One of the men was plump, the other wrinkled. My tall guide, who also seemed to be wearing a gown, stepped forward to join them. "I have the honor to present Mr. Wellington Stout," he said. "Mr. Stout, you see before you the Forceps—" The plump one bowed. "The Pelican—" A grave nod from the wrinkled one. "And I am the Elevator. This, of course, is Nurse Ruff." The woman, a brassy blonde, gave me a broad lipsticked smile and a wink. "Do you know where you are, Mr. Stout?" the Elevator went on.

"No, sir, I don't." I was feeling a bit light-headed.

"You're in a grand cavity near the center of the earth. We are quite safe here, even if the surface should be heated to the incandescence of a star."

"That's reassuring."

"Was that a question?"

"I don't think so."

"Do you have a question?"

"Yes, why is the light so yellow?"

"That's the cheesium, it collects down here," said the Forceps.

"I'm sorry, what is cheesium?"

This time the Pelican replied. "That's *two* questions, you naughty boy, but I'll answer anyway. It's a radioactive element allied to radon."

"Isn't that dangerous?"

"*Three* questions! Oh, yes, if you stay here for more than two weeks you'll be dead, but we can bring you back."

Something in the air was making me dizzy. "Do you mind if I sit down for a moment?"

"That's four questions, but it's perfectly all right." The Elevator patted the yellow white surface of the table and smoothed it with his palm. "Sit here and rest a moment. In fact, lie back if you will, and I'll show you something interesting."

The nurse and the Forceps helped me to lie down and straightened me out on the narrow table. "Look up there, Mr. Stout," said the Elevator. "What do you see?"

I saw people standing on the ceiling as if it were perfectly transparent. I saw the soles of their shoes, and their legs diminishing upwards. I saw the bottoms of the glasses in their hands. I saw the dusty undersides of tables, and the bare bulbs burning under lamp shades. When I listened closely, I could hear the murmur of their voices, or, at least, of somebody's voices. At first they didn't quite make sense.

—*Aloss for his brechen eggsilence!*

—*Aloss for his bald white tummyli!*

"How is that done?" I asked.

"Oh, it's easy when you know how. We can see any place on earth from here, whenever we choose. Are you comfortable, Mr. Stout?"

"Yes, quite."

"We're going to put part of you to sleep now, is that all right?"

"Oh, yes." I was trying to listen to the voices.

—*Foramen as God has joint these two together, let magnum put them arse-under.*

—*Debride first, you know, and then comes the groan.*

—*I sleep when I breathe, and I breed when asleep.*

—*O, well trickled, sir! See the lonesome sport of his nanogism!*

One of the others was doing something at the back of my head, I wasn't sure what.

—*Put us another bit in it. Burr, brrr! It's chili in here. I saw, I see, Signore. No, it's hoppelpoppel. Grackly! grungy! His testos are bleeding out the earbits.*

"You know," said the Elevator, "the Spaeth creatures are really pathetic upstarts. We've been here for thousands of years. The Spaeth creatures say they want to rule the world. Well, who do you suppose does rule the world?"

"The Dentists?"

"Oh, yes. *Oh,* yes. We're a very ancient order, we are. Why, we're so secret that nobody has heard of us, not even ourselves."

"Everybody has heard of dentists," I muttered sleepily.

"Oh, yes, that kind of dentists! But *we* are the Un-

derground Dentists. They haven't heard of us! Do you
know what 'the planet' spells if you rearrange the letters?
'Teeth plan, then plate.' "

—*Clips him up, clebs him down. Throw in the trowel,
boys, suit yourself, mortar most foul.*

"What are you doing to me?" I asked.

"Dental surgery," said the Pelican. "We've got to get
to the root of the problem." He giggled. "Do you get it? Do
you think that's funny? The root of the problem?" When I
looked up, I could see that he had put on a silly grinning
mask and a red fright wig.

"But what's the problem?"

"I'm glad you asked. Did you ever hear of dental or-
gasms?"

"No."

"You'd be surprised what a skilled dentist can do,
wouldn't he, Miss Ruff?"

"Don't get impertinent now, Doctor."

"She's repressed, you know, but we'll soon fix that."
He reached into the nurse's body somehow through her
uniform.

"Oh, Doctor!" she cried.

"It's all in fun," said the Elevator. He was wearing a
mask too. "All in fun, you know, and fun for all, isn't that
the way?"

Something was smoking with a most unpleasant odor,
like burning plastic in a toaster. "Condition yellow," said a
loud unemotional voice. "Execute Plan B, execute."

"What a nuisance, just when things were going so
well!"

"Never mind, there'll be another day. Is there room for everybody in the capsules?"

"Afraid not, and we'll have to draw straws. Nurse Ruff, you lose, as usual."

"But, Doctor, it's not *fair!*" she said. She drew a deep breath and began to scream.

"What can't be helped must be whelped. Strike her on the point of the jaw, will you please, Elevator? That's the manly way. Patient first, nurse after. Now let's roll him in, rolling spin, roll again."

Cradled tenderly

I've often wondered what it must be like to have some part of one's anatomy so delicate that it needs to be "cradled tenderly in silk and lace," as we say in our adverts. A man's testicles are not treated in the same fashion, although I don't see why not. In fact, although I don't travel in women's underwear as a rule, I do quite often wear tights at home. They are comforting under the trousers in winter, and the fabric gives the willy an occasional nudge, as if to say it's all right to have one.

I've worn other things in fun, including teddies, camisoles, and the archaic chemises of our grandmothers. I once got a designer to run me up a satin cache-sexe with a peekaboo cutout for the penis, actually just a ball brassiere. The designer was amused; she measured my equipment with calipers and made a delightful little apricot-colored sporran upheld by a silver chain, but it was not a success; the close weave of the satin made it hot and un-comfortable.

Anyhow, the testicles were designed to hang free in order to cool them in the breezes, because body heat would tend to sterilize one's sperm. But nature has provided two little hideaway pouches, one in each groin, and I was wondering about some sort of plastic device that would keep the testes from descending once you had tucked them up there; how long would you have to wear such a device in order to be sure of contraception? It would never be popular anyhow; we like to dangle.

On the other hand, from what I can gather, women consider their breasts a nuisance apart from attracting men. When the breasts are the wrong size or shape, as they usually are, they make women feel deformed and unworthy, and when they're too big they get in the way. The jiggle that men find entrancing can be painful to women, especially when they run; "sports bras" are not bras at all but bandeaux, designed to bind the breasts flat and hold them too tight to squirm. Well, the jangle of balls is painful too, or we wouldn't need jockstraps. Did the Greek athletes perform without them? I don't believe it. Once in a sleeping compartment between Nice and Paris we hit a bad section of track and my balls shook like castanets. It was not an experience I wanted to repeat.

That must have reminded me; at any rate I was dreaming about the first time I ever made love on a moving train. It was with Myra, in 1963; we were on our way to the South of France on our honeymoon. That was before the TGV, and the track was just uneven enough to toss us around a bit, but I couldn't quite get to the point of putting it in her, although I knew I was about to, and then the guard came and shook me by the arm.

I was in a coach seat, not a berth, and Myra was not there. In the dawn light, the train was drifting across a flat green landscape that could have been anywhere. Two or three cows lifted their heads to look at us, but zipped out of sight before I could make out if their expressions were French or German.

Two fat people in the seats opposite were looking at me suspiciously. The guard snapped his fingers. "Votre billet, monsieur." The old man beside me said helpfully, "He wants your ticket."

"Yes, I see." I fumbled in my pockets, found a pink pasteboard and handed it over. The guard glanced at it and gave it back. He said something I didn't understand and went along to the next row of seats. My helpful neighbor translated, "You are going the wrong way."

"What do you mean, the wrong way?"

"He says your ticket is for Bucharest."

"Bucharest!"

My neighbor nodded, gazing at me with eyes that were large, pale, inquiring, and watery.

"Have I been asleep?" I asked.

"Yes, I think so. Asleep."

"Where are we now?"

"Not far from Calais. I don't think we stop until London, do we?"

"Oh, well, that's all right." Had I really bought a ticket for Bucharest? I had no recollection of it, nor of boarding this train; and I knew I had forgotten something else that was even more important. I hit my forehead with the flat of my hand, but all I got for it was a headache.

My luggage was in the rack; I took my kit to the loo, where I swallowed a pill from the brown bottle and managed to shave without looking in the glass. When I came back, my neighbor was reading a Clive Barker novel, the two fat people were reading *Die Zeit,* and we were drifting past the dismal concrete blocks of Calais. Presently we dived into the Chunnel and the lights began to flash by. I tilted my seat, meaning to nap until it was over, but just when I was getting comfortable there was a squawk of static from my pocket, then distant voices muttering:

—*And what shall we say about the prepunderance of his tentophorial abits or ambits?*

—*O, he's guilty right enough. When he said he was fallen asleep, he slipped out and cabled Mrs. I.*

I found Roger's little black box in my pocket and took it out. Now the voices were clearer, though distant and feeble as crickets.

—*They say the rope they hang him with is worth twenty thousand pounds an inch.*

—*That's it in a pigshell. There he lies, the rotten king, with a candle attis hoyd and a syndal at his fate, where Ad led Amon and Ambie wet on Augie.*

Nobody around me seemed to be paying any attention to the voices; it was obvious that they were meant for me, and yet I couldn't comprehend one word in four. "Mrs. I" must be my housekeeper, Mrs. Islip, and I certainly felt guilty, but of what? While I was still thinking that over, we emerged in Folkestone, and rain was falling out of a leaden sky. I may have dozed again; it seemed no time at all until we were pulling in to Waterloo.

I was tired, confused and hungry; I went into a railway buffet and had scrambled eggs, but they were rubbery and cold. For some reason I couldn't remember what day it was. How long had I been in Milan?

A man was just setting out the newspapers in a stall as I passed: I was able to make out that the date was Thursday, October 21. The headline on the *Guardian* was something about scandal in the EEC, and on the *Sun*, Mongoids and bleeding statues. Out in the road, rain was flying like tinsel against the hoardings. People had their heads down under umbrellas, and there were no taxis to be seen. I set off on foot, carrying the suitcase in one hand, garment bag draped over my head to keep the rain off, but it blew stinging into my face anyhow.

Crossing the Waterloo Road I was nearly run down by a taxi; it careened away with a derisive parp of its hooter, leaving my trousers soaked to the knees. On the other side, outside a vast empty pub, I heard a voice at my shoulder, "Sir, if you'll forgive me—"

I glanced down: it was a brown little man, bareheaded and soaking wet, almost but not quite presentable. "Yes?"

He gave me a charming smile. "I know I shouldn't impose on a stranger, but the fact is I'm in some distress."

"You are, are you?"

"I am that. I've lost my return ticket and all my money. My name is Martin Gallagher and I'm from county Galway in the Emerald Isle, at your service, sir."

I glanced around to see if he had a confederate, but no one was loitering near us. "Will a pound be any good to you?" I said. I put the suitcase down and held it between my legs long enough to find a coin in my pocket.

He took it so dexterously that it seemed to disappear. "Very generous, sir, it will do me the world of good. And whom shall I be sending it back to?"

"Never mind about that." I walked off briskly, but he kept up with me. "Dear sir, I must insist, as an honest man. You'd do the same I know. Just your name, and a street will be all I'll need."

"Send it to James Morrison at the Carlton," I said, and left him saying, "Thank you, thank you sir, you'll not be sorry."

I glanced back from time to time after I turned off the main road, but the wet pavements were empty, and a few minutes later I was in front of my own building. The windows were dark except for the second-floor left; that was my flat.

I put my key in the door. At first it wouldn't turn, and then it did. The lobby was stale and silent, lit by one orange bulb in the ceiling. I glanced at my letter box; it was empty. I looked at Mrs. Islip's too, because she sometimes stuck yellow notes onto hers, to let the other tenants know what she was up to; but hers was as blank as mine. The tin lids of the letter boxes had the same familiar dents.

Coming home was always like this: a feeling of relief at having got here safely, and a touch of disappointment because it wasn't going to be any better than before. This block of flats was rebuilt in the seventies, and was the latest thing then. It had no lift, but otherwise every mod con. I had lived here nine years; a few more, and I would have matched the time I had spent with Jenny at The Willows. So joy recedes. On the wall of the stairway someone had scrawled ORANGE JEWS. I trudged up the Turkey-carpeted stairs, breathing the familiar staleness, and got to my landing at last. A strip of light peeped under my red door, but none under Peabody's to the left. Peabody was a cranky Northerner who kept odd hours; we never saw each other except when he was up too early or I was up too late.

I let myself in and shot the bolts behind me. Letters and magazines were heaped on the hall table, with one of Mrs. Islip's yellow notes on top. The sitting room door was half open, and I heard the murmur of a male voice. It was a BBC weatherperson honking about the jet stream; Mrs. Islip must have left the telly on, although it was not like her.

I carried the luggage down the hall (resisting the impulse to straighten the framed photographs) and around the corner to the bathroom to drip. I dried my face and hands with a towel. My legs were sodden from the knees down; I went into the bedroom to empty my pockets and take off my shoes, then my jacket and trousers and hung them over the shower rail to drip too. I threw my shirt in the basket while I was about it, then put on slippers and a red dressing gown and went back to the sitting room.

I stood outside the doorway there a moment, looking at the television and listening to the BBC voice. " . . . abducted in Camberley by two persons described as wearing reflective clothing. Several farmers in Cornwall . . ." I was shocked again to see the clutter, as always when I came home from a journey; the place was crammed with all the things I couldn't bear to part with when I left The Willows—chairs and footstools, sideboard, spinet, pictures, fire screen, writing desk, curio cabinet, knickknacks. The sideboard took up the most room, and there was nothing in it but some silverware that I never used and china that even Jenny didn't care about, but it was a handsome old rosewood piece in perfect condition, and it would have been like selling off a child. Perhaps, I was thinking, I could get rid of the spinet, which was always out of tune and which nobody ever played.

Then the television suddenly flipped to a view of a parade and began to blare martial music.

I felt as if I had been doused with a cold pailful of water. "Who's there?" I said in a hoarse voice that wasn't as loud as I meant it to be.

There was no answer. After a moment I pulled myself together enough to step into the room. As soon as I had done so, I saw the white-haired man seated on the far side of the fireplace. It was Tom, fatter and older than I remembered him.

"Hello, Welly," he said. He raised the control in his hand, and the sound from the television cut off. He was wearing a brown polyester suit and a purple shirt with the collar open; I could see the white curly hairs of his chest. His brown necktie was hanging out of the pocket of his suit coat.

"Good God, Tom," I said, with my heart in my throat, "what are you doing here?"

"Your housekeeper let me in."

"I see that, but I mean, what are you doing in London?" I sat down and folded my hands to stop them shaking.

"Heard you were in the hospital. Jesus, Welly, they never told me there was any danger. I raised hell with them, if that's any satisfaction."

"Who are 'they,' Tom?"

"I can't tell you that. I think they're just errand boys for somebody else, anyway. This thing is a lot more complicated than I had any idea. Anyway, I'm sorry." He drew a leather case out of his pocket. "Care if I smoke?" He took a cigar, bit the end off, and put the flame of a lighter to it, turning it round and round until it was going to his satisfaction. "You look like death warmed over," he remarked.

"So would you, if you were shot in the head."

He grinned with yellow teeth. "Rather it was me, huh?"

"Now that you mention it."

He nodded. "Truce until we get this mess cleaned up?"

"With pleasure."

"Okay, what have we got? The package was stolen from your hotel, but maybe it was a fake to begin with. They think the real stuff could have been on one of your business cards. Am I right so far?"

"I suppose so. Tom, I did what I was meant to do—or tried to."

"These people don't give you E for effort. Another thing, it wasn't smart to leave Milan without telling anybody. That may have been a signal that you're guilty, or that

you know something. Are you sure you had the right package in the first place?"

"Of course I'm sure. I mean, at least it was the one I
found in my letter box with your name on it."

"What about this Rosemary Sanchez?"

"I don't know. Roger said she hadn't come back to her
hotel. Or it may have been Willie."

"Who the hell is Willie?"

"Roger's cousin, or brother or something. Tom, listen,
I've had a bad week. I don't care about the parcel or the
business card or the Spaeth people or the Dentists, they can
all go to hell together as far as I'm concerned. All I want is
to forget the whole thing and get on with my life."

"You won't have a life if you don't find that card." He
looked at my face. "What's the matter?"

"Nothing really, it's just that I've got a bullet in my
head, I've missed Cicely's wedding, and the Secret Masters
of the Universe want to kill me. I don't blame you especially, but I can't help wondering, why me?"

After a moment he said, "Have you got anything to
drink?"

"Certainly." I got up and opened the liquor cabinet,
picked out the Laphroaig and poured two glasses. My hands
were still shaking. I handed Tom his whisky and took a sip
of mine, rolling a smoky drop on my tongue.

"Well, cheers," he said.

I sat down. "Cheers."

He was leaning back, holding the glass in both hands.
"Back in nineteen eighty-nine, I think it was, Eunice and
I were on a train coming home from Montana. We had a

sleeper, and we'd get up in the morning and go to breakfast together."

"What has that got to do—"

"Let me finish. We'd done this trip before on Amtrak,
and it was a lot of fun to meet the people we sat across from
in the dining car. One year it was a couple that were traveling across the country looking at farms and studying different farming methods. They thought the high desert was
a waste of space. Another year we met an actor and his wife,
the one who played Mr. Magoo. They were traveling
around the country playing golf."

"Get to the point, Tom."

"I'm coming to it. This one morning I overslept and
Eunice went down to breakfast without me, finished and
came back before I was up. When I went down there alone,
the only seat was at a table with three black people. One
of them, the one sitting across from me, was a man in his
forties who had metal hooks instead of hands. He could
hold a fork, but he couldn't pick up anything with it. His
wife put food on the fork for him, and she wiped his mouth
with a napkin. And I was feeling so sour, because if I'd been
with Eunice I never would have been at that table, that I
thought to myself, 'Why me?' "

"Oh, that's awful," I said after a moment. "Oh, Tom."

"This man couldn't feed or dress himself. He'd never
handle a woman's tits again. Welly, he couldn't even jack
off."

"I take the point."

After a moment he said, "You grew up with more

spunk than I gave you credit for. Don't go all weepy on me now. What about this Sanchez?"

I took another swallow of the Laphroaig. "She works for Diane Downey Fashions in London."

"You try to reach her there?"

"No. When the hell would I have done that, Tom?"

"Call her now."

"Oh, God," I said. I got up and went to the phone in the corner. I tried to look out the number in the directory, but the whole book was a blur, and I rang enquiries instead.

A robot voice, male, asked in a BBC accent, "*Which town, please?*"

"In London, a number for Diane Downey Fashions?"

"*Thank you.*" Another robot voice, female, recited the number, one clear digit at a time, and I keyed it in. Presently I got a male voice, Eton accent: "*Diane Downey Fashions, may I help you?*"

"Miss Sanchez, please."

"*Just a moment.*"

A female voice, North Country accent: "*Miss Sanchez's office.*"

"Hallo, is Miss Sanchez in?"

"*No, I'm sorry, she's gone to the country. Would you like to leave a message?*"

"Oh, too bad. Look, I'm calling for a friend of hers who's quite ill. He really wants quite desperately to talk to her."

"*Oh, I'm sorry to hear that. Is it a life-or-death sort of thing?*"

"It is life or death, yes. I'm sorry to trouble you."

"Not at all. I'm so sorry for your friend. Let me just see. Yes, she's gone to Oxfordshire to stay with a friend. It's 'Two Bears,' near Boxton. Do you know where that is?"

"Yes, I know Boxton quite well, in fact. Can you give me the telephone number?"

"I'm terribly sorry, they're not on the phone."

"Oh, I see. Thank you so much, you've been very kind."

"Not at all. I hope your friend feels better."

"I hope so too." I rang off and made a note on the pad. "She's gone to the country, some place near Boxton, not far from where I once lived. They're not on the phone."

"So you're going there?" he asked.

"No."

"Why not?"

"It's none of my business. If your mysterious friends want to talk to Rosemary Sanchez, they can wait till she gets back to London, or they can go to bloody Boxton with my blessing."

He put his cigar down carefully in the ashtray beside him. "Welly, I took the trouble to fly over here because I wanted to save your damn neck."

"You wanted to salve your damned conscience. Go home, Tom."

After a moment he said, "Well, that's that, then." He swallowed the last of the Scotch, put the glass down with a click and heaved himself up. "So long, Nelly-Belly." He walked out of the room; after a few moments I heard the door close behind him. I sat for a few minutes imagining him going down the stairs, out into the road, a fat lonely old man trudging towards Waterloo. I wished I had behaved better to him, but it was too late now. It always was.

With the telly off and Tom gone, the silence was cotton wool. I went into the kitchen and looked at the utensils hanging obediently in their rows. I put the kettle on, measured coffee beans into the Moulinex and ground them for drip, then walked up the hall to look at the post.

I couldn't read Mrs. Islip's note; it seemed to be in a worse scrawl than usual. Under it was a reminder from my dentist, a circular for some kind of punt with an automatic kent, and two or three bills. There was also an envelope with the Weybright logo on it, and a little air letter with a Swiss stamp. I seized the air letter and tore it open. I could tell it was in Cis's handwriting, but she had used a hotel ballpoint or something and I could barely make it out. There was an address in Rome, and it ended, "Love."

I opened the firm's letter; it was signed with a looping scrawl that I recognized as Louis Hostetler's signature. Above that I could make out the words "sorry" and "no longer required as of." The rest was a blur, and I was beginning to wonder how long I had had my contacts in. I went back to the bathroom, took the lenses out and cleaned them, put them back. The world didn't look any different; when I tried to read Cis's letter again it was still a blur, and Hostetler's too, not that I was in any doubt what that one meant. They had given me my congé, gold watch to follow, never mind that I was only a few months shy of retirement. That was the new young management for you, style all the way, and I ought to have known it was coming. Now they could get on with their rip-off of Lissom and join in the jolly game of mutilating women.

I heard the kettle shriek, and went to put it out of its pain. I dumped the coffee into the French carafe, poured the water, set the plunger on top. I put a cup and saucer beside the carafe and sat down at the blue table to wait. It was good to sit here quietly at my own blue table alone, not necessarily thinking about anything in particular.

I had found out about layered pleasures when I was a kid, about nine, reading a book called *The Mushroom Boy* and eating sliced onions. The soft fantasy of the story and the nip of the onions went together somehow, and I realized that the whole was greater than the sum of its parts. Afterwards I always had to eat onions while I read that book. I don't remember now what it was about.

Years later I found the same thing sitting on the beach at Hyères, wet in a canvas chair with Myra beside me, drinking an achingly cold Gibson and watching the sun go down over the Gulf of Lions. Incense and music are like that in church, I imagine. And cigarettes and brandy after sex, but I found out that you can't add to a really intense pleasure, you can only take something away, or turn it into pain.

The weather must have improved suddenly, because sun was flooding through the half curtains. When I poured the coffee in the sunlight, it had the golden greenish hue of clean motor oil.

Mrs. Islip had left some marshmallows in a clear vase on the table, small pinkish white blossoms in a spiral round the hairy stems, and there were bright magnified air bubbles on the stems of the flowers and on the glass; when I moved my head, the bubbles were like little prismatic stars. I felt cleansed somehow, as if I had just survived some awful accident or operation. It was one of those moments when you feel intensely how beautiful the world is and how lucky one is not to have to leave it.

I found myself thinking about the voices. I hadn't heard them since I got off the train, and what had they amounted to, anyway? I often heard voices, quite clearly—just a word or two, apropos of nothing. "Wash your hands," for instance, in my mother's voice. Just now when I came into the kitchen, I had heard the word *béarnaise*, spoken with the faintest suggestion of a lisp. French sauces had been the furthest thing from my mind. But that could happen to anybody; it was probably just random neurons firing. Perhaps the neurons had been firing more briskly than usual, because I was under stress and had been shot at in a foreign country, and so forth. Suddenly I felt quite sure that my ordeal was over, that life could begin again, and I felt so exultant that I had to get out into the air.

I put on another pair of trousers and an old tweed jacket, picked up my suitcase just as it was, and trotted downstairs. I went out the back way into the yard and unlocked the lean-to where the old grey BMW lived. For a wonder, she started like a lamb when I turned the key to "Fahrt," although I hadn't had her out since August. I opened the gate, drove through, closed the gate again, and headed down Blackfriars Road towards the sun.

It was the kind of miraculous day that England

sometimes surprises you with, but not usually in October: gentle breeze, robin's egg sky, drifting clouds. There was more traffic leaving London than coming in, and all the faces were smiling.

A flattened octopus

On the map, London looks like a flattened octopus, or perhaps like a shattered windscreen, with cracks radiating in all directions. I was tooling down one of these roads, or tentacles, feeling more lighthearted than I had in weeks. The clouds were layered like violet white zeppelins, all except for one noble column that started out brownish and turned creamy at the crest where it caught the sun. But that was no cloud, I realized, it was smoke from an open fire somewhere over towards Reigate.

I turned west as soon as I could, worked my way onto the M3 and ran down through Basingstoke and Stockbridge towards Salisbury, watching the needle tip of the cathedral grow taller against the horizon. If you had a good glass in a spire like that and knew where to look, it seems to me you could read a message in the spire of another cathedral fifty miles away, and so on across the island. Across the Channel, too, maybe, and intelligence could flutter from one church to another all round the Continent. If the churchmen didn't use them for that, before they had telegraphs, more fools they.

After Salisbury I turned north and west and passed Stonehenge behind its barrier. Sad that they had to put that

up, but tourists were chipping off too much of it and carrying it away. I didn't stop; it was the Downs that I wanted,
and I kept going north towards Tilshead, hearing occasional bangs from the old Westdown Artillery Range, until
every now and again I got a glimpse of rolling green hills,
the landscape that means England to me.

When I was a kid I had a special fondness for one of
the pictures in Stevenson's *A Child's Garden of Verses*. It
showed a counterpane turned into fields and gentle hills;
when I first saw the Downs I recognized that picture and
knew that I had come home to my childhood. Ta.

A good many of my ancestors on my mother's side
came from county Wicklow, where Jenny and I spent our
summers from 1978 to 1985. Green rolling hills manicured
by sheep; winds that you can barely stand against among
the heather on the heights. The wind seems to blow
through you, washing away all the stink of the city. And
the lilt of Irish grumbling. That's a country for horses and
sheep; all the Irish who could get out are gone.

We went to Kevin's Kitchen once looking for Gwynn
and McDonnell gravestones, but there's something evil
living in the ruins of that place, and I never wanted to go
there again. Jenny didn't feel it; to me it was a miasma thick
enough to cut with a knife. I've felt the same thing in some
cathedrals and not in others. Westminster and Chichester
are not bad, and the Sainte-Chapelle in Paris is a joyous
place, but cathedrals in Italy, the Duomo included, are
heavy with grim death. Do tall man-made structures attract
something besides lightning, and do they store it up in
some way we don't understand? The Duomo has lightning

rods now, but it didn't when it was built, and all those cathedrals must have taken an amazing number of hits during the last few hundred years. It's a wonder more monks were not sizzled.

The church my family went to when we lived in Potamos was called the Riverside Church, although it was nowhere near the river; it had tall stained-glass windows with pictures of Jesus and the apostles. At one time there had been a triangular window behind the altar with a picture of a big eye, but it made people nervous, and somebody broke it with a slingshot. The pastor took up a collection to pay for a new window, and this one turned out to be a picture of a lamb lying on the grass.

The pastor was named J. Snelling Penegor; I always wondered what the J was for. He was a thin pale bald man; his gums were the color of canned salmon when he smiled, and his fingers were cold. His sermons were usually about loving-kindness and getting along with your neighbors, not hellfire, but they went on about an hour too long. The singing was a relief in a way, because you got to stand up then, but qua singing it was awful—earnest and off-key. Why do Protestants all imagine that they can sing?

I asked my father once why the pews weren't padded, or why people didn't bring their own cushions. He smiled and told me that if we had cushions, people might fall asleep. "Some do anyway," he said. After my mother left him in Seaview, he never went to church again, and I gave it up too.

I myself don't think holiness is to be found where there are a lot of people; they get in the way somehow, and if they sing that makes it worse. I've felt I was in the presence of something holy on the Downs, and once sheltering from a spring rainstorm under a cart in county Wicklow, when a vagrant bit of sun came out and lighted up the streaming water. I think it's light that does it. I feel it very often and always unexpectedly, when the sunlight falls on something white. "Hush, hush, whisper who dares." But there's nothing like that for me in any church.

Another illustration in a book that had a great effect on me, though not the one the artist intended, was a depiction of the Sun as a large, jolly face looking over the horizon. For some reason I took the picture literally and dreamed about it; I used to have a recurrent dream of lying on my back looking up in darkness as something round and impossibly huge loomed over me. I couldn't see it, but I knew it was there. Robert Graves had nightmares when he was small about a mask he had been shown in the British Museum, because it was a face, and too large. There's something like that in Chesterton's *Man Who Was Thursday*, too, but this wasn't a face, it was a planet.

Pascal said that we ought to believe in God and heaven, because if it's true we win, and if it isn't we've lost nothing. I do believe there's something behind the appearances of this world, but I don't know how to make myself believe in anything more specific, and don't think I would if I knew how. I can't worship any God who's more petty and vengeful than I am.

I kept on through Devizes, a town that I never can see without thinking of the limerick: "The one was so small, it was no ball at all; the other won several prizes." When I

came to the junction, I turned west onto the M4, then
north on the A46 to Cirencester. The BMW was running
sweetly, and I kept on into Gloucestershire, meaning to go
as far north as Stratford, but the sky was blackening fast,
and I turned east at Ettington. It was too late; just outside
Banbury the rain came down like hoses.

I hadn't planned to stop there, but there was nothing
else for it, and I pulled up at the first pub I saw. As soon as
I had got out of the car and dashed across the pavement, I
knew where I was. It was called the Silver Penny now, and
the front had been painted a scabrous off-white, but it was
the same old Ox and Sparrow where I had spent many
happy hours in days gone by. Leonard and Glynis Home
owned it then, but that was long ago.

In the entry was one of those illiterate photo menus,
heavily emphasizing omelets and quiche. I went down the
stairs into the bar and found a young woman palely loitering under the hanging wineglasses. "Yes, sir?" she said.

"Can I get some dinner and a room?"

"Yes, I think we can manage that." She took a key off
the board behind her and handed it to me. "Like to go up
and get dry?"

"I'll fetch my suitcase first, thanks," I said. "By the
way, I don't suppose Glynis is still here?"

"Glynis? No, she hasn't been here for ages."

By the time I had gone out and come back with my
suitcase, I was much wetter than before. I climbed the tot-
tering stairs to a swaybacked landing redolent of mildew.
My room was small and dim, with a view of the rainswept
road. The walls were discouraged oak paneling; the bed,

more like a cot, looked to be the same one that had been there fifteen years ago.

When I unpacked, I came across the little black radio or whatever it was that Roger Wort had given me. I was surprised to see it, because I had almost made up my mind that it was part of a hallucination or dizzy spell I had had in Milan and again in the train coming home.

When I switched it on, I heard a scratchy voice: . . . *he brightens her on the bad. He rises, she rose. The moro the marrier! But can you love it when it pennythrates your perannium?* I turned the dials, hoping for something more sensible, but all I got was Les Paul and Mary Ford singing "On Top of the World" in several voices accompanied by a billion banjos.

I turned the thing off, put on dry clothes, and went down to the dining room, where I was the only patron and the bar girl waited on me. Distrusting all the dishes with foreign names, I ordered plaice and hoped for the best, but it was very dry. As I was pushing the remains around my plate, Glynis walked in looking large as life, with a bottle of wine in her hand. She didn't seem to have aged much. There was a lot of makeup round her eyes, and her hair was brassy blond, but then it always had been.

"They told me you were here," she said, and leaned down to kiss me. "How are you, luv?"

"I'm fine, Glynis. It's wonderful to see you. Is Leonard—"

She sat down and put the wine on the table. "No, he died four years ago. How long are you staying?"

"Just the night, then I'm going back to London."

"Have you been to see the house?"

"No. Haven't had the heart."

"Not in all this time? You ought to, you know."

"You think so?"

"Suit yourself, but I wouldn't let it fester." She poured the wine and we drank. "I can't stay," she said. "What room have they put you in?"

I told her and she said, "I'll look in later if I can." She kissed me again and left. I went upstairs, took one of Willie's pills for my headache, undressed and got into bed. A faint discolored light came through the blinds.

After a while, remembering what had happened, I was beginning to think it was curious that Tom had known about Roger Wort but not about Willie. Did that mean that Roger was real, but Willie was imaginary? If so, were the pills imaginary too? Was my headache imaginary? An hour went by, and I was about to drift off when I heard the door open and shut. Her tall form came towards me; her voice said, "Billy?"

"Here I am."

" 'Course you are." She sat down, and the mattress tipped me chummily against her thigh. "Feeling all right? Cheerful and friendly?"

"Yes, Glynis."

"All right then." She reached behind her and I heard the sound of a zip. After a moment she stood up, then folded back the bedclothes and got in. "Make room, luv."

She kissed me, and her mouth was hot and moist, but astringent somehow. I could see her big eyes dimly reflecting the streetlight from the jalousies. She put her dry cheek against my breast for a moment, then her head moved downward, and I felt her fingers below my navel. After a while there was a sharp click down there, and her voice said, "It's no good, you're turned off." I felt disappointed but rather peaceful. Her head rose into view again and she said, "Don't worry about it; we're still the best of friends, aren't we?"

"Of course we are. Bless you, Glynis." I think I saw her leave the room; then I fell into black dreamless sleep.

In the morning when I opened the blinds the milky light made the room look clearer but rather sad; it didn't seem possible that Glynis had ever been there. The girl at the bar brought me a soft-boiled egg, toast and coffee. I hadn't noticed before that she had a thin scar down the middle of her upper lip. By the time I had settled with her and got on the road again the sky was almost clear, with patches of sunlight when the clouds thinned apart, and I started off southward past Chipping Norton, but the BMW was not behaving at all well, and not long after we crossed the Thames it chose a deserted lane to sputter to a halt.

I got the tool kit out and put the bonnet up. When I had been tinkering with the motor for a while, a woman in an Irish hat appeared and gazed at me over the hedge. "Anything I can do?" she asked.

"It's very kind of you, but it's looking like a job for a mechanic."

She came out to the road and approached me, a woman in her forties with a broad humorous face and no makeup. "Let's have a peep anyhow. What have you tried so far?"

"I've cleaned out the float chamber as best I can. The ignition seems to be all right."

"Hum. May I borrow this screwdriver?"

"Certainly."

"Start her up then, would you?"

I got into the driver's seat, feeling a little overcontrolled, and cranked the starter.

"Wait a minute," she called. I waited.

"All right, again." I tried it once more with the same result.

"Again." The engine gave an encouraging sputter.

"Once more." This time the engine coughed, caught, and settled down to its business. "Mixture too weak," she said.

I got out to thank her. "These old BMWs can rattle themselves out of adjustment," she said. "I've put a bit of thread in the screw to hold it awhile, but you'll want to have a look when you get home."

I had an odd feeling; all this country round here was familiar to me, and I knew I was not far from Boxton.

"I don't suppose you know where 'Two Bears' is, do you?"

She replaced the screwdriver in my tool kit and straightened up. "This is 'Two Bears,' why do you ask?"

"Oh. I was looking for someone who was staying here, actually. Rosemary Sanchez."

"Are you a friend of Rosemary's?"

"Not exactly, but we met on a flight to Milan, and I think I may have given her something by mistake."

She looked at me skeptically. "I hardly know how to take that, but Rosemary's gone to the States," she said. "She's on the plane by now."

"Oh, I see. Thank you."

"Not at all. I think the carburettor's okay now."

"I don't suppose you could give me her number in the States?"

"I'm afraid it's put away. It's a place called Plymouth, if that's any help."

"Is that Plymouth, Massachusetts?"

"I don't think so. It's one of the other eastern states, but I forget which. Sorry."

I thanked her again and drove off with a mind more or less blank, but I must have been remembering what Glynis had said about going to see the house, because the BMW took a turning I hadn't intended, like a horse that knows the way.

All the hedges and trees were glistening with raindrops; the road grew narrower, and then I was bumping down a lane I remembered. I stopped at the gate and got out in the silence.

The white house looked shabby and unloved. All the shutters were closed, one or two of them hanging awry. Someone had mowed the grass recently, but the hedges were growing wild and the flower gardens were a sea of weeds in which a few marigolds were defiantly blooming. Under their stems I saw something dirty white. It was a bone button, and I put it in my pocket. The nets were down on the tennis court, the pool was empty and cracked.

When I went onto the terrace and peered in at the French doors, I saw that the rooms were stripped bare and the fireplaces full of trash.

I walked down to the river and sat on a stone watching the gray water hasten by. I may have expected some phantom from the past, but nothing of the kind happened, and I got up rather relieved, knowing that I needn't come back here again.

Driving south, I turned on the radio for some music, and heard the announcer say, " . . . bursting with a tremendous impact. Fragments of metal are said to have fallen as far away as Camberley. Early reports had it that organic matter also fell. In Woking, parishioners leaving St. Mary-in-the-Vale were said to have been deluged with blood and gobbets of flesh." He cleared his throat. "In the Midlands, extraordinary winds . . ." I changed the station several times, and finally got an orchestra playing dance tunes.

After about half an hour I realized that there was someone in the seat beside me, but I didn't want to look at her too directly. I heard her say, or perhaps remembered, "Bill, what part of the States are you from?"

"Pennsylvania and Oregon."

"Oh, are they close together?"

"No, three thousand miles apart."

"How peculiar! Will you take me there sometime?"

"You know I will."

Then we sat in comfortable silence together, and after a while I knew she had gone.

Tit for tat

When you make a woman laugh, she's done something absolutely honest and unpremeditated, and that makes a sudden intimacy. That's a good way to begin. If it's a sexual joke, so much the better, but it doesn't have to be. At a sales conference in Brussels one evening I was sitting in a bar with a pretty little Belgian buyer; we were in a group, and this one loud German was telling us how great he was, how much money he made, how many famous people he knew, and every time he wasn't looking our way, I'd put my two forefingers up to my head and wriggle them like antennae.

Of course she asked me why, and I moved closer to talk into her ear. "Well," I said, "it's this story about the ants who were rolling a great ball of dung up towards their nest. It was really the biggest ball of dung that had ever been seen, a tremendous prize, but the little worker ants were sweating and straining very hard indeed as they went up the hill, and the queen, down at the bottom, was waiting anxiously and cheering them on. But one of the worker ants slipped, and then another, and before you know it the great ball of dung was rolling down the hill faster and faster. And the queen, you know, was frantically waving her feelers." I put my forefingers up to my head again. "So if you ever see an ant doing this, it means, 'Stop the shit!' "

She told me later that she laughed so hard she pissed herself. In a minute we were holding hands, and then sitting closer, and it was duck soup after that.

Memories: what would we do without them?

I got back to London in a grey drizzle about half past twelve. When I let myself in, the first thing I saw in the glare of a ceiling bulb was a line of black and tan ulsters and rain-coats, hats, overshoes and umbrellas slashed and laid out on the floor like a massacre.

The letters that had been on the hall table were on the floor as well, opened and piled neatly with their envelopes. The closet was empty, wire hangers tangled to-gether.

I looked around and listened, but couldn't hear any-thing except my heart beating. All down the hall ahead of me, the pictures were on the floor, tilted against the wall in a ragged row. The ceiling light shade had gone, the naked bulb made a splash of yellow on the floor.

I took a few steps and listened. Still nothing. I could see now that the photographs and mats had been removed separately and were lying against their frames. When I looked in at the open door of the sitting room, I saw furni-ture upside down and rugs rolled up.

I put my head in at the kitchen door and saw pots and pans on the lino; knives, eggbeaters, the juicer, toaster, mixer, china, glasses, silverware, cereal boxes, jam jars, matches, paper napkins, plastic bags. There were other things on the floor that I realized I hadn't seen in years— the Mr. Coffee, the waffle iron, the popcorn popper, gifts from Tom that I'd put away and forgotten. In between were heaps of sugar, flour and cereal, mingled with clots of jam and mustard like blood and shit. Near the refrigerator black beetles were crawling over the golden yolks of five eggs broken in a row on the floor. The fridge door was open, shelves empty.

I was very frightened. I didn't really want to go into my study, but I knew I had to, and I pushed the door open. In the light of a table lamp that stood naked on the floor, I saw papers in rivulets, boxes of paper clips, razor blades, pencils and pens in rows. Cicely's picture was there, lying on its frame, and stacks of books from the shelves. The telephone and answerphone were there too, and the computer with its casing off and the brown bones of circuit boards yawning. The desk drawers stood upright like sentry boxes.

I had no sensation of falling, but found myself on the floor looking up at the stacks of books which seemed to have grown taller than houses; I could read the titles on their spines as if through a telescope: *A Collector's Guide to Games* by Goodfellow in scuffed half morocco; *The Real Italy*, a thick white paperback; *Gamekeeper's Gallows* by Hilton in its soiled white jacket; Ewing's *Dress and Undress* in green boards with the title pasted on; Legman's *Limericks* in monk's cloth stamped in raspberry. They seemed to have an immense occult meaning, and I stared at them until they faded into the darkness.

I dreamed I was lying in bed with my arm around a woman's cool hip and my mouth on her breast, pulling at the gorged nipple. Her milk was warm, sweet and rather thin.

I knew who it was, because Glynis was the only woman who had ever let me do that, apart from my mother. I knew when it was, too; it was 1974, and we were in her room over the pub one night when we had got chummy after hours and Leonard was away. The child was asleep in its crib. Glynis wouldn't let me suckle her for more than a minute or two, but I could tell by her squirming that it was a sexual thing for her; that had never occurred to me before for some reason.

It was fine to have her long naked body in my arms and to give her that private half-guilty pleasure, and it was nice to think that she got it from her baby too. It's tit for tat, after all, but it made me realize what a different thing it is to be a woman.

If we all went about naked, these flesh-to-flesh embraces wouldn't be anything unusual, and I suppose that must be the real, hidden reason for the nudity taboo. Holding a woman naked in your arms for the first time is thrilling because forbidden, therefore a special treat, but if we all did it with casual acquaintances every day, there would be nothing much in it.

Only a few ounces of a woman's breasts have to do with making milk; all the rest is for exhibition. I've heard it said that breasts as we know them evolved in imitation of the buttocks, in order to make the ladies equally attractive from either aspect, and perhaps that's true, but most of our simian relatives don't have large breasts, or buttocks either. Would purple ones have become popular, I wonder, if we hadn't taken to wearing clothes sometime during the last ice age? Bikini bottoms are the equivalent of baboons' bums, I think. Anatole France was right: the unclad female body is not half as erotic as the same body artfully dressed; the reason we cover up the breasts and bottoms is that they are the parts most likely to be disappointing when we see them.

It's gravity that does them in, pulling them down, stretching the ropes no matter what we do. I used to daydream about space stations, of women adrift in weightlessness beyond the Moon, their breasts as round as cantaloupes.

It is a bit degrading isn't it that a woman should be considered attractive because of these udders hanging off her chest, or a man because of his pecs or God help us, his "buns"? But that's Mother Nature for you, and the only thing that worries me is when it's silicone or steroids; what are we really doing then, if it isn't rutting after chemicals instead of men and women?

Pascal said that if Cleopatra's nose had been shorter, the whole shape of the world would have been changed. I never understood what he meant by that, unless it was Cleopatra's long snout that attracted her lovers. That's possible, I suppose. The noses of beautiful women have been getting shorter and shorter in my lifetime, until they're in danger of disappearing altogether. Why should we judge women's beauty by their noses, never by their fannies? Or by their eyes, which are usually closed when they give us most pleasure? It's because the eyes and the nose and mouth are on display, and we have to do the best we can. But it's a damn poor way of improving the breed, if you ask me.

Then the wet nipple popped out of my mouth and she said, or I remembered her saying, "That's enough, Bill, don't be a swine." We were kneeling up somehow, and when I tried to get a better look at the round golden thing in front of my eyes, I saw that it was not a breast but a doorknob.

It was the knob of the street door in the lobby, in fact, something I had seen a thousand times without taking any notice. It was a heavy brass thing, rather large, with a worn border of leaves round the rim. In the yellow overhead light, the parts between the leaves were dark brown, the rest gleaming gold.

I could not quite understand why the thing was so near my face, until I realized that I was kneeling on the carpet before the door with my suitcase in my hand, and that blood was dripping from my chin. I was sore in various places, especially my left shoulder and both knees. I had no recollection of getting here; it looked as if I must have fallen.

I was dizzy, but I managed to stand up by holding onto the doorknob; it was cold and waxy in my hand. I turned the knob and got out into the twilight. A black drop of blood fell to the pavement between my feet, then another. I found a clump of paper handkerchiefs in my mac and held it to my chin as I began walking. I didn't know what had happened, but I knew it was something serious, and that I had to get away.

A man stepped out of the house on the corner and saw me weaving across the road. He called something after me, but I went on without answering. At the corner of Waterloo Road I got into a taxi driven by a rat-faced Paki. "Heathrow," I said.

"Sure you wouldn't like to go to Guy's Hospital instead?" he asked. I must have looked awful.

"Just drive," I said.

When we got to the airport the dim sky had bright-

ened to the color of a water agate; evidently it was not
evening, as I had thought, but early morning, and I had lost
another day.

The concourse was brightly lit and full of well-fed
handsome people with somewhere to go. I entered the first
men's room and looked at myself in the glass. I couldn't see
very distinctly, but I could tell that there was dried blood
on my chin and down the front of my mac. I washed my
face with paper towels until it was pale and clean. The mac
was hopeless; I took it off and stuffed it into a trash basket.

Out in the mall I stood awhile looking at the an-
nouncement boards as they clicked over, rattling to change
one message into another. British Airways had a flight leaving for New York in thirty-five minutes. I went to the
counter; there were coach seats not yet booked, and I got
one.

The airplane was the wide-bodied sort, with four clusters of seats and three aisles, like the nave of a church.
When I got on, the aisle was full of busy sleeves and elbows
where passengers were hoisting their luggage into overhead racks. Eventually I found my seat in the right-hand
section on the aisle. As the plane continued loading, some
of the nearby seats filled up but others remained vacant,
and I saw that it was going to be an easy flight.

When we were all settled, a stewardess appeared in
our aisle to give us a dumb-show lecture about the emergency exits and the oxygen masks, accompanied by the
recorded voice of another stewardess who was not actually
here and might even be long dead. The air grew gradually
staler as we huddled strapped into our seats like candidates

for a mass execution. I stared at the upper part of the cabin, noticing that it was filled with grey plastic blocks of odd shapes which did not quite fit together.

After another delay the plane trundled off to the head of the runway and sat there for some time. Then, quite un-expectedly, the engine noise increased to a roar; the plane gathered itself like a cheetah and drove forward with a steady and implacable motion that seemed to go on forever. At last it tilted upward, and with a final bump was in the air.

As we rose into the atmosphere I looked in my wallet for Roger Wort's card, but it wasn't there, and I remembered that I never had had one for some reason. I wanted to call Wort, or somebody, just to let them know that I was making the effort to do what they wanted, but I didn't much like the idea of calling Milan and talking to an Italian telephonist.

The only card I had was Willie's, in fact, and there again I hesitated because I knew he and Roger were rivals in some way, but even so, surely he wouldn't refuse to give me Roger's number? I put a credit card into the phone slot, took down the receiver and punched in Willie's number. There was a pause, a click, and then the distant sound of a ragtime piano playing "Jellyroll Blues." I rang off and tried again; this time all I got was a cosmic hiss, and I gave it up.

My nearest fellow passenger spread his work sheets over the seat between us, unfolded a laptop, and began clicking keys. An invisible haze swelled up from the smok-ing section. After an hour or so two stewardesses approached pulling a heavy cart that was bravely painted and battered like a circus wagon. I lowered my tray table, and they served me a glass half full of hollow ice cubes, a plastic swizzle stick, a paper napkin, a foil packet of sugared peanuts, and two minibottles of Beefeater. In another hour or so two more stewardesses came along with another cart, and served me an omelet, a little cake, and a slice of melon. With the cake I got something called Better'n Butter, and synthetic coffee in a plastic cup.

Whilst we were unwrapping the meal, I glanced over at my neighbor and pulled a face of comic dismay. A youngish man with polished skin and hair; he looked vaguely familiar. He smiled in return, leaned towards me and said, "Don't think of this as food, think of it as an eating experience." The voice was familiar too, but I couldn't place him for the life of me. He buttered the cake and popped it into his mouth, letting the crumbs dribble down his chin. After the stewardesses took the trays away he went back to his laptop and didn't glance my way again.

I was looking through the airline magazine when a man came up the aisle and knelt beside me. I had to look twice to be sure that it was Roger Wort, in a Campbell plaid shirt with the sleeves rolled up, exposing his blond hairy arms. He had one pink hand on the arm of my chair to steady himself, and the other held a half-empty highball glass.

While I stared at him speechless, he said, "You won't get anywhere running away like this, Bill. In fact, I'd say it's definitely a no-no."

"I'm not running away," I said, and looked around.

Nobody seemed to be listening, even my neighbor, but I lowered my voice to a sort of hiss. "I'm going after Rosemary Sanchez!" I said.

"Who's Rosemary Sanchez?"

"She's the one I gave the card to!"

"Don't get excited. Where is Rosemary Sanchez now, Bill?"

"Someplace called Plymouth."

"Massachusetts?"

"No, a different one. In another state."

"How did you find this out, Bill?"

"From a friend of hers in Oxfordshire."

"But she didn't tell you what state Plymouth is in?"

"She couldn't remember."

"What's the name of this friend, Bill?"

"She didn't tell me."

"She didn't tell you her name?"

"No."

"How did you know she was a friend of Rosemary Sanchez, Bill?"

"She happened to mention it."

"In Oxfordshire?"

"Yes."

"And that's all you know?"

"Yes, damn it."

He got to his feet with a grunt, and stood there tucking his shirt in with one hand. "We have to talk when we get to New York, hey."

"Fine."

"Some things have got to get straightened out."

"Good. We'll straighten them out."

"This isn't good enough, Bill."

"I know it isn't, Roger."

He shook his head sadly, turned and walked back down the aisle out of view.

Into geological time

Studies of successful people show that they have three things going for them: a good start, some talent or ability, and luck. Most of them believe they got where they are by sheer ability, but you never hear of the people who had a good start and some talent but no luck whatever.

When I think of all the improbable things that had to happen to bring me where I am, I'm almost tempted to believe that everything in the world is arranged to suit me and that the whole shooting match will end when I'm done with it. Begin with Caresse Crosby, let's say. Then add Tom getting a job in the garment industry and marrying the boss's daughter. Then he offered *me* a job, which he wouldn't have done if he hadn't thought it would be amusing to watch me fail. And so on, all the way up the line—my friendship with Alec Weil, which led to getting the ear of Hugh Rosenzweig. Everything good that happened to me had some element of astounding luck in it. And except for Jenny's death, there had never been a cloud until now.

Dozing as I was, I realized that somehow we had drifted into geological time. In the early Paleozoic the drinks cart came round again, and I got another gin; it made me drowsy again, but not quite enough. In the Cretaceous the stewardesses reappeared with clusters of blue plastic headphones. The curtains were pulled and a movie dimly unreeled on the screen at the front of the cabin. It was a Canadian adventure story, marred by a streak of light from a window where a passenger hadn't closed his curtain; I followed it to the end anyhow.

Except for the drone of engines, the illusion of non-motion in this huge metal cylinder was perfect. It would be better if they had bicycle seats and the passengers had to pedal part of the way; they could help to propel the airplane and would arrive cheerful and in better shape. The company would have to furnish more air, though; it was like a drowned submarine in here, one of those films when they've got to ration the oxygen until the crew is rescued. (Waiting for the hollow thump on the hull.)

The stewardesses came by handing out customs cards which I couldn't read, but I filled mine in as best I could. I was drowsy, although it was still early morning. The shadowy interior of the airplane, with its scattered dim lights, seemed to have grown as vast as a cathedral.

I was floating away, half asphyxiated, imagining that the hull had been breached and all the pale oxygen tubes were swaying down from the ceiling like cobras while menus and flight magazines drifted brightly along the aisles. Then I dreamed I was a child again, too young to know how old I was, and I had just fallen out of a boat into the river. I had been told not to stand up on the seat, but had done it anyhow, and this was the consequence. Apart from the surprise when the water lipped over me, what I noticed especially was the brown darkness and silence. It was quite different down here to anything I had been led to expect. For one thing, there was no bottom to it, and it was hard to tell where the top was, or how to get there. I thought of this later when I read *The Water-Babies* by Charles Kingsley, but in the book the children liked being underwater and felt at home there, whereas I felt I was condemned to stay in a place I did not like at all.

Then someone came down in a cloud of bubbles and lifted me into the boat. I thought it was my father, but he was still at the oars. It was my mother who had saved me, and she said, "Ladies and gentlemen, this is your captain." I was so surprised at this that I came awake in my seat, and heard the voice go on, "We have been advised that all international flights are being diverted from Kennedy because of an emergency situation. We are diverting to Logan Airport in Boston, and our ETA there is oh-six-twenty local time. We have no more information at the moment. Passengers who need assistance in Boston please see your British Airways representative on arrival. Thank you."

All over the cabin I could see that people were sitting up; some of them were in the aisle, clumping around a stewardess near the toilets. Eventually they dispersed and she came forward, pausing to speak to passengers every few rows. When she got to me, she said, "We hear that a meteor has struck Manhattan near the Williamsburg Bridge. All air traffic is being diverted. We have no more details yet."

Two rows ahead of me a man turned and asked, "But how am I supposed to get to Long Island?" I didn't hear the stewardess's reply.

The sound of the engines changed in some subtle way and I felt that we were descending. Off to the side I heard a whining noise, like the sound of an electric drill. It stopped and came on once more, and then a third time. Someone had told me once that it was the sound of the hydraulic pumps lowering the landing gear. But why did they have to do it three times?

Eventually through the window I could see the horizon, and then the gray ocean rushing by, and I knew that we were about to crash in the water. I tried to remember all the instructions about flotation gear and rubber boats, but I had forgotten it all. I put my head between my knees. After a long time I felt a slight bump, then another. It was not what I had expected; we had not tilted arse over teacup and did not appear to be sinking, but were running along as if nothing unusual had happened. I raised my head and looked out the window. Airport buildings were drifting past; we had landed on solid ground after all. People were standing up with a rustle, putting on jackets, lowering luggage from the bins.

In the aisle ahead of me as we waited for the queue to begin moving stood a tall cowboy-hatted man with the sad brown face of an outdoorsman. He was leaning over to talk to someone still seated, and I saw that his wallet was sticking up invitingly from the back pocket of his jeans. The wallet was attached to a metal chain that looped halfway down his thigh and then rose to his belt to which it was attached by a rivet.

I was thinking that if I were a pickpocket I would see that as an easy challenge. The only ticklish part would be lifting the wallet from his tight jeans; then one clip with a pair of bolt cutters and away. But perhaps he had some alarm device in his pocket.

If I were a pickpocket, I would slide some little bibelot in as I pulled the wallet out, something to serve as a con- solation prize and also a calling card; it would be stamped with a haloed stick figure. And of course I would share my gains with the poor.

Then we were all trotting up the covered incline. Even though the crash landing had been a false alarm, I was feeling the way one does after a narrow escape, hollow in- side and a bit out of place. I used to imagine that everyone had a fixed number of lives like a cat and that you didn't die until you had used them all up, whatever the number was, but that you could tell every time you had lost one by the sense of something missing.

A uniformed man stood at an intersection diverting us away from the Customs area; there was a stale smell of smoke in the air. One or two younger men gave me side- long looks as they passed me, and then we were surging out past the barriers into the concourse. I waited till all the pas- sengers were off, but I didn't see Roger.

Down at one end of the mall someone was shouting. Some people had stopped and were looking that way, oth- ers were running, shoes clicking on the tiles. I carried my suitcase in the other direction, past a giant jack-o'-lantern made of orange honeycomb crepe paper, and found a Hertz place manned by two bearded Sikhs in white suits and turbans who ignored the constantly ringing phone on the counter behind them. The counter was packed with customers, and there were more coming up behind us. I kept turning around, looking for Roger.

"*Attention all passengers,*" said the loudspeakers. "*All flights to destinations in Connecticut, Maryland, Virginia, Washington, D.C., and New Jersey have been canceled for the duration of the emergency. Service representatives are waiting at the north end of the concourse to help you make alternative travel arrangements.*" Then it began again in Spanish, and after that in French.

When it was my turn at the counter I signed all the papers. I paid with a credit card, then went to get some dollars from a blue money machine. Afterward I went to a phone booth, put my card in and punched for Directory Assistance in Plymouth, Massachusetts. The screen lighted up with WHAT NUMBER, PLEASE? I typed in 1) DIANE DOWNEY FASHIONS, 2) ROSEMARY SANCHEZ.

SEARCHING . . .

1) NO LISTING FOR DIANE DOWNEY FASHIONS

2) NO LISTING FOR THE FOLLOWING:

ROSEMARY SANCHEZ

R. SANCHEZ

I hung up and punched for Directory Assistance, U.S. cities, then PLYMOUTH. I got eighteen entries and a map display; the nearest Plymouth was in Connecticut, but I knew it was no use trying to get there, and I thought I'd try the next, which was Pennsylvania. I punched it in, then the same two requests. The screen gave me a number for Diane Downey and another for R. Sanchez. Then it said:

2) R. SANCHEZ HAS CALL PROTECTION.
YOUR CALL, PLEASE?

I typed in R. SANCHEZ, and picked up the handset from its cradle. There was a buzzing in the earpiece, a click, and then a female voice: *"You have reached the home of R. Sanchez. At the tone, please state your name and the nature of your call."* Beep.

I said, "Hullo, I'm trying to reach Rosemary Sanchez. My name is Wellington Stout, we met on the plane to Milan, and it's quite urgent. I'm in an airport phone booth at the moment, can you tell me how to reach you?"

There was a pregnant pause, then a hum and a click. At that moment I heard a voice racketing off the ceiling: *"Mr. Wellington Stout, please come to the Hertz counter. Mr. Stout, your car is ready. Please come to the Hertz counter."*

I swore, ran back, waited again, and one of the Sikhs waved me outside. I stood shivering on the pavement while another Sikh drove the car up; the jacket that had been all right for chilly England was not warm enough for the north-eastern U.S.

The car was an agressive-looking white Buick with fuel injection, power windows, air bags, blue mohair upholstery, and an onboard computer. The Sikh showed me how to turn it on. In a quiet feminine voice it said, "Your name, please?"

"Ah, my name is Wellington Stout," I said.

"Wellington, will there be anyone else acting as my driver while you are the primary driver?"

"No, I don't believe so. Ah, thank you."

"Not at all, Wellington."

The Sikh explained, "Now you just drive narmally, you see. Each time you start the car, you see, it will ask who you are. Therefore nobody can steal the car from you."

"That's very reassuring. Ah, will it talk to me a good deal?"

"Only in case of emargency, or to answer your questions. For example, if you ask it to choose a route to your destination, it will do so and display it on the map screen here on the dashboard."

"Will it really!"

"Yes, sir."

"I must say that's marvelous. Well, thank you."

"Not at all, sir. Enjoy your drive."

As I pulled away from the curb, a man came forward waving at me and tapped on the offside window. At first I thought it must be Roger, but it was a small brown fellow in a green madras jacket and hat. Because he looked familiar, I lowered the window and said, "Yes?"

He put his head in with a smile. "Mr. Morrison— no, sorry, Mr. Stout—you don't remember me, do you?"

Then it came back to me. "You asked for some money in London."

"Sure and I did, your honor, and you gave me it like the generous man that you are." He opened the door and was inside before I could object. "Pull up there at the TransAm terminal."

Cars were honking behind us; I followed his orders because I didn't know what else to do, but I was alarmed and angry. "Who are you, and what the devil do you want?" I said.

· He had settled himself comfortably into the upholstery and crossed his legs. "Mr. Stout," he said, "certain people believe you may be responsible for the disappearance of a valuable object. Do you understand me?"

"Yes, but it was nothing to do with me."

He waved his hand. "I believe you entirely. The question is, how are you to convince *them*? As long as they think you might be guilty, I'm sorry to say, the possibility remains that they will hang you from a hook."

I stared at him speechless, too frightened even to bluster. He said, "Not immediately, of course, because the possibility also remains that you will lead them to the stolen object. But as time goes on, the latter possibility grows dimmer and the former more certain. Now it's important that you understand me and believe me. Do you?"

After a moment I said, "Yes."

"Very good. Now in your opinion, who does have the object?"

"I don't know. If it was in the business card, maybe that woman has it."

"Rosemary Sanchez?"

"Yes."

"Do you know where she is?"

"I'm on my way to look for her in Plymouth, Pennsylvania."

"A very good place, too. Persevere, Mr. Stout. Never say die." He smiled and opened the door. Before he got out, he dropped something on the seat, a little gold-colored coin. I picked it up: it was a pound.

My *favorite letter*

The dashboard of the white Buick had three circular clusters of readouts and dials; they reminded me of the letter O, my favorite letter, repeated three times. O has a perfect shape, the shape of the mouth that makes it; it's the first letter of "one," and as a numeral it's zed, so there you have the two numbers that make all the rest in binary notation. As a word, it expresses awe, pleasure, and joy. It's also the first letter of "open," "orifice," "orgasm," and "ova." There are three Os in my name, Wellington Nelson Stout, like three open eyes in a row, and I used to think that was why I could see further round corners than most people.

We are told that we used to have a third eye in the tops of our heads and that it later migrated into the brain and became the pineal gland, a story that I find harder to believe than the Resurrection, but if we did have an eye up there at one time, I think we lost it because it kept getting poked out by twigs.

Potamos has two Os, like Oregon, and so has London, but Seaview and Eugene have none. Boston ought to have been a lucky name for me, but on the other hand the Ospedale San Carlo Borromeo ought to have been even luckier.

"How do I get out of here?" I said more or less to myself, but the car's feminine voice answered, "I am displaying a map of the exits from Logan Airport, our present location. What is our next destination, Wellington?"

"I want to go to Plymouth, Pennsylvania."

"I am displaying an itinerary, Wellington." The little dashboard readout glowed. It was pulsing red at one of the exits.

"You want me to take One A North, is that it?"

"Yes, Wellington."

"All right. You needn't call me Wellington quite so much, by the way."

"I will call you Wellington and sir on alternate occasions, sir."

"It isn't anything personal, of course."

"I understand that, Wellington."

"It's a bit warm in here. Can you lower the heat?"

"Certainly, sir."

"How do I turn on the radio?"

"I can do that for you, Wellington. What would you like?"

"Some news, please."

A voice erupted from under the dashboard: " . . . a direct hit on one of the greatest ports in the world, Carl, one of the chief nerve centers of this country. Just for openers, it will tie up both air and ocean traffic in and out of New York City indefinitely."

"Indefinitely?"

"Yes, because shipping has been destroyed, the docks have been destroyed, warehouses are underwater, the streets are full of mud and debris. If our worst enemies—"

"Like the Soviets—"

"Yes, if we had still been locked in cold-war conflict with the Soviet Union, or, let me say, any other hostile nation, and they had wanted to inflict maximum damage on us by an air strike, Carl, they couldn't have done any worse than this if they tried."

"But Boston and Philadelphia, and other seaports up and down the coast—"

"They're not going to be able to take up the slack, Carl, not for months or years to come, believe me. And we're not even talking about the damage to the economy of the eastern seaboard and the whole country. There has never been a disaster like it. Never."

"We're talking with catastrophe buff Fred Hoffman about the meteorite that struck Manhattan early this morning, and the two others later in the day, one off Pensacola and one in the Gulf of Mexico north of Veracruz that caused lesser damage. Mr. Hoffman, what are the chances that three meteors, or I should say meteorites—" The voice faded, came back in. "—space of time—" It was gone again.

"Turn it off," I said. I began thinking about *The War of the Worlds,* by H. G. Wells, where the meteorites had turned out to be Martian spaceships. What time of year had that happened in the story? I knew it wasn't winter; that was *The Invisible Man.*

Here in Massachusetts it was midmorning, bright and warming as the sun rose higher, with a little wind whipping the bare trees and a few clouds moving slowly above the northern horizon. It couldn't have been less like Britain, even apart from driving on the right side; the dimensions were all wrong, everything too big and too grimy. Even though I had never been in this part of the country before, I felt in a disturbing way that I had come home.

We drove north until we got clear of the Boston suburbs, then turned west, and after an hour or two found ourselves on a scenic route that took us past one blue lake after another under a smiling sky. I had expected all the trees to be bare by this time, but those I saw were almost fully fledged in papery yellows, oranges and reds, every leaf sharp-edged and fluttering, each tree gracefully waving her fans around the naked stems of her emptiness as we passed. Leaf confetti was strewn along the highway, and clouds of it rose now and then, whirled, descended against us and were gone.

As we approached the New York line we began to encounter increased traffic coming the other way, mostly sports cars, luxury sedans and limousines; but we had our side of the highway almost to ourselves. The car handled so easily that my attention wandered once or twice, and I had to swerve back into my own lane. The shadows shortened, then lengthened again, and I began to realize that I was very tired; it was early afternoon here, but I had been up since about six o'clock London time. Shortly after we crossed into New York State I saw a motel on the right; its NO VACANCY sign was lit, but a car was just pulling away from one of the cabins, and I turned in. The driver of the other car glanced at me as we passed; he was a pasty-faced man in a gray slouch hat.

"We have no vacancies," said the man behind the desk in the little office. "None." He was a bony pale man in a white shirt and black tie; he wore rimless glasses so smudged that I could not see the color of his eyes.

"Sorry, but I saw a car leave just now, and I thought—"

"That unit isn't ready. The maids haven't been in there. Come back in an hour."

"That will be fine. Can I leave you my credit card in the meantime?"

After a moment he took my card and put it into the reader. "You know why that man left?" he said. "It was a family of four, the parents and two children, boy and girl. Boy about nine, girl five or so. He said he didn't want them to occupy the same bed. Wanted me to bring in a rollaway for the boy. Well, I didn't have a rollaway available."

He handed me back the credit card and leaned closer over the counter. "I said, 'Why don't you sleep in one bed with the boy, and your wife in the other bed with the girl?' Well, he turned white. Said, 'That's out of the question.' I said, 'Well, work it out to suit yourselves. You can sleep with the little girl and your wife with the boy, if you like that better.' I was deliberately rude to him. That's not the way I usually am, but I knew he would be mad enough to go, and he did. Isn't that amazing? With every motel full, up and down the highway? Some people!"

"They might have slept on the floor, and let the children have the beds," I said.

"Why, certainly! Some people would have been glad

to *have* a floor to sleep on, but not him! Why, they could have taken the mattresses off the beds, and the children slept on the springs, but he said, 'I never heard such an indecent proposal in my life. You ought to be ashamed,' he said. Well, *he* was the one that had indecent thoughts, if you ask me. About his own children, too, standing right there listening to every word. You come back in an hour, and I'll rent you that unit."

"Thank you very much. Is there a restaurant nearby?"

"The Eyehop is all, south of here about a mile."

"The Eyehop" turned out to be the International House of Pancakes, a low brown building with a very large chimney. A number of people were waiting just inside the door, but the line moved fairly rapidly and in about twenty minutes I found myself at the counter looking at a glossy illiterate menu with pictures of waffles (Belgian and domestic), pancakes, ham steak, salad and french fries.

"You from New York?" asked the man on my right. He was fat and elderly; his denim jacket was buttoned up wrong and his hands were shaking.

"No, from Boston actually."

"How'd you get *here*? You're going south, aren't you? You're going the wrong way. You better get north as fast as you can."

"Yes, I'll do that."

The waitress came, and I ordered the Belgian waffles with strawberries, although I was not really hungry. The man on my right muttered at me until my order came, then finished his coffee and left, to be replaced by a teenager in a blue suit. The waffles were quite good, and the coffee was excellent.

The motel cabin had the air of a building under construction. The carpeting smelled aggressively new, and one of the two queen-size beds had been dismantled and was stacked against the wall behind the chests of drawers. A cot on wheels had been set up in its place.

There was a strong smell of paint in the bathroom, although part of it was bare plasterboard. Across the toilet seat, preventing it from being used, was a strip of paper lettered LO GO GRI PHON. A white plastic hose was crudely set into one wall; it ran diagonally down over the medicine cabinet and disappeared into the corner. Leftover green tiles and grout littered the floor of the shower stall, and there was a disinfectant spray can on the toilet tank. I picked it up, squirted and sniffed; it smelled like canned bog gas. I could not reconcile all this with the story the manager had told me, and I was feeling uneasy, but I undressed anyhow and got into bed.

I dreamed I was in a huge bare room with tall windows in brown varnished frames. Outside, the sun glittered on fields of snow as far as I could see. There was snow on the window frames, and a little had drifted in over the sills. It was very cold in the room. There was nothing to wrap myself in, and nowhere else to go. In the dream, I felt melancholy because I knew I had risen into the remote future, and was the last man alive in the world.

I was awakened by a clattering sound. In the faint highway glow that came in around the window drapes, I saw a man carrying something bulky across the end of the room.

When he disappeared into the closet, I got up and switched on the bedside light. Almost immediately, the man emerged from the closet, blinked at me, and picked up another piece of the dismantled bed. "What are you doing?" I asked.

He said something indistinct and carried his burden towards the closet door. He disappeared inside with it, although I couldn't see how, and came out again a moment later. He was a short dark-haired man in striped overalls with a sort of motorman's cap on his head. "You wouldn't believe the mess in there," he said. "Come take a look."

I followed him to the closet, and he gestured towards the pipes that filled it, mostly vertical but some every which way. "Would you build a motel like this?" he said. "Come on, tell the truth. Would you?"

"No."

"Damn right you wouldn't, or me either. But I've got to lug this goddamn bed in there just the same, and do I get paid overtime? No. Out of the way."

He crowded past me and came back in a moment staggering under the footboard of the bed, the last piece. I stood back to give him room, and he disappeared into the closet with his burden. I looked in after him; he was gone. From somewhere in the darkness to my left I heard a thump and an exclamation; then nothing. I closed the door and went back to bed.

In the morning I looked into the closet, but it was not full of pipes and there was no sign of the bed. When I returned the key, I showed the manager the strip of paper I had removed from the toilet. "Can you tell me what this means?" I said.

He adjusted his spectacles to look at it. "Where did you get this?" he asked after a moment.

"It was on the seat in the bathroom."

"Oh no," he said. "Was it really? Oh no. This is not one of ours. It must be some kind of a joke. Now that's interesting. Wait just a minute." He disappeared through the doorway behind him and came back with a large dictionary, which he opened on the counter.

"Now this I *do* know," he said. "Logograph, that's a puzzle word. Not many people know that word, but I do. It means a word puzzle, something like an anagram or a palindrome. See right here?" He turned the dictionary around and showed me the entry, which I unfortunately could not read.

"But then," he said, "the end of it says 'griphon,' which might be the same as 'gryphon' with a *y*, you know, or 'griffin' with two *f*'s, and either way it's a kind of fabulous monster."

"Yes, I know what a gryphon is."

"It has the head and wings of an eagle, and the body of a lion."

"Yes."

"But I'd say there's even more to it than that, because if you look at the derivation, now, 'logograph' comes from the Greek *logos*, word, and *griphos*, a fishing basket."

"A word in a basket."

"Yes, or a fish in a basket. Or the Logos in a basket, either way, that's Our Lord Jesus Christ who made the sun and the stars. But it isn't just any basket, now, it's a *reed* basket, and that sounds like Moses, doesn't it? His mother laid him in a papyrus basket daubed with pitch and bitu-men, and left him among the reeds. I don't know why any-body would put that on a toilet seat, though." He watched me fold up the strip of paper and put it away. "Honestly, I don't know how that happened. I'll ask our maids, but I know they'll say they don't know a thing about it. Strange things happen sometimes, don't they?"

"Yes, they certainly do."

"Well, have a nice day. Enjoy your trip."

It was a cool, crisp morning. Tired old family cars with furniture roped on top and U-Hauls behind were streaming northward in a haze of blue exhaust, but we had the other lane to ourselves. I spent some time thinking about the odd manager of the motel and seeing his pale, astonished face whenever I closed my eyes. His was a strange occupation, gatekeeper to strangers who paid him every night to dream and go.

At a crossroad south of Albany we encountered DE-TOUR and ROAD CLOSED AHEAD signs and had to turn off onto secondary routes. For an hour or so we were able to work our way south by avoiding large towns; then a flash-ing light and a siren came up behind us, and I pulled over. A state trooper walked up and looked in the window. "Where are you headed, sir?"

"Potamos, P.A. It's my hometown." I realized as I spoke that it was the truth; I had always intended to stop off in Potamos, even though it would mean a delay in get-ting where I ought to be going.

"You live there?" the trooper asked. He had a serious beardless face.

"No, my family."

"Where are you coming from?"

"London."

"London, Connecticut?"

"No, England. Sorry."

He said, "This is a rented vehicle, is it not, sir?"

"Yes, it is."

"Where did you rent the vehicle?"

"Boston. Massachusetts."

"And where are you going when you leave Potamos, Pennsylvania?"

"Plymouth, Pennsylvania."

The trooper wrote something on a pad, tore off a pink slip and handed it to me. "Sir, you may proceed. Sign this and keep it on your dashboard for inspection. If you attempt to travel toward New York City, or in any direction not indicated on this declaration, you will be stopped, and your vehicle may be impounded. There may also be civil penalties. Have a nice day."

I thanked him and pulled out onto the blacktop again. In the rearview mirror I could see him standing in the sunlight beside his cruiser with its actinic flashers, watching us until we were out of sight.

Half an hour later we crossed the humming Matamoras bridge. We had gone only a mile or two into Pennsylvania when I saw that it was all different now, there was a new concrete highway that crossed the Delaware north of town, and I didn't see any of the old landmarks. I kept an eye out for the high school, but it was gone and there was a three-story hotel there in its place, stucco, absolutely inappropriate for the climate, with a red-tiled roof. I pulled off on the gravel, parked beside a white Cadillac and got out to have a look anyway, remembering where the school building used to be, and the football field and the tennis courts and the flagpole going *chink, chink* in the wind.

Not far off, a woman in a black suit was walking on the grass. She looked at me as if she thought she knew me but wasn't sure. I began to feel the same way, and I crossed the driveway towards her. "Nelson?" she said.

"Yes! Who are you?"

"I'm Karen Woodland—Karen Slayter. For goodness' sake." She came forward and hugged me—a sturdy body in a good foundation—then held me at arms' length. She smelled of verbena. "What in the *world* are you doing here?"

"Just passing through. You're looking good, Karen." It was true: she was a matron now, but she had aged well; there were lines of humor in her face, and her thick dark hair didn't look dyed.

"You're not here for the reunion, are you? That was last month."

"No, I didn't know about it. I had to come over un-expectedly."

"From England?"

"Yes."

"It's too bad—it was our forty-sixth reunion. We had fifty-eight people here, two from California and one from Maui. Tell you what, a few people are still hanging around. Let's go and see them—have you got the time?"

"Certainly, delighted."

She put her arm in mine. "You sound English your-self. Have you lived there that long?"

"Funny, my English friends say I sound American." We were walking towards the hotel entrance. "Karen, so you married Dick Woodland?"

"Yes, forty years ago, and we're still married. Three children, two grandchildren. What about you?"

"I was married, but not anymore." No one seemed to be about; we went into the large yellow-carpeted lobby and crossed it to a pair of double doors marked POWWOW ROOM. Karen pushed them open and I started to go in, but two swaying bodies intervened. They were men in dark suits; their polished black shoes didn't touch the floor, and their faces were grey, eyes rolled up, mouths hanging open.

"Don't mind them," Karen said. "Halloween, you know." She pushed by the cadavers and drew me after her. "There's Vic Hegarty," she said. "Oh, and Randy Spence."

These two seemed to be alive, at least, and I recognized them vaguely; they had been in my class, but I had never known them well. I was still trying to remember who the other two looked like.

Hegarty was the skinny pale one; he had milk blue eyes and ruffled almost-white hair. Spence was an un-healthy pink, too plump for his clothes. They were both smoking. Karen introduced me, and they transferred their cigarettes from right hands to left in order to shake hands. "Well, well," Hegarty said in a cracked voice. "All the way from England, huh?"

"That's right."

Spence showed me his yellow teeth. "Too bad you didn't get here for the reunion, Nels," he said. "We had one person from Maui and two from California."

"Is that so?"

"Our forty-sixth high school reunion," he said. "You never came to a damn one of them, did you?"

Karen took my arm and drew me away. "Nelson has to go now. He just stopped in to say hello." We brushed by the hanging corpses and went out into a dark room; somehow we had got into a cloakroom or something and missed the lobby.

A man stood up as we came in; he had been sitting at a little wooden table with some papers and an inkwell on it. "Nelson?" he said in a familiar scratchy voice. It was the superintendent, who had an office in the high school, Mr. Mapleton. We used to call him Marblenose.

When he came a little closer I could see that his face was clenched in anger. "I'm *surprised,*" he said.

"Surprised at what, Mr. Mapleton?"

"I'm surprised that you would show your face here." He waved a sheet of paper at me. "Do you know that this is a lie from start to finish? You never graduated from this school."

"Sure I did. Don't you remember?"

"Lies," he said. "Lies." He turned away and went back to his desk, but I didn't see him sit down. Karen stepped in front of me, held my arms, and looked at me sadly. "Don't feel badly about it," she said. "It was a long time ago."

Then I was alone in the room, and I couldn't see how

to get out except the way I had come in. I pushed through the door; the hanging corpses had gone now and the room was filled with folding chairs set haphazardly, and ashtrays full of stale butts.

Another vivid hallucination

I walked out and found the lobby. It was empty. Outside, Karen's car was gone, but as I stood on the gravel I heard her voice say, "It isn't real, you know."

"I suppose not." Near me on the lawn I could make out some sort of bronze plaque, half hidden by creeping weeds. As I stood there feeling the breeze chilling my ears, I heard the crunch of gravel underfoot, and when I turned around it was Eric Mulligan walking towards me, big as life, smiling his rueful smile.

"Bill, I had to stop and say a word to you," he said.

"You left us so suddenly," I said.

"I know. Believe me, I understand."

"What did you want to tell me, Eric?"

"Why, nothing at all. There's nothing to tell."

"And that's it?"

"That's it," he said with another rueful smile. "Goodbye, Bill." He turned and walked away, as he had at the funeral. My eyes were a bit moist, and when I blinked he was gone.

I knew that I must have had another vivid hallucination. How many of these episodes had I been through already? I felt the tender place in the middle of my forehead;

it seemed a little spongy, but wasn't painful. They had
changed my medicine in the hospital because it was giving
me hallucinations; could it be that those pills of Willie's
were having the same effect? Perhaps I ought to stop them;
there were only a few left anyhow.

I walked out to the highway and along the steep hard-
top a little way, looking for I didn't know what. I saw a
creeping dusty-green weed by the roadside; it had roundish
leaves like a miniature geranium, and little green buttons
that we used to eat when I was a kid; we called them
cheeses, but I never knew what the name of the plant was
until I noticed it in England and Jenny told me. I picked a
couple of the buttons and put them in my mouth; they were
crisp and chewy, with several aftertastes, first bland, then
spicy. I walked back to the car and got in, relieved to be
cradled in its plush support again. "Your name, please?" the
computer said.

"Wellington Stout," I replied.

"Welcome back, sir," said the computer. The motor
started when I turned the key, and we drove on majesti-
cally into town. The outskirts were cluttered with new construction, but some of the old landmarks were still here. We
passed the humble yellowstone building that had been the
courthouse in colonial times; later it was the county jail,
but it was boarded up now, apparently no longer used.
Across the street, an inn called the Jim Bunch commemo-
rated a famous frontier scalper of Indians.

Wandering alone one day in the hills above the town,
I had found the fieldstone foundation of a settler's cabin,
one small room, just the stones, the silence, the leaves on

the ground, the trees growing inside the magic rectangle, and the sunshine. I felt a presence there, but it was something too transparent to be seen or heard. Trees barred the old logging road, too, slender then; they must be thicker now.

I drove down to Patterson's Landing. It was chained off, with a PRIVATE—NO TRESPASSING sign, but I got out anyhow, stepped over the chain and walked down the graveled slope to have a look at the water. The grey river flowed easily and smoothly here; that hadn't changed, nor the bristle of branches like a stained toothbrush on the other side. A dog was barking frantically somewhere upstream. This was where people used to come for boating and swimming; down a little farther, I thought (but I wasn't sure), was where I had nearly drowned. Later, in my teens, I remembered wading into the cool water with snorkel and flippers, swimming out into the current and then lying there facedown, not seeming to move at all, surrounded by curious trout, until I fetched up at Balmer Point a mile and a half away.

Still later, down along the riverside, hunting with Mike Will the albino justice of the peace, I had watched a buck come out of the trees into the clearing where Mike had stationed me. I raised the shotgun and put a slug into its shoulder, watched the steam come out of its nostrils as it fell, not dead, its wild cow eye looking at me as I approached. I shot it again in pity and revulsion, saw it jerk, tremble and lie still, and Mike complained that I had spoiled too much meat.

I got into the car again, backed up the hill until I

could turn, and drove up to High Street. The business center was still two blocks long, but most of the signs were different. I stopped at Phil's Pharmacy, on the corner where Potamos Drugs used to be. The phone book hanging from a chain in the outdoor booth was pancake thin, but the phone was a Touch-Tone with a bright chrome front plate. I picked up the phone book and looked for familiar names. I found a Robert Woodland, but no Richard or Dick. There was no Hegarty or Spence. There was a George Swenson, who might have been a classmate of mine, but it's a common name. Then I saw Stout, Althea, and the address of our house. I thought it must be an old phone book, they had left it there by mistake, or else somebody had hung it up for a joke, but I put my thumb in it to mark the place and looked at the date on the cover: it was this year.

I went into the drugstore and found a dark-haired man in a white coat behind the counter; he reminded me a little of the waiter in the Flavo in Milan. "Yes, sir?"

"I was wondering, do you happen to know Mrs. Stout?"

"Mrs. Stout? Yes, she comes in here. Nice lady."

"Yes, but isn't she dead?"

"Dead? No." He backed away from the counter.

"But I went to her funeral."

"You must be mistaken." He picked up the phone and began to dial, looking at me nervously.

"Sorry," I said. "Sorry." I turned and went out, and walked down the hill past the library lawn, two blocks to Third, then east three blocks to Mary Street, scuffing through piles of papery brown leaves and smelling their sharpness. It was quiet along here, no lights in the windows and no smoke from the chimneys. No children were playing behind the picket fences.

Our house was still there, although newer ones shouldered close on either side. The porch needed paint; bare wood showed in places through the battleship gray. The porch ran the width of the house and was really a veranda, I suppose, although we never called it that. The white paint was peeling on posts and trim. A big pot with a dead plant in it stood beside the front door. Nobody had taken the screen door off yet, and there was a big tear in the top half of the screen. A yellow cat came around the corner, stopped and looked at me. I was thinking about the hours I had played on this porch; sometimes it was a galleon, sometimes a spaceship going to Mars. I climbed the two steps, crossed the porch, opened the screen, and twisted the brass handle of the doorbell. The *skringg, skringg* echoed inside.

After a while the door opened. She was taller and younger than when I had seen her last; there was a network of tiny wrinkles in her face that would make her an old lady before long, but the good bones were there and I could see, as I always could, that she had been beautiful as a girl. She wore a dark red dress and a crocheted blue shawl. "Yes?" she said, looking at me.

My throat had closed up and it was hard to talk. "I'm Welly, Mom. I've come back."

"Welly's in England. He's younger than you. You look

like him, though." After a moment she said, "Come in."

I followed her into the dark living room. There was one lamp at the end of the old maroon couch, next to the radio. Its little yellow light was on, although no sound was coming out. She turned on the floor lamp beside the rocking chair. "Sit there where I can see you," she said.

She settled down on the couch and looked at me. "Now let's see who you are, Mr. Wellington Stout. What's your middle name? No, that's too easy. What was your favorite toy when you were little?"

"It was really just a rolled-up napkin with a face drawn on it. Dad made it. I called it Jimmy."

She nodded. "I have to believe you are Wellington, then. But how can you come back—what does that mean?"

"I don't think I can explain it, Mom. I didn't think you'd be here, but I just came."

"Then I won't try to understand it. I'm glad you're here, whoever you are. Are you going to stay long?"

"I can't, Mom."

"All right. Shall I get you something to eat?"

"No, Mom, I'm not hungry. Let's just talk."

She smiled. "What shall we talk about? Are you a ghost or am I?"

"I don't know. How have you been, Mom?"

"Fairly well. I had the flu last month."

"It's so cold in here, Mom," I said.

"Yes, there's something wrong with the furnace, and Mr. Phillips can't come until tomorrow."

"Let me see if I can do anything."

"Better just leave it alone."

"No, maybe I can fix it."

"Take off your good coat, then. There's an old duster of Don's hanging on the door."

The yellow kitchen was warmer than the living room; the old wood-burning range was lit, and a kettle was steaming on the back. Two chairs were pulled up to the scarred wooden table with its blue-painted border. Two plates and a cup were in the drainer beside the sink. I opened the door in the corner, put the duster on, flicked the light switch and went down the steep wooden stairs.

The furnace was a coal-to-oil conversion, and it always had been cranky. I opened the door, pressed the red button, waited for ten minutes, then lit a wad of newspaper and threw it in. Nothing happened. I tried once more, then opened the fuse box and pulled out the little saber fuse. It looked okay, but I found another and replaced it. I pressed the button again.

While I was waiting, I glanced around the basement. There were garden tools stacked in one corner, a few shelves with flowerpots and glass jars, and an old brass-cornered steamer trunk that I didn't remember seeing before. When I lifted the lid, a puff of dust and mold came out. There were water stains around the edges of the yellow figured-silk lining, and spots of white mold here and there. The tray on top, lined with the same cloth as the trunk itself, was full of neatly folded handkerchiefs. I lifted it out in another puff of dust; underneath were packets of letters held together by faded ribbons. I was looking for my high school diploma, although I knew it couldn't be here, and I kept going through layers of old dance cards with little pencils attached, theater programs, ticket stubs and postcards of Niagara Falls.

Below these I found a layer of photographs, rich plain sepia or iron-colored tintypes, of people in absurd costumes, probably dating from the turn of the century. Their eyes gazed out soullessly; whatever thoughts had been in their heads, they had all evaporated into the ether by now.

The farther down in the stack I went, the more I noticed something troubling about the proportions of the figures. It was as if they were getting smaller, turning into gnomes or dwarves, while still dressed as normal people. Had people really been that much smaller then?

I climbed into the trunk in order to reach the next layer more conveniently, and found large yellowed envelopes full of canceled postage stamps. They were larger than modern stamps, some of them as big as the palm of my hand. Under them I found rolled diplomas, none of them mine, then school yearbooks. The dates on the covers were from 1905 to 1910.

I put them aside and uncovered crayon portraits and watercolors framed in passe-partout; then deeds and stock certificates of companies I had never heard of. Below them I found garnet jewelry and gold rings or bracelets, cameo brooches in ivory and coral, then Civil War notes as big as newspapers. Burrowing under these I found ruffled cloths of indeterminate use, then knapped flint projectile points large enough to slaughter mammoths. What light there was came from high overhead; I was covered in dirt and mold, but I dug deeper and found bits of paper half dissolved in the soil, some bearing huge single letters; then fragments of brittle brown armor not designed for human beings.

While I was examining these, I heard a distant sound and looked up. Far above, dim yellow light came from a rectangle that must have been the top of the open trunk. As I listened, the sound came again; then the light flickered and went out with a crash.

I groped forward in the dark and found myself in a tunnel barely big enough to hold me. I followed it for what seemed miles; eventually it turned upward and I climbed out into light and air. I was standing in the yard of my mother's house, beside a fresh molehill. The treetop sky was apple green. The house was dark, and I knew there was no one inside.

I felt dizzy and my head was buzzing, as if I had just wakened from an unhealthy sleep. I wanted to return to my car, with its enfolding upholstered seats and its comforting voice. I knew which way I had come, and I walked up side streets and alleys until I came to the garage beside the county library. Beyond the library lawn, across the street in the dusk in front of the lighted drugstore, a man in a brown suit stood looking at my car with a notebook in his hand.

There was nothing obviously sinister about him, and yet I felt a stab of fear. I stepped towards the wall of the garage where I was half hidden by rustling hollyhocks, and backed away slowly down the alley until I was out of sight.

I couldn't be sure whether or not there had been something familiar about the man's face. I went back to the cross alley, turned and walked behind the garage to the

back entrance of the library. Because of the slope, the
ground floor could be reached only by a black-painted flight
of stairs rising against the white clapboards of the building,
almost as tall as I was, then a narrow stoop and a tall shiny
black door with a lamp glimmering on a curled standard beside it.

I climbed the stairs. This door had always been locked
when I was young, but I tested it anyhow, felt it yield, and
slipped into the cool darkness of the back hall. No one was
there, and no sound came from the library room in front.
The hollow air was scented with dust and furniture polish.
I went along to the tall dark-varnished newel post of the
stairway, rounded it, and climbed slowly to the second
floor, trying not to make the stairs creak.

On the bare bowed boards of the landing, I tried to
look through the windows at the drugstore across the street,
but the glass was clouded by years of dust and vapors.

A narrow stairway led to another floor, or to the attic;
I had never been so high, but was sure I remembered that
there were windows up there too. I climbed the bare steps
to a door that opened on a curious narrow space, really
nothing more than a packing box on its side. I had to lie
down to get into it, and when the door closed behind me
in the spider-smelling enclosure, I could see a thread of light
above. I pushed open the coarse pine of the box far enough
to climb out. Someone took my arm and helped me over
the side, and I found myself in a long dim corridor full of
people I did not know. They looked at me incuriously as I
walked down towards a glow of light at the end. The light
came from two wide glazed doors, and when I opened them

and stepped out, I saw that I was on the porch of a building just above the sidewalk of a busy street.

When I walked to the curb and looked up at the
building I had just left, I saw the words U N A • A R R A •
A N U in gold letters over the entrance. Then someone jos-
tled me, and I moved along towards the corner.

The sun was low, casting a theatrical glare on walls
and windows. Near the avenue, sidewalks were crowded
with pedestrians. Many of them were crying children. Their
faces, in the strange light, looked hardly human; some were
wolflike, some porcine. There were lines outside restaurants
and fast-food places; other shops were closed, some boarded
up. One of these was a clothing shop with BACK TO SCHOOL
signs in the windows, which I thought a little odd, since we
were already in late October. Another, a barbershop, displayed a sign that read: GONE FISHING.

I found a row of phone booths with people waiting
outside them under a shelter. Metal-backed telephone
books hung in a frame beside the booths; I seized one and
turned it upright. It was the directory for Plymouth, Pennsylvania. Half dazed, I looked up the addresses of Diane
Downey and R. Sanchez. Sanchez was not listed, but the
sleepwear shop was on the avenue I had just come from,
and proved to be only a few blocks away. It was a rather
chic little shop, with a lot of maroon and green silks on display. At first I thought it was closed, but when I tried the
door it opened.

"Yes, sir, can I help you?" said a plump redheaded
young clerk. She was wearing a green silk blouse, a size too
small; I could read every lump on the hem of her bra.

I waited for the door to jingle shut behind me. "Yes, as a matter of fact. I'm looking for Rosemary Sanchez; I wonder if you could tell me where to find her."

"May I ask your name, sir?"

"Wellington Stout. We met in Italy."

"Just a moment." She went behind the little counter, dialed a phone, and after a moment began a low-voiced conversation, glancing over at me from time to time. Presently she beckoned and handed me the receiver.

"Hallo?" I said. "Ms. Sanchez?"

A woman's voice. *"Yes, hello?"*

I felt a sudden excitement at hearing her on the wire. Was it really her voice? I tried to remember what she looked like, couldn't. "Ms. Sanchez, it's Wellington Stout. I'm sorry to trouble you, but we met on the plane to Milan last month, and I gave you my card, I don't suppose you remember—"

"Yes, I do remember, Mr. Stout. I saw that card just yesterday, oddly enough."

"Oh, you still have it, then?"

"Well, not exactly. I sold them all to a collector—I had hundreds. Boxes and boxes full, I'd saved them for thirty years."

"Oh dear. I wonder if you could tell me the collector's name."

"Well, his name is Morris Gelb, but he's in Montana. May I ask what this is about?"

"It's terribly inconvenient, I know, but it seems there may have been some information on that card. If you could give me Mr. Gelb's address—"

"There wasn't anything written on the card."

"I know. It wasn't that kind of information. There may have been a microchip in the card, you see. The information isn't mine."

"*I see. How thrilling.*"

"I'd be very happy to offer Mr. Gelb another card in exchange, or several cards."

"*Look, I really haven't got time, but some of those boxes are still here. Yours might be among them, but I doubt it. If you'd like to come over and look around—*"

"That would be marvelous."

"*All right, then. Cherry will give you the address. Let me talk to her.*"

I offered the phone to the redhead, and she had a low-voiced conversation with Sanchez. She hung up. "You want to go to Rosemary's house?"

"Please."

"Well, you go out the door, turn right, right again at the corner and go seven blocks. Turn left and it's the gray house in the middle of the block on your right."

I found the address without trouble: it was a tall house, probably built in the early part of the century, square-shouldered and high-ceilinged but quite narrow, as if it had been part of a row of Victorian houses now all gone but this. Lilacs were rank in the yard, and dead hollyhocks stood beside the porch.

I went up the gravel walk, noticing a rag doll lying disconsolate in the grass, and climbed the creaking porch steps. I pushed the antique bell beside the door. I heard nothing, but after a few moments the door was opened by a short dark-skinned woman with black hair parted in the middle. She was wearing a flowered housedress and an old sweater; her ankles were swollen over the tops of her black shoes. "Yes?" she said.

"I'm here to see Ms. Sanchez. My name is Stout."

"Yes, Mr. Stout. Come in." She led me down a carpeted hall to a room whose single window was covered with a patterned cloth pinned to the window frame. "Wait here, please," she said, and went away, closing the door behind her.

I looked around. The room was cluttered with threadbare overstuffed furniture, maroon and green, almost black in the feeble glow of the sconces on the walls. In one corner was a sort of shrine, with a picture of the Virgin Mary in a gilt frame, and several little cups with candles in them.

There were religious pictures on the walls, too, and various bits of bric-a-brac on the end tables. One of them was a cylinder of glass, rather heavy, filled with paraffin wax. The bottom narrowed a bit, like the nozzle of a rocket. The wax took on a bluish tint from the decorative border that was printed on the glass, and it was full of air bubbles, big ones in the middle, little ones at both ends. A white plastic wick was stuck in the top. Cemented to the front of it was a picture of the Virgin Mary in flowing blue garments parted in front to reveal a red T-shirt, on which could be seen a flaming red heart encircled by white roses. The Virgin was pointing to these sternal aureoles with her right forefinger to make sure they were not overlooked. Around her were four angels each consisting of an Italian child's head and a dove's wings, and below her was a scroll reading *Immaculate Heart of Mary* together with a yellow

machine-readable label. On the other side was a prayer in
Spanish and English. The English part read:

OH, SACRED HEART OF MARY

REFUGE OF ALL SINNERS

OPEN THE DOOR TO YOUR HEART

AND RECEIVE

IN IT ALL THE SINNERS

AND INTERCEDE BEFORE GOD FOR THE

SALVATION OF OUR SOULS.

Up the side ran a warning, in English only, about
putting the candle too near inflammable objects such as
curtains. I was thinking about this in connection with the
tapered bottom of the tube when I heard someone come
into the room. I turned to see a slender little woman in a
white blouse, black bolero and skirt. Her dark hair was
drawn back; her lips and fingernails were bright red.

"You like my candle?"

I put it down. "Oh. Yes, very much. But you're not
Rosemary Sanchez, are you?"

"No, her sister Lola. Are you disappointed?"

"Certainly not, Miss Sanchez. Quite the contrary, in
fact."

"Call me Lolita, or Lola—I like that better. You want
to see Rosemary's cards, is that right?"

"Yes, if it wouldn't be too much trouble. My name is
Wellington, by the way, but my friends call me Bill."

"Yes, you look like a Bill. Come on." She led me out
into the hall and down a dark staircase. Halfway down

something happened that I didn't understand. She seemed to be gazing up at me, as if she had abruptly turned her head clean around like an owl's; then I was looking at her dark hair again. We emerged into a large basement, with partitions that did not quite reach the cobwebby ducts and pipes under the ceiling. I followed her into one of the rooms; it was lined with unpainted shelves and worktables from which scraps of black fabric were spilling over. Somewhat to my surprise, the room was dry; when I sniffed, I detected no damp or mildew, only wood shavings, glue, and burnt metal.

On the bare concrete floor were three large pasteboard boxes taped shut around the edges, with white address labels stuck to them. "These are what we have left," she said. "The others were mailed yesterday, but there wasn't room in the van. You can open them if you want." She took a large X-Acto knife from a shelf and handed it to me. "Be careful, it's sharp."

The floor was strewn with little grey nodules about the size of a pinhead; they crunched and scattered and were painful to my knees. I cut the first box open, noticing as I did so that it was addressed to Morris Gelb at a box number in Billings, Montana. I spread the top back. Inside was a layer of gray wadded paper; when I removed this, I saw ranks of cardboard trays containing business cards. They were packed tightly; it was hard to get a tray out, and I pricked my finger on something sharp before I managed it. I pulled up a card or two at random, then moved another tray and looked at a few of the cards in that one. "These are all Ts," I said.

"Yes. It says on the box what's in each one."

I hadn't noticed, but when I turned back the lid and looked, I saw that it was marked in the corner, "T–V." I looked at the other two boxes: they were marked "L–P" and "C–D."

"Then it's no good looking for 'Stout' or 'Weybright,' is it?"

"No, I'm afraid not."

"I'm very sorry." I dropped the knife and stood up creakily. "I've put you to all this trouble for nothing."

"It's perfectly all right, and I'm sorry we couldn't help you."

A thought occurred to me. "Didn't your sister keep any of her cards—just a few, for sentimental reasons?"

"I don't know. Maybe. She's in Two-Ply now, but she'll be leaving there tomorrow."

"I'm sorry, did you say 'Two-Ply'?"

"Plymouth, Indiana."

"And she'll be there until tomorrow?"

"Or early Monday, and then she's flying back to England."

"Thank you, you've been very kind." I put the X-Acto knife back on a shelf. She stood watching me. Her eyes were dark and knowing.

"Do you want to stay here tonight? You won't find a motel room anywhere."

"Well, if it wouldn't be an imposition—"

"Certainly not. There's a cot right here, and a little bathroom behind the stairs. Are you hungry?"

"No, not at all. I'll just settle in here, if that's all right."

"Sleep tight, then, and I'll see you in the morning."

I looked around the room. Apart from the tables and the cot, there was an upright chair in one corner, in front of a professional sewing machine. The scraps of fabric on the cutting tables were thin silk, and must have been hard to sew. I looked into the small pasteboard boxes at the back of one of the tables; they had notions in them, buttons, snaps and the like. One box was half full of glass eyes. I picked one out curiously: it was a doll's eye with a golden iris. As I held it, the pupil widened and turned to look at me.

I dropped the thing as if it were a poisonous insect, and heard it click and roll on the floor. My heart was thudding absurdly. After a few minutes I was able to nerve myself to turn off the light. I took off my shoes, pulled the blanket over me and slept.

I'm Dr. Peabody

I dreamed I was in a confined narrow space, lying on a cot surrounded by green drapes. A young man opened the drapes and said, "Hi, I'm Orderly Green, and I'm here to clean you up a little." He dipped a sponge into a basin and began to wash my naked body. When he squeezed the sponge, I saw that the water was red. As he was drying me with a scratchy towel, I said, "I wonder if I could have my clothes?"

"You want to get dressed? I don't see why not. Wait just a minute." He closed the drapes and went away. When he came back, he laid out my clothes on the cot and helped me sit up. I was very weak, and he had to help me on with every garment. When I was fully dressed, except for shoes, he helped me stand and supported me across the room, which was lined with large filing cabinets.

We went down a hall and into a small office where a man in a white coat was sitting behind the desk. He had straw-colored hair and a little mustache. "Well, hello!" he said. "I'm Dr. Peabody. I see you're feeling pretty well." He waved me to a chair.

"I'm not really, but things could be worse," I said.

"Of course they could!" He was looking at the screen of his computer, tapping keys occasionally. "Now, you've had a serious injury to the brain, Mr. Stout. We don't want to take any chances with that."

"I understand."

"Apparently most of the things that have been happening to you are hallucinations or delusions of one kind or another. Some are delusions, some hallucinations, except when it's the other way around. That's because of the movement of the bullet in your brain. It's still in there, you know."

"Yes, I know."

"*And,* it's going to be a little tricky, but it might be dangerous to wait any longer. I'm going to schedule you for dental surgery this afternoon, will that be all right?"

"No!" I said, and stood up. "I don't want any more surgery, I want to go home." The doctor, looking vexed, was pushing a button repeatedly. The orderly was nowhere in sight, and I tottered out into the hall. Several people in

green hospital blouses were there, and I thought I had better hide in a broom closet. I closed the door behind me, sat
down and went to sleep.

Sometime during the night I really woke up, turned
on the light and went to the bathroom under the stairs. I
was aroused much later by sounds coming from the next
room—clickings, and a noise like shoveling gravel.

I put my shoes on and went through the doorway. Lola
was there, standing in the middle of a small room hung
around with gray canvas like the inside of a pantechnicon.
Wearing a sort of pinafore over a blue cotton dress, she was
doing something with a scoop in a large brown paper bag.
Behind her, filling one wall, was a cage of welded metal
bars, and behind that was a giant mouse. I had to look up
to see its eyes. They were as big as my head. It was a brown
field mouse with pink naked feet like a pigeon's. Its moist
nose quivered at us, and it nipped the bars with foot-long
yellow teeth.

"Where did you get *that?*" I said.

"My mother used to breed them. Diggy is the last one,
poor thing. They're a lot of trouble and expense."

"I can imagine. Does he have space to run?"

"She. Yes, she has a tunnel, but she's love-starved, and
of course she can't mate with normal mice."

"That's rather tragic."

"It is, isn't it? Do you think it would be kinder to put
her to sleep?"

"I can't say, but does the Academy of Science know
about this?"

"No, we've always kept it quiet—we don't want any

publicity. You won't tell anyone, will you?"

"No—no, if you'd rather not."

"That's a good boy. Let's see if you're telling the truth." She came close to me and pulled my head down. Her eyes came so near mine that I could see the yellow and green streaks in her brown irises. The pupils seemed to contract, but the irises kept on expanding until they merged into one great eye the size of a small planet, over which I was helplessly adrift.

Then I went somewhere far away, and when I came back to myself I was sitting on a box with my head down. Her warm palm was on my forehead, and I could smell her scent, partly orrisroot and partly sweat. "All right now?" her voice said.

I straightened up, feeling a little dizzy and disoriented. "I think so."

"Stand up and see."

I obeyed her, and after a moment I really did feel all right. She said, "You didn't tell the truth, you know, but I'm going to let you go anyhow, just because of how much I like you. Don't abuse my confidence, though."

"I won't."

"It's a good thing you said that. Do you know how lucky you are?"

"I do, Lola."

"No, you don't, but you will. Go this way, it's shorter." She drew a section of the canvas aside, revealing a little door. I tried the handle; the door opened into a dim hall. "Thank you again," I said.

She smiled. "Oh, it's nothing at all."

She closed the door behind me, and I saw that I was in an earthen tunnel rather than a hall; the ceiling was lost in darkness, but the shape of the excavation seemed to be oval, like that of an egg standing on end. The curving walls were of earth packed around roots and pebbles. There were no timbers or posts; it was like a tunnel dug by an animal rather than one made by man.

The light came from little brownish yellow bulbs strung at intervals on the floor. There was a smell of damp earth and mouse. My scalp was prickling. I tried the door handle, but it wouldn't turn; I knocked and no one answered.

I stood a moment listening to silence, then shouted, "Ms. Sanchez! This isn't amusing!"

There was no reply, not a sound, and I had the feeling that the room on the other side was empty.

I set off to the right at a pretty brisk pace and walked for some distance before I heard a sound behind me in the darkness. I paused to listen. It was like the sound of two men running in felt snowshoes, and with it was an urgent grunting noise. I understood at once what it meant: the mouse knew I was here.

I ran for all I was worth, ran until my heart broke, but the thing was after me like a freight train. The string of lights ended abruptly and I was running into the darkness. I ran until I felt a hot breath of decay and heard a moist snuffling noise just behind me; then I tripped over something, fell downhill and hit my head a sickening crack against a stone.

I got to my feet and fell again because the ground

was not level; I was on a slope in the midst of damp brush
and trees. I could hear a heavy body crashing through the
undergrowth somewhere above me, and I got up and ran.
I don't know how many times I fell. After a while I realized
that the sounds of the beast were more distant, but I kept
on going through the wet blackness; I was afraid to stop.
The land led me down and up again, sometimes so steeply
that I had to climb holding onto the slippery trunks of
young trees.

Eventually I found a deep ravine that led me downwards to a little brook, and as the sky lightened and I could
see again, I followed the stream hoping it would lead me
to some inhabited place. Near the bank I saw two ivory
buttons lying on the moss; I was surprised to find them
at this elevation. The box in my pocket was muttering
and sputtering occasionally, like a radio tuned to a police
channel.

The stream was a pretty little thing, the color of ice
water and just as cold, swirling and gurgling as it fell over
brown rocks between ferns and moss. The sharp curving
edges of the ripples glimmered like rinds of clear glass. I lost
my balance, fell in, and climbed out again with my shoes
full of water.

As soon as I could find a place to sit on a fallen tree,
I took the shoes off to empty them out. It crossed my mind
that they might be the ones the Spaeth people had put
locator devices in, but I was too cold to worry about it
now. I put the shoes back on, although they were still
wet.

I heard voices through the trees, went in that direction and came upon a little roadside rest area with a single green-painted picnic table on a slab of concrete. A mulberry-colored sedan was parked in the shade, with canvas bundles on top. A white-faced old couple, sitting at the table with a thermos flask and a cooler between them, watched me with suspicion as I came limping and squelching towards them. They both had cheeks pouched like chipmunks', and wore straw fisherman's hats with grommeted airholes in the sides.

Realizing how odd I must appear, I approached them bowing and nodding. "Pardon me," I said, "I wonder if you could tell me how far it is to Plymouth?"

The man put his hand on the thermos flask and scowled. After a moment he said, "Pierceton, you mean. It ain't far. We just passed it, didn't we, Mama?"

"About five miles back."

I said, "No, I'm sorry, I meant Plymouth, Pennsylvania." I would have liked to sit down and smell the coffee, but the couple looked so dour that I hung back, feeling like a petitioner or a runaway slave.

"This ain't Pennsylvania." The man took the plastic cup from his wife and screwed it onto the thermos flask.

"I beg your pardon, I think I must be lost. Where are we, exactly?"

The man said to his wife, "Put that cooler in the car, Mama."

She opened her mouth, showing two rows of perfect teeth, then shut it again and picked up the cooler by the handles. It was a metal cooler, tangerine-colored with a white top. She hefted it with some difficulty—it looked quite heavy—carried it to the car, set it down, opened the back door and slung the cooler in.

"Get in the car, Mama," the man said. He stood up, gripping the thermos flask, and backed away.

"I don't suppose you could give me a lift to the nearest town?" I said desperately.

"No room." He followed his wife into the car, slammed the door. The motor started in a moment; the car backed rapidly, turned, ran down to the highway, turned again and was out of sight in a moment. I heard a faint backfire, then nothing.

It was early in the day, the air was warming a little but not much, and everything was perfectly still; I was all alone in God knows where. My head was aching ferociously. I felt myself over: there was a new lump high on my forehead, and the bullet wound below it seemed tenderer than before. My clothes were muddy and torn, my pockets ripped, and my wallet was gone; I must have lost it in the woods.

On the picnic table the old couple had left a waxed paper with a few crumbs in it. Someone had carved in the tabletop in inch-tall letters the word S U C K E R. The radio in my pocket said distinctly, *"Can you hear"*—sputter— *"freezing rain, urk."*

In the trashbin at the edge of the apron I noticed a discarded newspaper, wings spread like a dead gull's among the orange rinds and sandwich wrappers. I rescued it and looked at the dateline: it was the *Fort Wayne News-Sentinel,* and the date was Friday, Oct. 29.

I knew that couldn't be right. It had been Saturday

the twenty-third when I left London, still Saturday when I arrived in Boston; I had slept one night in Sanchez's basement, and therefore this ought to be Sunday the twenty-fourth. Moreover, if I was anywhere near Fort Wayne, I must have traveled some three or four hundred miles during the night, which was clearly impossible.

I had lost a day once or twice before, but this was nearer a week. I considered that I was justified in feeling alarmed. On the other hand, if this was Indiana, at least I was in the right state.

I carried the newspaper with me down to the verge of the blacktop and sat with it on the grass while I took off my shoes and socks. The banner headline on the front page said ALIEN TROOPS EXIT CRATERS. There was a blurry picture of men with weapons moving through a cloud of dust, and a vignette of two craters seen from above. They were terraced craters and looked deep, although it was hard to tell because of the want of scale.

The story began, "Armed soldiers were seen advancing westward from the crater in Arizona's Painted Desert Thursday, sources said. Six new craters rimmed out in Arizona and New Mexico on Wednesday and Thursday, bringing the total to forty-three. A Department of Defense spokesperson said, 'We are watching developments closely and will respond at the appropriate time.' "

I looked through the rest of the paper but didn't see anything about problems with the calendar. Was the rest of the world going along from one day to the next as usual—was I the only one out of step?

An old Ford pickup came into view; the driver was a

dour-looking man in his fifties. I stood up and showed him my thumb, but he went on by without a glance. When half an hour had passed without any further traffic, I put my shoes in my pockets and spread the socks on my shoulders to dry. The old couple had turned right, and they had said there was a town five miles back the way they had come; therefore I turned left and began trudging barefoot down the road.

I had forgotten how long it took a man on foot to get from point A to point B. The sun was noticeably higher when I reached a bend in the road that would have been less than a minute away by car. The next bend was also a good distance away, but there was a footpath in the brush that seemed to cut off a loop. I headed that way, and after a few minutes I saw a pale flag of fire through the trees.

It was a campfire in a clearing, and beside it sat the little Irishman, Martin Gallagher, roasting a frankfurter on a stick. He was neat and clean in a pink shirt and brown gabardine suit, but was unshaven and wore no necktie.

He looked up with a grin. "Top of the morning to you."

"What are you doing here?" I said.

"Waiting for you, to be sure. Come and take a seat, there's nothing to fear." He had an open knapsack beside him, and other things strewn around within reach: a paper plate with blackened hot dogs on it, a package of buns, a pot of mustard, a canteen.

I sat down half unwillingly, and he passed over the dog on the stick. "Have this, it's the hottest. Mind your fingers."

"Gallagher, what do you want?"

"Only a bit of talk between friends. Are you thirsty at all?"

"Yes, I am."

"Here, then." He passed me the canteen, and I drank. It was water, cold and very good. I took a bite of the hot dog; that was good too. Gallagher seemed to know that I wouldn't want the buns or mustard. He leaned back with his hands clasped on his knee, the picture of comfort, and watched with a smile as I ate.

I said with my mouth full, "You wanted to talk. What about?"

"One thing and another, cabbages and kings. To begin with, do you have any idea in the world what's happening to you?"

"No."

"I thought not. Do you sometimes wonder if you've lost your wits?"

"Sometimes."

"Let me tell you that you're no crazier than meself. Man dear, that bullet in your brain has given you a glimpse or two of the real world. You can't see the whole of it, of course, and it would drive you mad if you could, but what you're seeing would make you a dangerous man if only you understood it."

"It doesn't make sense."

"All the better; it's why they haven't killed you yet. Take my advice and don't try to make sense of it."

"But what can I do? What's going to happen now?"

"Now? You're going to have a ride into town and go

to Diane Downey, and find that Rosemary Sanchez has left a little something for you. And then we'll meet again."

"How do you know all that?"

"Why, because we're brothers under the skin. Did you think we weren't?" He got up and dusted off his clothes. He walked around me, and when I turned my head he was nowhere to be seen, although I stood up and revolved in a circle. I listened, but there wasn't a sound anywhere.

I thought I might as well make the best of it, and I used Gallagher's stick to hold my socks to his little fire. When they were dry and warm I put them on again, and my shoes too although they were damp still.

I poured water on the fire and shoveled dirt on it with a paper plate. I wanted to bury the plates and so on, including all five hot dogs he had left behind, but had no tools for that, and I put them in the knapsack instead. In doing so, I discovered four five-dollar bills lying in the bottom of the knapsack: just what the pound I had given him was worth. Was it because the gift had been so niggardly that he was reminding me of it in this way? I put the bills in my pocket and followed the path until it joined the highway again.

When I had been walking on the blacktop for ten minutes or so a car came around a curve from behind, passed me and stopped on the shoulder; it was a white Chrysler with West Virginia plates, and had two people in it. The driver was leaning out the window. "Where you headed, partner?" he called.

"Plymouth!" I said.

"No problem." He reached back through the window and opened the rear door for me. "Move them magazines, make yourself a place to set."

The backseat was so narrow and crowded that I had trouble getting in. I tried to rearrange the clutter while the driver took off, but there was so much of it that I ended up draped like an odalisque over a pile of suitcases.

The driver was a brown-haired man of about thirty in a yellow nylon jacket; the woman was a little younger and had permed auburn hair. "This is very kind," I said. "About how far is Plymouth, can you tell me?"

The woman said, "Can't be more than thirty miles, can it, hon?"

"Naw. We'll have you there in no time. I'm Bob Fallon and this here is Linda Joy. Fall in the creek, did you?"

"Something like that."

"Look like you was sleeping in the woods, too. Got leaves stuck to you. No business of mine, though."

"Ah, thank you," I said. I brushed at my hair and clothing, and found a few wet leaves. "I was lost in the woods overnight, in fact."

"How that happen? No business of mine, don't tell me if you don't want to."

"Hon," said the woman.

"Well, I said he don't have to tell me, didn't I?"

"I'm afraid it's too long a story," I said.

"That right? Say, what do you think about these space aliens? That weird, or what?"

"It is, yes."

"What you say your name was?"

"Wellington Stout."

"You a foreigner?"

"Not really, but I've been living in England."

"That right? What do you think of this country?"

"I was born here."

We chatted in this way until the outskirts of a medium-size town came into view. "Whereabouts you want to go in Plymouth?" asked the driver.

"Actually I'm looking for a shop called Diane Downey Fashions."

"It's on the avenue, hon," said the woman.

"Sure, I know where it is. No problem."

When he turned his head, I saw that he was a different man. His skin was olive and his hair black and straight. "Mr. Stout," he said in a new voice, "you know that the bullet in your head is making some trouble."

I said something, I don't know what.

"It's better if you go to a hospital and ask them to make X rays and perhaps CAT scans or other tests."

"Doctor—," I said. My throat was dry. "I don't know your name."

He was turning to watch the road, turning again to talk to me. His wife didn't seem to notice anything amiss. "My name is Dr. Parravicini. We were not introduced."

"Are you my doctor in Milan?"

"Yes, but not now. I came to tell you that you are in danger because of your head."

"But how can you be here, driving this car?"

He smiled charmingly and shrugged. "I don't know."

"Stop the car, I want to get out."

When he turned around, he was Fallon again. "How's that? We almost there."

"Let him out, hon."

He pulled over and double-parked, grumbling, "Damn fool."

Something I didn't like

As I watched the Chrysler pull out into traffic, it seemed to me that I had had a definitive kind of shock. Until now I had been able to believe that Roger was really there on the airplane and Gallagher at the airport, but the Italian doctor could not possibly have been in the driver's seat of that car. Therefore I was having full-fledged hallucinations and should probably be taking advice from a psychiatrist.

What shook me was that I absolutely had not been able to tell the difference between the real and the imaginary. What had Gallagher meant by saying that I was having glimpses of the real universe? "Real" in what sense? Was Gallagher himself real or imaginary, in that sense or any other?

I felt in my pocket for the four bills I had found in his knapsack. If I was able to spend them, would that prove they were real?

These speculations were driving me towards something I didn't like to think of, and I made myself pay more attention to the street I was walking on. This looked to be a run-down section of a once-prosperous small city: everything was slightly shabby, vaguely out of plumb, not quite conspicuously in need of repair.

It reminded me a little of Stroudsburg, Pennsylvania, when I was a child: wooden marquees cast a gloom on this side of the street, and red gum machines stood like Martian children in front of the corner buildings. The people I passed on the sidewalks were decently dressed for the most part, but they didn't give me a wide berth, as I thought they might have done in a more prosperous part of town.

I came to a sleepwear shop, and didn't realize for a moment that I had found Diane Downey Fashions, it looked so different from the other one. The display windows were set in wooden frames whose yellow paint was peeling; the robes and pajamas in the windows looked not only unfashionable but threadbare.

A bell jangled when I walked in. "Yes, sir?" said a middle-aged clerk behind the counter. She wore a shapeless wine-colored dress with a lace collar. Her expression was disapproving.

"I'm looking for Rosemary Sanchez," I said without much hope. "I don't suppose she's here?"

"Your name, sir?"

"Wellington Stout."

"Oh, Mr. Stout. Rosemary isn't here, but she left something for you." My heart jumped. "Just a minute." She rummaged in the shelf under the counter. I noticed the little greyish fuff of mustache across her upper lip, almost invisible but not quite. Something you had to overlook. Why not shave it the way they did their legs? Afraid of coarsening the stubble, maybe. It would have to be freshly shaven all the time, or you'd feel the bristles when you kissed them. Women feel men's bristles, say they like it. That's hard to imagine. Women's body hair is always a problem, like the giantesses in *Gulliver's Travels*, hair, pores, emblems of disgust.

I've thought it over many times, and I wouldn't be a woman for anything. Never mind all the mess and gore, the fussing with underwear and makeup, the second-class citizenship, pregnancy, PMS and all that, a woman's fate rests largely on her looks when young, and for every pretty girl there are a thousand unattractive women grimly getting along.

She had found something and was looking at it, front and back. "Yes, here it is," she said, and handed me a sealed white envelope with my name written on it.

"Thank you very much. Pardon me." I ripped open the envelope and found a business card inside. It looked like mine at first glance, but the typeface was wrong and the card stock was of poor quality. The y was missing from "Weybright."

I was elated, then stunned. "Is this all?" I asked.

"All she left you? Yes, sir."

"Where has she gone, do you know?"

"Well, I think she's gone out West. She didn't really say."

The door jangled, a woman came in, and the clerk turned to her. After a moment I left the store and stood on the sidewalk with the card in my hand, staring at it in disbelief. The thing was a crude forgery. I turned it over and saw that something was written in pencil:

Okra dokra, smart-ass

Whatever I had been expecting, it wasn't this. Rosemary Sanchez had eluded me again, and I was stranded in the arse-end of Indiana—without any money except the twenty dollars Gallagher had left me, without credit cards, phone cards or any ID.

The only thing I could think of was to call Tom in New York and ask for money. It would be the worst sort of humiliation, Tom would love it after the way I had talked to him, but I couldn't see any other way.

I went into a drugstore and asked for change of a five. The clerk, a pasty young man with hair over his forehead, did not look directly at me; he took the money and put four dollar bills and three quarters on the counter.

"Four," I said.

Without speaking, he added another quarter. I took them and went to the old-fashioned wooden phone booth near the entrance, but a man in a trench coat, just leaving, had hung a sign on it: OUT OF ORDER.

I went looking for another phone. I had not walked half a block when someone behind me said in a familiar voice, "Just a moment."

As I turned, three men crowded close and held my arms. I felt a hand pulling open my shirt above the belt, and next moment something oleaginous and dull slid into my belly. I saw what it was: a transparent hose was swaying down in front of my face, barely visible in the sunlight, but I could see it pulsing while vague corpuscles swam up it, and every time it twitched, I could feel it move a little in my gut.

The three men stepped back; two of them were strangers, and the third was the little Irishman. The jolt had knocked the breath out of me, but I managed to say, "Gallagher—why?"

"I did warn you," he said. "Did I not?"

"Yes, but. I'll go to Montana. I'll find the card for you."

"Indeed." He smiled at me, and all three of them walked away without looking back.

The tube was tugging me in the opposite direction, and I took a step to ease the pain, then another. In a moment I was walking down the street, past people who didn't seem to notice anything odd about me. The tube was almost invisible in the sunlight, but it was perfectly solid to the touch. I tried to get hold of it to pull it out, but it was hard and slippery. I saw now that it was drawing me towards an antique Checker cab that was discharging passengers at the curb. A woman with a fox fur round her neck was about to get in. I moved ahead of her in spite of myself and sat down in the far corner. The tube went through the roof of the cab without any resistance. The woman climbed in and closed the door.

"Where to, ma'am?" asked the driver. He was a pasty-faced man in a leather cap.

"The railroad depot, please."

The driver pulled out into traffic. "There's nobody back there," he remarked after a while.

"Well, that's right," the woman said. She did not look

at me. After about ten minutes we pulled in to the curb at a railway station, one of those low hip-roofed red-brick buildings that you see everywhere in the U.S. While she was paying the driver and getting out one side, I got out the other and the tube pulled me into the building.

Whether it was the irritation of the tube in my belly or not I don't know, but I had a sudden fierce need to urinate. I went towards the sign that said MEN, and after a moment the tube relaxed and let me do it.

By instinct I went into one of the stalls, although none of the men in the room gave me a glance. Once I got in, I saw that it was lacking one partition, and in the space beyond it three little men in grey overalls were watching me as I took down my trousers and sat on the commode. I wondered at the time why I was behaving in this way, but it was the sort of thing where you start to do something and don't like to stop.

But when I was well settled and pissing away, the three men came into the stall. I saw now that they were dwarves, the kind with large heads and very short arms and legs. They wore heavy work boots with lifts, more like pattens or orthopedic shoes, one much higher than the other. Their belts bristled with tool handles. Their broad faces were all alike, as if they had come from the same egg; they had bulbous noses and pale blue eyes. They pressed close around me, and I could hear the breath whistle in their hairy nostrils. Two of them began stripping off my jacket and shirt; another knelt before me with what looked like hedge clippers and began to cut the tube where it went into my body.

"This may hurt," he said. There was an explosion of

pink light and a sharp pain in my abdomen. The end of the tube was thrashing around overhead emitting a loud hiss.

"Don't do a thing to that, it will heal on its own. Keep it from air." He pulled off my trousers and underwear and stuffed them into a canvas sack, then my shoes and socks. The others had done the same with my upper garments, and I was naked as a baby. Now they were dressing me again. They worked without speaking and very quickly, as if they had been drilled, and they did not smile. The one in front of me was pulling trousers up over my legs. He put socks on my feet, then oxfords that almost fitted. The others were unzipping bags, hauling equipment out, putting it away again and zipping up, all in silence except for their breathing.

"What is this all about?" I asked.

One of them answered, "If you can stay out of their range for three or four days, they may lose you for good. Take care when you cross a stream."

"A stream? Why?"

"They're smart. They can stand at the mouth of a stream and spot you miles off."

"But what do they want? What do *you* want?"

"They want to freeze the Earth. They come from an ice world; you don't know the name of it. Go west."

One of the others handed me a suitcase that looked a good deal like my old one. "Take this bag. We put some clothes in it, things you'll need. Good luck."

"I don't know what to say."

One of them looked up at me with a scowl. "Don't thank us. It's our *job*."

They took my arms and we ballooned suddenly five times as big as the room. Looking down, I could see what looked like my own body seated on the commode, and the tube above it, but we were drifting away like blimps through the transparent station. Then somehow we were in another space full of low-hanging oily pipes and the sound of machinery. The air smelt thin, as if we were very high. I had to stoop to avoid banging my head on the pipes. The little men, who could stand comfortably, led me to a curved aluminum wall, slid a door open and pushed me into a space like a tiny elevator. The door closed and I felt a slight momentary pressure on my feet.

When the door opened again, I stepped out into what looked for all the world like the central part of a revolving restaurant, with seats and small tables arranged under the big tilted windows around the rim, a serving station, dumb-waiter and elevator in the center. The decor was Victorian, with red plush, wrought iron, and lots of mirrors.

Three men were sitting at one of the tables directly in front of me. "Ah, Mr. Stout," one of them said. "Please come and sit down, make yourself comfortable. Mind your step."

I looked down and saw that the circular part of the floor I stood on was turning very slowly with respect to the rest of the room. When I stepped over the line I felt a sort of fuzzy jolt in my abdomen, as if I had crossed from one electrical field to another. I didn't like it, but it was done now; I walked to the table and sat down. The three men smiled cordially at me. Two were in well-preserved middle age, the third a little older; they all had brown wind-creased faces, like outdoorsmen or golfers. They were dressed in comfortable-looking casual clothing of a cut and weave I had never seen before, and they all wore inconspicuous jewelry.

"Since you know my name," I said, "would you mind telling me yours?"

"I'm afraid we don't have names of the usual kind," replied the one who had spoken before, "but you may call us Smith"—he pointed to his chest—"Brown, and Jones." The other two nodded and smiled, and I sat back in my chair feeling relaxed and welcome, but rather puzzled. I saw now that the room was not revolving, as I had supposed, but was drifting forward above a desolate landscape while the wall of tilted picture windows revolved very slowly.

"You probably want to know," said Brown, "what you are doing here. We'd like to know the same, wouldn't we, gentlemen?" They all laughed, and I laughed too, although I couldn't quite see the joke.

"The fact is," Brown said, "we happened to notice that there was a null period when we could bring you up here as easily as not—it won't make any difference later, of course. In a virtual sense, we are cruising at two thousand feet over what used to be the state of Indiana."

"Indiana?" I said. The landscape below was a brown wasteland, like a giant strip mine. In the distance I saw what looked like two or three tornadoes swaying above the surface.

"Yes, this sector was almost totally destroyed. The Engineers didn't skimp hereabouts, would you say, gentlemen?" There were murmurs of agreement.

"I don't think I understand," I said. "I've just come from Indiana, and it wasn't like this."

"Of course not," Jones answered. He was the oldest and hairiest one; grey bristles sprouted in the folds of his cheeks and in his nostrils. "Of course not, but it will be. Yes, yes, it will be."

"Let's have something to drink, shall we?" said Smith. A mechanical-looking waiter rolled over. It was dressed like a musical-comedy bellboy, in a red uniform with a great many brass buttons and a little pillbox cap held on by a chin strap. Its face was that of a Disney puppet, with a round spot of rouge painted on either cheek. "Yes, gentlemen?" Its voice was tinny.

"You first," said Smith with a slight bow to me.

"Something cool," I said. "A kümmel collins, perhaps."

"What a capital idea!" said Smith. "We'll have the same. And some of those little snacks, Carl."

"Excellency," said the waiter; it bowed and went away.

"You see, Mr. Stout," said Smith, "this little planet of yours is of interest to several galactic powers. There was a friendly contest, and the winners are in the process of adapting the planet to their requirements. It's nothing personal, I assure you."

I opened my mouth to reply, but just then the waiter appeared with four drinks on a tray. They were in tall stemmed glasses, sweating cool, each with a maraschino cherry and a slice of orange. The waiter put the glasses down before us on little doily napkins, and gave each of us a blue ceramic dish piled with nuts and crisp sugar biscuits.

"When did this happen?" I asked.

"Oh, it hasn't happened yet."

"It may, though," Jones put in.

"Can I do anything to prevent it?"

They looked at each other. "Well, that's a fair question," said Smith. "Isn't it?"

"And we have to answer?"

"I'd say so." To me he said, "Excuse us a minute." They leaned their heads together, and a grey fuzzy screen appeared between their faces and me. I could see their heads dimly, and for a moment I thought I could make out tentacles waving between them, like the conjugation of snails or slugs.

The screen disappeared, and Smith said, "Well, Mr. Stout, we agree that we owe you an answer, although not a complete one. So I'll tell you this much: The devastation that you see here will be caused by a coalition of forces that hasn't come into being yet. If you wanted to prevent this version of reality, you'd have to keep that coalition from forming. Is that satisfactory?"

"A coalition of what forces?"

"You don't know their names." Jones leaned over to whisper to him. Smith frowned as he listened, then said, "All right, you do know one name for each of them. They are the Spaeth People and the Mongoids."

"Not the Dentists?"

He frowned again. "No," he said. "But I've told you too much, and that's all I'm going to tell you. Forgive us if we seem inhospitable, Mr. Stout, but this interview is now concluded." He nodded to the waiter, who bowed and conducted me to the elevator. The door closed behind me. When it opened again, I was in the oil-smelling lower space where the little men were gathered around a glass-topped table. Over their shoulders I could see what looked like a deserted road far below. A yellow dot in the center of the table was moving against the highway; then it stopped, and a bell rang.

"Wait a mo," said one of the little men. The yellow dot went out. "Now then." They hustled me over to the open end of a tube that seemed to be made up of metal rings, or else of a spiral like a Slinky; light glared from it in radial patterns. The little men pushed me into the tube and around a right-angle bend like an elbow; there was a sense of strong resistance and of a kind of shrinking, although the size of the tube did not seem to change. Then we were out into a space just like the other one, except that there was a round trap in the floor, and before I could protest we had all tumbled through it together. When I looked up I could see what looked like a vast beige Frisbee. Then the disk was receding into the high clouds and the Earth rose around us like a catcher's mitt.

The old Chevy

I had the distinct impression that I was sliding down a sort of nebulous funnel, being squeezed smaller and smaller as I went; then I landed, and when my head cleared I found myself behind the wheel of a car, not the Buick but a much older one. The car with its engine running quietly was parked at the side of a country road with cornfields on either side, an unnecessary silo on the horizon. The windows were open; the air was fresh and cool. I didn't know where I was or how I had got there. The dashboard in front of me had only a few dials on it, and the steering wheel was oddly narrow. It reminded me of the old Chevy Art Fleishman drove, that summer he took me around his territory, and in fact there was an order book on the seat beside me. I picked it up and looked at it. On the first page was written:

> Don't wait for me. Good luck.
>
> Art

His presence was so strong that I could almost see him, tall and scrawny in his three-piece black pinstripe. Thin hair carefully combed over the top of his head, a whiff of Bugler tobacco, Carstairs and Sen-Sen. Watery blue eyes with a humorous glint in them. "Billy boy, never trust a woman," he used to say. I hadn't thought of him in years.

I got out and stood looking across the cornfields. The car was Art's dark green Chevy, all right, well kept but dusty now. The leather suitcase in the backseat looked like mine. Tom had lent me the money to buy that suitcase before I got my first paycheck. "Art?" I called, and listened. I couldn't hear anything but the leaves of corn clattering faintly together. "Art?" He was gone.

I got back in, started the car and pulled out onto the road. The Chevy was a stick shift, hard to get into second gear. I drove slowly, looking and listening, then as the miles passed by I speeded up. I came to a road sign, the old-fashioned kind with a white arrow-shaped marker,

GROVERTOWN 23 MI. Now I knew where I was; this was the edge of my old territory. The first store Art ever took me to was in Grovertown: Miss Fannie's Foundations, Maude W. Hainline, Prop. A wonderful old woman, smoked cigars when she was with friends, liked her schnapps. She had written some kind of corset memoir that she told me I wasn't old enough to read.

It was about eight or nine in the morning, I judged, but there was no traffic on the highway and no signs of life around the houses I occasionally glimpsed across the fields. The highway was a two-lane, even when I got close to Gary, and it was deserted. I followed it north and began to see cars parked on the streets and in driveways, but not a single one in motion. They were all fifties models or earlier, too, and this potholed road was nothing like a modern highway.

I stopped the car in the middle of the road and got out to listen. There was not a sound except for birdcalls, not even a dog barking. I didn't dare turn off the motor in order to hear better; I was afraid I wouldn't be able to start it again. I was afraid of being stranded in a world where no other human being was alive.

I got back in the car and kept going north through East Chicago and then along Indianapolis Boulevard. Some of the shops looked open, but they were all empty. I couldn't see the Sears Building anywhere. The expressway was gone, and I got lost for a few blocks before I found Elston Avenue sidling off to the northwest.

I wanted to get out of Chicago very badly, and I ran on through Mount Prospect and Palatine under a cloudy sky. By midday I was passing through the outskirts of Madison, Wisconsin, south of the two lakes they have there, and it was just the same—empty streets, vacant shops. I kept heading northwest, and in late afternoon, when sleet was beginning to spit out of the sky, I crossed the Mississippi at La Crosse.

Once I got on the far side of the bridge, the wind and sleet had risen so that I could barely see the road. I pulled in under a sign that said LA CRESCENT TOURIST COURT. There was a light in the little office; I went in and rang the bell on the counter. Nobody came, but there were keys with long wooden handles on a board behind the desk. I went around and took number 10. The sleet had turned to snow, but it was still blowing hard. I found the cabin, unlocked it, went in and lay down on the bed. I was very tired.

I dreamed that the wound in my forehead was feeling swollen and tender again, and that I had been putting circular Band-Aids on it, but then they got too small, and I went into a drugstore to buy gauze. I happened to glimpse my face in a bit of shiny chrome, and I saw that the lump on my forehead had taken on the appearance of a closed eyelid; I could even see the eyelashes at the bottom, and feel them, too when I put my fingers there. Then I was so afraid of what I might see if the eye opened, that I woke up sweating.

My feet were cold, but there was no trace of snow outside; the room did not look like the one I had gone to sleep in. Cars were passing on the highway when I went to the office to return the key and pay for my lodging. The woman there pretended not to understand what I wanted. "Where did you get that?" she said when I handed her the key. "It's an old one, isn't it?"

When I offered her a credit card, she waved it away. "No, that's all right," she said, looking at me as if I were a harmless idiot.

The cars passing on the highway looked like a normal mixture of old and new. When I got into the Chevy, it seemed to be subtly different, but I couldn't say how.

Evidently whatever had been happening yesterday had stopped after I crossed the Mississippi. I remembered one of the little men saying, "Be careful crossing rivers," whatever that meant.

I bought a road atlas in a Texaco station where I stopped for gas, and dreamed of going to earth in some little Canadian town with a romantic name: Ste. Anne, perhaps, Île des Chênes, or St. Jean Baptiste. I drove to Minneapolis, thinking I might turn north and cross the border at International Falls, but there was a tremendous pileup on Route 10, and I learned from the radio that a big crater had appeared during the night, covering highways and railroad tracks, burying overpasses and breaking gas lines.

I kept on driving west, hoping to get out of the heavy traffic that was now moving away from the crater area. Eventually I realized that I was following my old route back to Seaview—my father's, too, more or less.

When my father drove across the country looking for a place to move to, he took the shortest route and stuck pretty close to the forty-first parallel. That was in September 1945, just after gas rationing ended. He made the trip alone, driving his old Nash touring car. He had the back loaded with supplies and camping stuff. He drove ten hours a day, camped where he could, slept in the car when he had to. He crossed the continent in ten days; the roads were not as good then. The car broke down twice, once in Boulder and once in Salt Lake City. He fetched up a little north of where he was aiming, but that was just the way the roads ran. He didn't stop until he had got as far west as he could, and that turned out to be Seaview.

Once when I got out to piss on a fence post and looked down the road behind me to make sure I was alone, I could see the world curving away, a thousand miles back to Boston, a twenty-fourth part of the arc around the equator. For the first time I was able to think of the earth as a planet like Mars or Mongo. It gave me a shocking sense of the weight and heft of this globe, round as a sea urchin's egg, spinning through space with me on its back like a mite.

There's nothing like this endless plain of wheat in Europe, although that's a big continent too. It's something about the tectonic plates. Northern Europe doesn't have the deserts, either; it's a civilized place, cultivated everywhere. In Switzerland the mountainsides are mowed like lawns. It's really true that the sky is bigger here. No wonder some visitors are captivated, changed forever by this landscape. Being small makes them feel more important.

When I was young I always liked the start of a journey. I was excited, I thought, "I'm going *away*." I didn't like the preparations, packing, writing ahead, but I liked the moment when I actually got into the train or the bus or the airplane and sat down and started. Then I knew that if there had been any mistakes in the packing it didn't

matter, because it was too late now, and I could lean back
and just enjoy the sensation of going away. Never mind
where to, that wasn't the point. I liked watching the scenery
go by, even if it was only clouds, and I liked the little personal attentions, people serving you drinks and meals, of-
fering you magazines. Life on the road cured me of that
fairly quickly, and I learned to take a more measured view
of airports and railway stations and hotels in general, but I
still had the idea deep underneath that someday I would
go on a journey to some wonderful far-off place and never
come back, never write a postcard, never be heard of again.

Now in a curiously unpleasant way that wish was coming true. I felt cut off from my adult life, set adrift, almost
as if I were a boy again, traveling by bus, going to Oregon.
I had traveled this way every summer from the time I was
twelve until I graduated from high school. Going to stay
with my father, following his path across the country. Hoping for something that would never happen.

As for the job, that was all over anyway, and the last
few years hadn't been a great deal of fun. My working life
with Weybright had been a scramble to stay at the top
middle of middle top management, trying not to get sucked
down to rot alive among the men in industrious limbo,
who at my age would have been rubbished and forgotten
long ago.

What I felt now was not the lack of employment or
status, so much as the miserable loneliness of existing in a
continent and a country where I was a stranger now, where
not a single person knew if I was alive or dead, or would
care if they knew. The Romans, instead of killing citizens

(which was forbidden by their laws), exiled them. They were still doing it under Mussolini sixty years ago. The British did it too in the eighteenth century; exile to Australia was cheaper than building prisons. The next thing would be for us to fire off our undesirables to distant stars; but it looked now as though someone else had beaten us to it.

We're a gregarious lot; no matter how much we like to work alone, to be accountable to nobody but ourselves, we need to rub noses every now and then. Some of it is just ritualized self-interest, networking, favors and obligations, but some of it fills an unspoken need that is almost like sex.

People who live alone turn a little strange, maybe because they're keeping inside them all the bits that ordinarily fly out and attach themselves to other people. All the connections clipped off, like water pipes not connected to anything, dripping in the darkness.

From the car radio, and from the television in motels, I learned that craters were still forming throughout the West and Northwest. A big one had erupted in the Cotton Bowl stadium, forcing the cancellation of a game between Texas A&M and the Dallas Herons. I heard a televangelist shouting, "They're here, they're large, they're armed, they're rude. And the *real* Organization has yet to rim out! My friends, these messengers are here to *deposit toxin of comets* on our fair earth!"

There were scattered reports of soldiers emerging from the craters in the desert, but they never seemed to make contact anywhere and there were no casualties.

From Aberdeen, South Dakota, I had to turn south

to avoid a crater. Just before nightfall I reached Pierre, a little town on the Missouri River, which on the map is like a coiling dragon. Great swaths of purple and red were lighting up the western horizon, and the lights of the town were pinpoints.

I stopped at a modest motel and checked in for the night. When I emptied my pockets, I noticed that the clothes the little men had given me were almost identical to my own, labels and all. Several things were missing, my key ring for example, but I still had several dollars in loose change. There was a wallet that looked much like the one I had lost, but its contents had been streamlined a bit; three ID cards instead of a dozen, and no bills except the twenty dollars I had got from Gallagher.

The contents of my suitcase looked unchanged; even the little *karakuri* I had meant for a wedding present was still there in its box, and its head nodded when I looked in.

I put everything away in the chest of drawers and drove down the road to a place called The Spur for dinner. A waitress served me an Ox Spur Enchilada (stuffed with chicken, beef, pork and watermelon), a scoop of rice and beans, and a wilted lettuce leaf with a slice of exsanguinated tomato.

I was able to eat about half of it; I left the greasy plate, paid and went back to the motel. It was close to sunset now, and the sky was covered in a layer of lemon custard, shading in the west to a sullen avocado. I was a little unwell, perhaps because of the food: dizzy, a touch of nausea. As I entered my room, I managed to bump my head some how; the pain was so intense for a moment that I nearly fell.

Somebody grasped me under the arms, shoved me forward and made me sit in a tall wooden chair. It was like a child's high chair; my feet didn't reach the floor. When my vision cleared, I saw that my room now contained a metal desk, behind which sat a gigantic man in uniform. It was only because I was perched so high that I could look him in the face. His head was bare and shaven and was half again as big as mine; his eyebrows and lashes were color-less, and so were his eyes; he looked like a civil servant from Aberdeen. The uniform jacket was gray-violet twill, and had a dark leather Sam Browne belt, which creaked every time he shifted his weight. There were three silver crescent moons on each of his epaulets, as well as a dusting of stars, unless that was dandruff.

"Mr. Stout," he said, "I am Deputy Commander Willard O'Leary of the Space Patrol." He had a faint ac-cent, something like border Irish. There was a movement to his right, and I saw a strange deformed creature, also in uniform. It was hairless like the giant, but hunchbacked and four-armed. Its face and hands were pale yellowish green, like a decomposing courgette. It looked at me with pink mouse eyes.

"This is a routine interrogation," said the giant. "You are not in danger as long as you answer correctly. Take a moment to compose yourself."

Surprisingly enough, I was feeling better than I had a moment or two ago. "Excuse me," I said, "but there isn't really any Space Patrol, is there?"

"There isn't now, but there will be," he said indiffer-ently.

"Well, are you one of the soldiers from the crater, or what?"

He made a contemptuous gesture. "No, they are only subfactual appearances caused by gravitational stress. They will be gone in a few months. Mr. Stout, let us begin. What were you doing in Milan?"

"If you really want to know, I was asked to drop off a packet there."

"Who asked you to do that?"

"My brother Tom."

"Give his full name."

"Thomas A. Stout, but he didn't know what was in it."

The adjutant produced a little pad and wrote something down.

"What *was* in it?" the giant asked.

"I don't know." The adjutant was apparently writing with its forefinger, which had extruded a kind of pen.

"Who did you give it to?" asked O'Leary.

"Nobody. I mean, I was supposed to give it to Roger Wort, but I left it behind in my hotel room, and then it was stolen."

"Do you know that of your own knowledge?"

"Well, no, but Roger told me."

"Where is the packet now?"

"I don't know."

The giant glanced at the adjutant, which put away its pad and retracted its fingerpen. "Mr. Stout," the giant said, "are you aware that you are lying?"

"No. I mean of course I'm not lying."

"Our instruments show that you are. Give him the injection, Igor."

The deformed servant approached me with something bright protruding from one finger. I struggled, but there seemed to be straps holding me to the chair. A momentary sting in my arm, then I felt rather peaceful and calm.

"Now then," the giant said. "Who did you give the packet to?"

I had a sudden vivid recollection of that night in the restaurant. I was sitting opposite Roger, and he had just withdrawn his hand with something in it.

"I gave it to Roger," I heard myself say. I realized that I had suspected it all along: Roger had stolen the thing, relying on my lost memory to cover his tracks, and everything he had done and said since then was an elaborate lie.

"What was in the packet?" the giant asked again.

A kaleidoscope of images came: Roger's face, and then the faces of the Pelican, the Forceps and the Elevator in the yellow cheesium-lit cavern underground. "It's a component for the world-freezing device." I hadn't known this until I said it, but I realized it was true.

"Why were you chosen to carry it?"

Another kaleidoscope. "It kills everybody who handles it unless they are protected."

"Will it kill you?"

"Yes. I am already dead."

"Mr. Stout, I am going to tell you something, although I will break a regulation when I do so. In a sense you are right, but in another sense you will survive a struggle in which whole planetary systems will perish." His pale shaven face was earnest and correct. "More than that I don't know. This concludes the interrogation."

The adjutant came forward and helped me down from the chair. It then stepped back, and kept on stepping back, or rather, I saw now that it was receding towards the far wall along with the desk and the giant, as if they were all on wheels. They kept on drifting away until they were only tiny dots that hurt my eyes; then the wall closed in front of them and I was standing in my motel room just as it had been before. The lifeless air in the room told me that there had never been anyone here.

As I opened the drapes, the highway lights suddenly flared brighter and went out. The lights in the room behind me were out, too, and all the buildings opposite were dark against the smudged orange sky glow. Sparks were dripping from one of the light standards. Somewhere in the distance I heard the sound of tires squealing, followed by a metallic clang and thump, then silence. High over the fading sunset two lazy pink contrails hung like the tails of spermatozoa. No more cars passed on the highway.

I always used to wonder what it was like to be George III during the Regency. That was the period when everybody in England seemed to be having a terrific time and old George was shut up in Windsor Castle, stone blind and mad as a hatter. Did he know he was insane? What if he forgot about that when he was asleep only to realize it again every morning?

I was feeling such distress that I picked up the bedside telephone, punched for an outside line and then Tom's

home number in Scarsdale. His sleepy voice answered on
the third ring.

"Tom, it's Wellington."

"Welly, for God's sake, where are you?"

"Tom, listen, I think I've gone mad."

"Where are you calling from, Welly?"

"I've just been interviewed by a Space Patrolman. He
said his name was O'Leary. He had a sinister assistant
named Igor."

"Calm down, Welly."

"I'm all right now. I just wanted to talk to somebody."

*"Tell me where you are. Give me the number and I'll call
back."*

"Good-bye, Tom." I rang off, feeling better, and began
undressing for bed.

When I went to the bathroom, I found a paper strip
over the toilet seat. It said I NEVER KNOW WHEN YOU'RE
KIDDING.

It's them Martians or Mongos

Casper was a ghost town, evacuated because of earth-
quakes and flooding. In Buffalo, where I stopped for the
night, my motel was a large affair, three stories tall, nearly
empty, with a dark parking lot as big as a department
store's. The paper strip over the toilet seat read YOU COME
HERE OFTEN?

Across the highway, a rancher who was having
coffee and cherry pie in Arby's told me he had lost five hun-

dred head in the last ten days. He said, "I've been through windstorms you wouldn't believe, and snow over the chimney twice, but when the ground begins to raise up and bury your cattle, I believe it's about time to admit you're licked."

I asked him what he attributed these disasters to, and he said, "Oh, it's them Martians or Mongos or whatever you care to call them. I've got as much fight in me as the next fella, but when they start comin' down from outer space to spoil a man's livelihood, why, I throw in my hand."

His eyes were bleared, and his lower lip was shiny with spit. "Hell of a way to end up," he said. "They use to call me H. V. in the army. You know what that stands for?"

"High Velocity?" I said.

"That's right. Was you in the army?"

"No, unfortunately."

"Nothing goddamn unfortunate about it." He turned his head and seemed about to spit on the floor, but changed his mind. "They called me that because I was always movin', never quit movin'. You know what they call me now?"

"No, I don't."

"They call me Hard Shell. Hard Shell Van Os, that's who I am. Ask anybody around here. But don't call me H. S. You know why?"

"Yes, I believe I do."

He stared at me with his phlegmy eyes narrowed. "What makes you so damn polite?"

"I'm from England," I said.

He looked at me for another moment in silence. "Hell,

go on home." He turned his round back on me, and I left
the restaurant. Judging by the newspapers in the machine
outside, it was a Sunday.

Shortly after I went back to my ground-floor room,
there was an agitated knocking at the door. I thought it
might be the rancher wanting to continue our conversation, and I called, "Who is it?" An unfamiliar voice answered; I couldn't make out the words. I opened the door
and saw a little dark-haired man standing there. He was
wearing a brown polyester suit and tie, but no topcoat, and
he was shivering.

"Excuse, please," he said, "I am your faucet."

"What?"

"I am from Italy losted. My name Jeppy. You know
me?"

"I'm afraid not. Oh, Geppi, the astronomer? Is that
who you are?"

"Of course. I am from high to low. Excuse me, I
come in?"

"By all means. Please forgive me." He sat in the armchair, still shivering, and I got the duvet from the bed to
give him. "How do you come to be here, Professor Geppi?"

"I am your faucet in Mongo," he said. "You understand?"

"No."

"They told me to make balloon, and so I come, but
we paf!" He struck his hands together. "And so I am here,
thank you very much."

"Professor, do you mean that you crashed? In a balloon?"

"Oh, very much paf!"

"But now about the faucet—"

"Faucet yes!" He laughed. "I find him on Horace, great faucets!"

"On Horace?"

"Oh yes. The planet that I find, he is fauceting."

Suddenly a light dawned, and I said, "Professor, do you mean Horus the god?"

"Oh yes, very much Horus. You know before, we have Roman pavilion only."

"The names of the planets. Mars, Venus, Mercury."

He laughed with delight. "Jupiter, Saturn, you know them. Yes, very much. But from far, Horus."

"Egyptian, isn't he?"

"Very much. So I name him not Roman."

"Good. And you say he has faucets?"

"Very many faucets, he is like Mars. I find him."

"You discovered the planet. So you had the privilege of naming him. It."

"Yes, but not Mongo." He shook his finger. "Not a serious for newspapers."

"No. No Mongo."

"He is here." Geppi pointed to the ceiling.

"Here?"

"Here in the sky. You see him?"

"No."

"Come, you will see." He got up, abandoning the duvet, and beckoned me to the door.

"You'll get cold again."

"No, not important." He led me out into the parking

lot, away from the scattered lights of the motel. We stopped in the darkest corner. "Now you see? Look up, almost crooked. You see Eridanus?"

"No."

"You don't know names of sky?"

"Not really. Well, the Big Dipper."

"All right. Come." He took an instrument out of his pocket and led me to a light stanchion. He fastened the instrument to the stanchion with a clamp, adjusted it, peered through it, loosened the clamp, tightened it, and so on, while I was beginning to wish I were back in the warm. At last he stepped back. "Good!" he said. "Now you look."

I bent to the little instrument, a squat device with a great many knurled rings, and peered through the eyepiece. At first I saw only swimming lights, then it all came into focus, and right in the middle was a pale sphere about the size of a grain of rice, shadowed in a crescent along one edge. "Is *that* it?" I exclaimed.

"You see him?"

Surrounding the tiny planet, veils of opal spectra came and went. "What's that around it!" I asked.

"We don't know which. They are making something new, it is fabulous. Perhaps they will hurt us." He giggled.

I straightened up, and Geppi removed the little telescope from the stanchion, put caps over the lenses, and handed it to me. "This is for yours," he said.

"Oh, no, I couldn't possibly," I said, but he pushed it on me, giggling, "Yes! Yes!"

"Well, look, let's discuss it indoors," I said, and I led the way back towards the motel, but halfway there I glanced back and saw he was going the other way around a parked van. I waited. When he didn't appear again, I walked back, and called, but he was gone.

Later the moon rose, and in its light, looking out the window with Geppi's instrument, I saw pale grey lines wavering down from the sky. When I increased the magnification, I could see that each line was made up of little men in overalls, falling hand in hand. I wondered if I would see them in a microscope too: little men in overalls, serious and deformed, holding the world together.

There was always, in leaving a place for the last time, some sweetness to take away the sting. When I left Potamos where I had grown up and lived most of my life, I remember that I thought, Well at least I don't have to see Mr. Hanfield anymore. Hanfield was the druggist's son; his white-haired father was addressed as "Doc." The two of them stood behind the counter agreeing with each other about politics (they were both Republicans), Doc in grunts around his cigar, young Mr. Hanfield in a nasal whine, implying a complaint no matter what the subject was. It hadn't occurred to me, until the day I left, that I would be glad never to see him again.

The old man died a few years later, while I was in college; I heard that when they cleaned out his back room, they found drugs that had been there since Richard Nixon was a boy. The drugstore was sold to the mother of a young pharmacist who wanted to set him up in business; what happened to young Mr. Hanfield I never found out. I had left him behind forever, just as I was leaving each of these

Midwestern and Western towns. Forever. A solemn thought.

As I drove onward between buttes like melting sphinxes with shapeless falling bodies and a hundred toes, I began to have the feeling that I was growing continually rounder and harder, and eventually that I was like an egg rolling down a long tunnel towards some dimly apprehended destination. I even began to imagine that I had speckled markings on my shell, and to wonder what would happen when I was candled. At the same time I knew quite well that I was still my usual shape, a little stouter perhaps because of lack of exercise, but the delusion grew so strong that I hesitated a long time before tipping myself out of bed every morning, for fear that I might fall and break.

Beside the road somewhere north of Sheridan, I saw a little T-shaped red sign that said in white letters FREE—FREE. I watched for the next one; it said A TRIP. The next was TO MARS. Other signs came into view one after another:

FOR 900

EMPTY JARS

BURMA-SHAVE

Those signs used to be everywhere. Where were they now? When was the last time I had passed a Burma station?

South of Billings, thousands of frozen grasshoppers glittered in the headlights and crunched under my wheels. They had come out of the glacier, the motel manager explained to me when I stopped for the night. How long had they been in the glacier? She didn't know.

I unpacked, turned on the television and listened to a greenish tenor sing "Ridi, Pagliaccio" until he came to the ha-ha-has. The only other channel was showing a rerun of *I Love Lucy,* and I clicked that off too.

The usual movie list was on a card beside the TV; one of the attractions was an adult film called *Space Virgins.* I turned it on and lay back against the pillows to watch it. After a brief introduction, the astronaut hero zipped open the heroine's blouse and pulled it down over her shoulders, disclosing two very large pink-centered silicone breasts. Not much finesse there, and no brassiere. I couldn't help contrasting it with a long-ago film in which Sylvia Kristel played the governess of a teenage boy. She had unfastened the bra behind her back and then held the empty garment crumpled to her very modest breasts, looking down at the boy with a sort of bruised expression.

The astronaut was kissing the young woman's nipples, making her squirm in quite a convincing way. He pulled off her skirt.

At that moment I became aware that someone else was in the room. When I turned my head, I saw that it was one of the space soldiers, sitting stiffly upright in the armchair by the door. I recognized him by his wooden complexion and brown battle dress, although he was not wearing his helmet or any weapons.

"Why is he removing her clothes?" he asked in a monotone, without looking at me.

After a moment of panic I decided the best thing

would be to reply as if the situation were entirely normal. I said, "Because it gives them both pleasure."

He asked in the same way, "Would it not give them pleasure if she removed her own clothes?"

"Yes."

"Then I don't understand."

"No."

"Would it give us both pleasure if you removed my clothes?"

The panic returned. "No, I don't think so."

"Is it because I am a stranger?"

"No, because you're a male."

"But you are a male also."

"Yes."

"Then I don't understand."

"No."

In the screen, both actors were now nude and were apparently engaging in vaginal intercourse, although the camera stayed resolutely above their navels, leaving chaste apertures below. The soldier stood up and removed his blouse, revealing two rows of brown nipples, about twenty in all. I was up like a startled deer and made for the bathroom. When I looked back, he had taken off his trousers, and I saw a rubbery gray strip of reduplicated penises and scrotums sagging down his thigh like an elephant's trunk. I got into the bathroom, closed the door and latched it. The strip over the toilet seat read URANUS IS OUT.

A crackling sound came from the ventilator over the commode, then old-lady voices:

—He's three-faced, he be; grease him as you please, put

him in the to-and-fro cart, you'll never see his like entire.

—He's got an album in his short drawers, and there's a fingularity in the vifinity of Fagittarius.

—He's Jeff as a journal, but he hears every wort.

—Low be his green! A frog ought to speak less and croak more.

Frustrated, because I was trying to listen at the door, I climbed on the commode and hit the ventilator with my fist. I heard a final cackle, and the voices stopped.

When I went to the door and listened again, I heard murmurs and stifled moans from the TV, but no other sound.

"Are you gone?" I called.

"I am gone," his voice said faintly.

When I opened the door, his body was lying like a log on the floor. I saw that there was a faint wood grain in his skin, even in his half-open eyes. He was too heavy to lift, but after five minutes he began to sink into the floor, and half an hour later the carpet had closed over him leaving nothing but a brown stain.

I sat down and closed my eyes for a minute, and when I opened them I was back in the sitting room of my flat, seated across from my brother Tom. He was dressed as he had been that day in London, brown polyester suit and purple shirt, with his necktie hanging out of the pocket of his suit coat, and he was looking up with the sleepy expression he used when he thought he was making a fool of me.

As we were talking, I noticed that with a slight effort I could look at the edge of my vision without actually moving my eyes. I had never been able to do this before, and I was interested by the way the image broke up into prismatic colors just before it gave way to darkness. I pushed a little further and was surprised to find that I could look into the darkness itself, leaving my field of view behind. The second or third time I did this, going further and further, I glimpsed *another* coruscation of colors.

When I slid into this field of view, I saw my own face looking back at me. It looked startled, like someone trapped by a flash camera in a dark room. The feeling that welled up somewhere behind my eyes was amused contempt mingled with a little affection, the sort that you might feel for a dog.

I was offended in a very remote way, and I drifted out of Tom's little circle of light wondering if there was anything else beyond it—Peabody in the adjoining flat, perhaps—but when I found the next circle of brightness it was my own, and I was looking at the man-shaped brown stain in the carpet.

Thinking about this afterward, I was sorry that the experience had not lasted longer; if it had, I might have been able to learn more about what Tom was thinking and how his convoluted mind worked. But probably it had been nothing more than an exceptionally vivid hallucination, or else I had fallen asleep without knowing it.

So many curious things had been happening to me since I left England that I was sure only a few of them could be real, but the puzzle was to find out which. Was I the mandarin dreaming of a scarlet dragonfly, or the dragonfly dreaming of a mandarin?

In the morning even the stain was gone, and I was half

convinced that the soldier too had been part of my dream experience, but when I went to the office to return my key, I found that I had been charged for the movie we had watched together.

I found Morris Gelb's name in the Billings directory, but there was no address and his telephone didn't answer.

Every night the voices muttered from the little radio.

—*Here's his cane and here's his tubals. He's a farinher, he has a chased peggo. The rounder he rise, the fatter he fall.*

—*Look out, here's the preposition of his four fiveskins. Those are cheese that were his shies. If a trefoil's in the forest, can the son be saved?*

—*Let him drain, he's young yet, you can't make a hamelet without breaking higgs.*

Sometimes it was that sort of thing, and sometimes it sputtered with fragments of the police band or CB: "*manager of the Shallow Bell Inn . . . known to be traveling west . . .*"

The radio wouldn't stay turned off anymore, and even if I hid it in the bathroom or the closet, I heard it just the same. Twice I tried to leave it behind in a motel, and both times I found it in my pocket later that day. I was desperate, but I felt now that if I could just get all the way west, get to Seaview, I would be saved.

I remember the first time I knew that my parents were going to die. I was in a waiting room somewhere, and another kid across the room said something about his father's funeral. Until then I had known that everyone died, but for some reason I hadn't realized that my own family were included.

In a general way, I knew later on that I would have to die too, but I told myself that it wouldn't happen till I was eighty or some such incomprehensible number, almost the same as forever—anyhow, I told myself that I wouldn't have to worry about it for a long, long time.

And there was a long, long time when nobody died— nobody of my age, nobody I knew. We had all escaped mortality, we had found the secret that nobody talked about. Then that ass Cornelius Nye keeled over—nasty old bugger, nobody liked him. And next it was Jenny. It was utterly unexpected and unfair. She was forty-seven, a healthy, vigorous woman.

Leonard and Glynis were at the funeral, of course. A year later I sold the house and never went near the place again. I was away one summer when they came to town; I didn't answer their invitations. After a while even the Christmas cards stopped.

After Jenny it was Eric Mulligan, heart attack in the early nineties. The only time I ever saw a ghost—a possible sighting, I'd call it—was at Eric's funeral in Shropshire. It was a graveside service, and after it was over, on the way back to the parking lot, I could swear I saw Eric walking ahead of me. You couldn't mistake that broad back. When I blinked and looked again, he was gone.

I used to believe he had let me see him for an instant, just as a way of saying, *Don't worry, I'm not really dead.* But was he telling the truth?

After Eric it was Tony Seely, emphysema; poor Lauren Tobias, drugs and pneumonia; Brian Fennimore, Colin McKay . . . The only ones left of that jolly crew were

Glynis Home, Jack Pearcy, and Susan Steinberg, none of them talking to each other anymore. How did it happen? It was as if when Nye died he broke some sort of compact, and then the rest of us were fair game too. What if we'd never met him? Small loss to anyone, and then all the rest of us would be alive.

What if I never came back, never was heard of again? The lease was paid up till the first of the year; after that I suppose the landlord would dispose of my belongings somehow (at auction?) and let the flat to someone else. How long would it be before I could be declared dead and my estate parceled out? How many would remember me a year after I was gone? Five years? "Poor old Bill" every now and then for a while, then nothing?

At Great Falls there was a downpour of yellowish fluff that looked like upholstery padding. East of Idaho Falls, rivulets of muddy water covered the highway for miles where a massive subsidence had diverted the waters of the Snake.

It must have been fun to give names to so many geographical features, like Adam naming the animals. I think that's where Western pride comes from, and the Western guilt under it; we know there were other people before us, and other names.

A huge fire was raging at Burns, Oregon, and that meant another detour, south past the two lakes of Malheur, and then at last up through the forests towards Bend on the Deschutes River.

There was a vast commercial pseudopod between Springfield and Eugene, and the city center was altered be-

yond recognition, streets closed, huge new concrete structures in the middle of town. I had to go all the way out to
the suburbs on the other side to find a motel with a vacancy.

Urban sprawl had sent a tentacle northwest into the
orchards, too, and now I discovered it was possible to walk
from River Road across a footbridge that would take me to
a jumbo shopping mall called Valley River Center. (Why
not River Valley, or Center River?) On one of the winding
paths a man on skates was being towed at a good clip by a
police dog on a leash. The river was gray and choppy; autumn water. I felt that I had been suddenly dumped out of
a world of motion into a world of quietness.

At the near end of the footbridge there were big signs,
UNSAFE FOR DRINKING OR SWIMMING, and an illiterate icon
of a diving figure with a red slash through it. A toxic river.
Three or four big white-and-gray gulls were sitting on the
weathered handrail, herring gulls probably, world travelers.

On the other side of the bridge I followed a bike path
eastward. There were trees to my left, then the parking lot,
then the tops of the monstrous mall buildings; on the other
side, Queen Anne's lace and blackberry brambles. A little
flock of joggers passed me, their faces sheened with sweat,
then two bicyclists from the other direction, moving almost
silently on the blacktop, not even a grunt out of them, only
the swish of their wheels as they passed.

I kept on walking east along the river to see how far
the trail would take me, and wound up in the middle of a
peaceful sunlit clutter of Quonsets. Beyond them was a
busy highway, and when I crossed at the traffic light I found
myself deep in the campus.

The trees along the paths were almost bare; they had left the ghosts of maple-leaf prints in dark brown on the concrete. The students I passed wore T-shirts, lumberjack shirts, dashikis, tunics, golf jackets, everything hanging out and nothing tucked in. Crouched in the sun on steps and in doorways, they looked as if they had fallen there by accident and would have to be helped up.

I passed the King Complex, a cluster of alpine dorms where I had wasted many an ejaculation. My roommate, Dave Hooper, author of *The Incest Epistles,* wanted to die in battle but did not think much of the options available to him at that time. He said when he graduated he was going to get flight training from the navy, then abuse himself just enough to earn a medical discharge, and go to France where he would form the Dave Hooper Escadrille and die gloriously fighting the aerial Hun.

Dave was the inventor of the Hooper cheese cramp, made by combining processed cheese with bacon bits, chopped green peppers, onions, ketchup, mustard and other things smuggled out of the cafeteria. Dave sprinkled the cheese with all the other stuff, folded it over, tucked it into the liner from a cereal box and rolled it flat with a beer bottle; then he extracted the cheese, formed it into an ithyphallic knobkerrie, and cut it into sections which he hid under the socks in his closet.

His girlfriend, later mine for a bonnie semester, was Gloria Dunkel; she wanted to go to Australia, she said, and perform the Seminole dong rub on all the dogs in Melbourne. I don't know if she got there, or how this affected the Melbourne dingos. The last I heard of Dave, he was a

tour guide in Patagonia, which he described to me in a postcard as the "Oregon of Argentina."

There were a dozen new buildings, all in pink brick
that harmonized with the old buildings and all in broken-
elbowed architectural styles afloat somewhere between new
and old. A silly brick arch, like a giant ivy-covered metal
detector, guarded the path to the library. The library itself
had undergone an Ozlike internal transformation; a huge
new staircase spiraled dizzily around a well in the middle,
and nothing was where I expected to find it. The corridors
were pale peach with aqua cornices and pale aqua lights,
and went on for miles, like an infinitely extended 1920s
powder room.

As I was leaving I passed an elderly man who was trying to hold a briefcase under his arm and stuff some papers
into it. I recognized him as my old design teacher; he looked
about ninety, but then he always had. I turned back and
said, "May I hold that for you, Professor Knoebel?"

He stared at me with his pale blue eyes, but let me take
the briefcase. "I don't know if you remember me," I said.
"Nelson Stout, fifty-seven."

"Oh, Stout, yes," he said. "Thanks." He crammed his
papers into the briefcase and took it back. "Tell me, whatever happened to you?"

"I went into the women's undergarment industry," I
said.

"Did you! Architecture of a different sort, eh? Ha!
Well met, well met." He took my arm. "Come with me,
Stout, I want you to look at something." He led me down
the walk to the lawn between the library and the art

museum. Tree shadows flickered over the grass. In the middle of the lawn rose a large metal sculpture composed of a rust-colored tube on spindly legs. The tube was three feet in diameter, and the top was about chest-high; a twelve-foot length of tube came out of the ground and descended into it again.

Knoebel urged me close to the tube and then threw a hinged section back, uncovering an oily green-brown stream and releasing a foul odor. Every now and then some small object shot by, too quick to see what it was.

Several students in green-and-yellow sweatshirts had gathered around us. "Now this," Knoebel said, "is our latest wrinkle, our dernier cri as it were. You might think to look at it that this pipe is metal or ceramic, but it isn't, it's a very strong lightweight polymer. This piece is part of the campus sewer system, but we're designing buildings in which fluid-filled pipes like this will be used as structural members."

"Full of shit?" I asked.

"Sometimes," he said, nodding. "Sometimes. Remember what I taught you about overlapping function, Stout. When it *is* sewage, of course, it will be odorless. We're working on that. Even this isn't as smelly as you think. Lean a little closer, get a good sniff."

Before I could protest, two large undergraduates had lifted me and thrust me headfirst into the pipe. I thought I heard them laughing or saying something, but the water had closed over me and I was shooting along in darkness, first horizontally and then straight down. I was holding my

breath without any discomfort, and as time went on I began
to feel proud of my endurance and wanted to see how long
I could last.

If it had not been for the luminous specks in the wall,
I might have had no sense of motion; I seemed to be hanging in space, surrounded by orbiting bits of trash that approached and receded like little planets. One of them was
a yellow teardrop shape, perhaps a urine bogey. Another
was a wad of paper. It drifted past my face, then unfurled,
and I could read on it YOU ARE BEING before it darted out
of range.

A little disoriented

I could smell the ocean when we were still miles away,
that wind that seemed to blow through my body leaving me
shaved and clean. The bus was lumbering past yards that
were increasingly sandy, and every now and then I glimpsed
a line of sunlit yellow dunes with a clear blue sky beyond
them. When I was thinking I couldn't sit still any longer,
we pulled into the sandy main street. I climbed down
squinting in the hard light. I was wearing my glasses, for
some reason, and felt as if I had lost a good deal of weight.
Nobody else got off; in a moment the door clattered shut,
the bus grunted away from the curb, turned the corner and
was gone in a blue exhalation.

I felt a little disoriented, out of place, but all the stores
I remembered were still here: the jewelry shop with its

wonderful window full of agates and jasper, the candy store with the chromed arms of the taffy machine endlessly revolving around each other.

The hardware store was cool and seemed dim inside, although when my eyes got used to it there was plenty of light. The wooden floor looked as if it had been soaked evenly with oil, drop by drop over the years. Brass numbers were inlaid in the floor so that you could measure a piece of rope or wire just by laying it down the aisle.

Plumbing and electrical goods were up front, hardware in the back—nails in bins, screws and other small fasteners boxed in little cabinets. Tools hung on one wall, toilet seats and mirrors on the other. The room was silent and empty.

I went into the back room, but no one was there either. This was a storage room for doors and windows, big sheets of plywood and plasterboard, stuff that would have cluttered up the front room. The door was standing open, and I crossed the yard to the brown-shingled house in back, but the doors were locked, even the one at the top of the outside stairs, and no one answered the bell.

I left my suitcase on the porch and went back around the store building, past the garbage cans and bottles, to the empty street in the hot sunlight. No one was on the sidewalk when I walked back to the taffy shop. Inside, broken chunks of different pale colors lay on paper doilies behind the glass. No place else in the world had saltwater taffy like this, not chewy but crunchy and brittle. After the machine finished pulling the thick ropes of taffy, they crystallized somehow, and when you ordered a pound, or a half pound,

the people in the store would break it off with a silver ham-
mer the way you'd break a chunk off an icicle. I wanted a
quarter pound of the blue raspberry kind that was right in
front of me, I could almost taste it, but no one came when
I tapped the bell on the counter, and after a while I turned
to go.

As I crossed the threshold, there was a sharp flicker
and a clang that shook the walls sideways. After a while I
found myself leaning back against the front of the store,
holding my head in my hands. People were bending over
me, and a large sign overhead was swaying from one hook.
It was shaped like a teapot, and I could make out the words
THE STAR CAFE. There was a smear of blood on the spout.

A middle-aged woman put her hand on my forehead.
"Now you just sit right there," she said. "Don't try to get
up."

"What on earth happened?" another woman asked.

"Why, the wind blew that sign down just when he
walked out the door. I never seen such a thing, did you,
Edna?"

A third woman muttered, "Hope he don't want to
sue."

"I'm all right," I managed to say.

"He can talk, anyhow. What's your name?"

"Wellington Stout."

"From out of town, are you?" An inquisitive face came
nearer.

"I'm staying with my father, behind the hardware
store." As soon as I said this, I knew it was wrong.

The face receded. Three heads whispered together.

"He ought to be in the hospital."

"Dorothy, don't be a fool—how would we get him there?"

"Well, he can't stay *here.*"

"Look, there's the Girone girl, she'll know. Yoo-hoo, Celia!"

A sleek Latin-looking teenager appeared. She was wearing a halter and shorts of many colors and carrying an armload of books. She took off her round purple sunglasses to look at me. "What's the matter with him?" Her lipstick was too red for her dark skin tone; she had tilted almond eyes, and dusky hair pulled back into a ponytail.

"Sign knocked him down. Says he lives in your house, Celia. You know anything about that?"

"I *used* to live there," I said. "My father was Charles Stout, he owned the hardware store."

"That's who my grandma bought the house from," said the girl. She peered into my face. "So how do you feel?" She had a faint lisp that reminded me of Jenny's; her esses sounded a little like effs.

"All right, I think."

"Well, can you stand up or what?"

I got up, found I could stand, and walked a few steps. One of the women plucked at my sleeve. "Mr. Stout, will you come inside a minute? There's a paper we think you ought to sign."

"Oh, for goodness' sake, Aunt Marian," the teenager said. "Where's your car?" she asked me.

"I don't know. I don't think I have one. I came in on the afternoon bus."

"There hasn't been a bus in here since last Sunday." She put her sunglasses on and stared at me like a purple-eyed insect. "Do you have friends in town? Any place you can stay?"

"I guess not, but please don't bother." I started towards a bench on the sidewalk; my head was buzzing. She caught up and took my arm. "You come with me," she muttered. We went down the street together, an odd couple; she was a quarter my age, and hardly came up to my shoulder.

"May I carry your books?" I asked idiotically. She did not reply. She led me to a clapped-out black Cherokee at the curb, opened the door and pushed me in, slammed the door, then went around to the driver's side and dropped her books in the back. She started the engine like a giant coffee grinder and we went around two corners, up an alley, turned into a graveled space and choked to a halt. I saw that we were behind the hardware store, but there were sacks of fertilizer piled at the rear of the store building now, and the house was covered with siding painted yellow.

As we got out, the girl glanced up and made a rude gesture. I looked over the fence on the other side of the alley in time to see a woman's kerchiefed head disappearing from an upstairs window.

"Who was that?" I asked.

"Mrs. Crabapple. Come on." She got her books from the back of the Cherokee and we climbed the stairs to the high porch. "Is that your suitcase?"

"Yes." At least it looked the same, although I didn't see how it could be when the house was so different.

"Leave it here for now." She unlocked the door and led me into a room dominated by a huge round oaken table. The room was half kitchen, half parlor; it was full of restored Victorian furniture, including a vast sideboard whose shelves overflowed with books and games.

"Okay, now you can sit down," she said. She dropped her books, plastic purse and sunglasses on the table, and pulled out a wooden chair for me. "What kind of tea do you want? We have rose hip, chamomile, peppermint, sassafras, St. Helena's, Red Zinger, or Lipton's."

"I don't care for any, thank you."

She frowned. "You have to have *some* kind of tea."

"Lipton's, then."

She put a kettle on, poured hot water from the tap into a teapot and tossed it out, then ripped open a tea bag with her fingernails and dumped the tea into the pot. She poured water from the kettle into the teapot, brought the pot and a cup to the table. Then she went to the scarred refrigerator, came back with a Coke, and sat down fluidly with one leg under her. She put her chin in her hand and looked up at me. Her eyebrows and lashes were thick and dark. "All right, let's get going. What's your name?"

"Wellington Stout."

"I'm not going to call you Wel-ling-ton," she said scornfully. "What's your real name?"

"People call me Bill."

"Okay, and my name is Celia, but my friends call me Tinker. It's short for Tinkerbell, but no short jokes, okay?"

"Tinker, if you don't mind, how old are you?"

"Seventeen. How old are you?" She looked barely nubile; there was nothing much in the multicolored halter.

"I'm sixty-four. Are you here all by yourself?"

"With my mother, but she went to Portland last Friday and couldn't get back on account of the earthquake. Don't worry about it." She took a long drink of the Coke and wiped her mouth delicately with the side of her thumb.

"I was wondering if you ought to have me here, actually."

"Just like Mrs. Grouchpot next door. Let her wonder. You want to stay a couple of days? There's a guest room upstairs."

"The one with the tin roof?"

"Yes, how did you know?"

"That's where I used to sleep when I was a kid."

She gave me a calculating look. "All right, I'll buy that." She poured from the teapot and pushed the cup towards me. "You want sugar or cream?"

"No, thanks, this is fine." The tea was lukewarm and rather weak.

"Okay, let it settle a minute, then drink it and give me back the cup." I did as I was told, although the tea was bitter. Several nasty-looking clumps of tea leaves were left in the bottom and on one side.

She turned the cup three times and peered into it. "Now let's see. Number one, you aren't here by accident. Number two, what are you here *for*? That's harder, but don't tell me."

"Are you a fortune-teller?"

"Oh, yeah." She was studying the cup. "Well, this is different. This says you've come a long way, like years and

thousands of miles. Got to go all the way back, too. Hm.
You came from some place named for a river."

"Potamos, P.A."

"I never heard of it. What kind of a name is that, In-
dian?"

"Greek. It means 'river.' "

"Uh-huh, like in 'hippopotamus.' See, everything ties
together. Now if you go back there, you'll have to do it all
over again."

"Do what again?"

"Life. You'll have to live through high school, college,
getting married, the whole thing, blech." She looked up.
"You think I'm crazy. And you think *you're* crazy, don't
you?"

"Not right now."

"No, but you've had moments?"

"Yes."

"Well, there's a reason for that. Let's find out what it
is." She got up and fetched a deck of cards from the sideboard, tipped them out of their worn slipcase, shuffled them
and held them out in a fan. "Take one."

I did so and turned it over: it was the eight of penta-
cles.

"Oh, poop, you can do better. Close your eyes and
draw again."

I humored her; this time it was the Magician that I
laid faceup on the table. "Oh, yeah," she said, and tapped
it with her red fingernail. "Skill, injury, craziness. Now we
know which way to go." She gathered the cards, put them
back in their case, and left the room.

When she hadn't reappeared after a few minutes, I went out to the porch for my suitcase and carried it up the outside stairway to the little attic room. This time the door opened; warm air puffed out in my face.

The room was smaller than I remembered; I could stand only where the ceiling was highest. The bed under the steep cant of the ceiling was covered by a red and white checked quilt. Beside it on a three-legged table stood a spindly brown-glass lamp with a fake-parchment shade. There were three books in the wobbly bookcase: one was the *Boy Scout Handbook,* one *God, the Invisible King,* and the third was a novel by someone I had never heard of. The room was hot, and I leaned over the bed to crank open the one little window. A fly or a yellow jacket was buzzing somewhere in the room, but I couldn't see it.

I left my stuff in the varnished pine bureau and walked out to the sidewalk, then down the hill to where Ocean Street opened onto the beach. The tide was about three-quarters out. The smell of the air was like nothing else on earth. In spite of an occasional whiff of fish, it was clean, achingly clean. Virgin air. It seemed to come straight from the empty blue sky over the ocean, unsullied, never breathed before.

The air was cold, but the water was lime green, the sun bright on the marshmallow breakers, and gulls were circling where the skim ran frothing up the beach. Only a couple of people were in sight, so far away that they were little black mites. I took my shoes and socks off and rolled my trouser legs, left the shoes under some driftwood and started walking in the warm sand.

South of Ocean Street the bluff rose higher and or-
anger. The bluff face was compacted sand and sandstone,
sometimes it was hard to tell which. The bluff line had been
moving inland forever, but it was slow. The easy access to
the beach was at Ocean, where a big creek used to run, but
you could get down from the tourist hotels at the top by
switchback wooden stairways that sometimes had to be rebuilt after a big storm, or else down one of the steep ravines,
if you wanted to leap like a goat.

At the foot of the bluff it was all loose rocks and driftwood, then dry sand, too hot to walk on with bare feet in
the summer, and after that wet sand, glistening like the hide
of the world elephant, and then the water in its different
moods, grim or flowery. The dry sand was pretty much
level, but the wet sand tilted down like the floor in an old
house. I never knew why that was.

The sand above the tide line was littered with the
usual junk, small pebbles and bits of broken shell. I picked
up one fragment; it was dead white, about the size of a
tooth, worn so featureless that you couldn't tell what kind
of a shell it was. I kept an eye out for starfish or sand dollars; I didn't see any, but you never knew. Sometimes people found blue glass floats that Japanese fishermen had lost
from their nets five thousand miles away. I did see a long
strand of kelp lying sand-draggled and brown as a medicine
bottle. Kids used to swing them like whips, or pop the air
bladders by jumping on them. Kelp was also good to run
with, leaving a long sea-serpent trail behind in the sand.

I always thought there was something barren and
melancholy about the coast, even in its brightest weather.

As if something necessary had been cleared out of it and most of it hadn't been filled in yet. There was something missing in the people, too, regardless of sex and/or gender, and that's one reason I never felt I belonged here. They were all transplants, even those who had been Oregonians for a hundred years.

Something white was bouncing along ahead of me. When I caught up with it, it turned out to be a torn plastic wrapper with one half-frozen pea rolling around inside. I couldn't figure out how it had got here, unless it was garbage spilled too near the top of the bluff. I was sorry to see it; in the old days people didn't litter on the beach, or up above either. I dug a hole with my foot and nudged the wrapper in. Things buried in the sand never seemed to come up again, although you'd think they would; maybe they just kept on going down.

After a while I began passing half-submerged stumps of rocks that the ocean had worn away. Those rocks were covered with mossy seaweed, barnacles and anemones, and you could find things swimming in little rock hollows, trapped there every time the tide came in and went out again, but I would have had to wade to get to them today, and the water was shockingly cold.

After a storm the beach would always be littered with junk the ocean had coughed up, sandy draggles of seaweed, eggwhite froth, broken bits of shell, waterlogged driftwood of all sizes up to and including stripped trees two or three feet in diameter. After a really big storm some of those logs, each weighing a ton or more, would be found sticking like javelins out of the bluff. In a winter storm the grey waves would come up pretty near to the top of the bluff, which was kind of hard to believe even when you saw it, but in calm weather, like now, the breakers curled over about as high as your crotch. When one hit you there, it was like a wet towel even when you were numb with cold, it hurt unless you turned your hip to it. The water when it curled up and over was pale bottle green with the light inside it, and the froth at the top was thick as frosting. But it was so cold even in August that grown-ups seldom went in.

I kept walking until I could see the silvery tide rising in the inlet, then I turned around and walked back in the dry sand. Under the bluff where big logs of driftwood were scattered, I came upon the half-buried body of the wooden space soldier. His features were eroded, damp, encrusted with sand, but they were still recognizable. The wood was orange brown, the sand where it was heaped up was dull khaki in the parts that were wet.

I had a strong disinclination to touch his face, but I scooped up dry sand and piled it against him until his features were hidden; otherwise I was afraid someone would see them and excavate him. I wasn't sure what they would do with him—put him in a museum, maybe, or stand him in front of a novelty store as a curiosity. I carried grey antlers of driftwood and piled them up around him until he was almost entirely concealed. The next storm would rearrange the pile and perhaps uncover him again, but until then he would be safe.

My feet were sticky with sand when I got back to Ocean Street; I wiped them with my socks before I put my shoes on, but I knew I would feel every grain that was left.

The crown of my head was getting warm, too, and I thought I would be sorry tomorrow that I hadn't worn a hat.

Walking back up Ocean Street, I passed the building where my father's hardware store used to be—it was a garden store called Fetzer's now. Up where the taffy shop had been, the café sign was back in place; I noticed several faces watching me through the window.

As I approached the crest of the hill I could see a tall yellow brown earthwork rising against the sky. When I got close enough I was able to make out that the barrier was caused by some sort of massive earth slippage; the street was impassable, and several roofs on the other side were crazily tilted. Yellow ribbons fluttered between sawhorses on this side. I could see part of a yellow tractor pointed up at an angle, as if the earth had collapsed under it.

A black-and-white car pulled up on the opposite side of the street. I heard the brake ratchet into place; then a stocky man in grey uniform squirmed out and stood spraddle-legged with his hands on his hips. He was about fifty, grey-faced, and looked as if I was the worst thing he had seen today. The star on his breast said CHIEF; he was hung about with weapons and radios. "Your name Stout?" he said.

"Yes, it is," I said.

"Mixed up with that little tart Celia Girone?"

"I'm staying with Ms. Girone, yes."

"Let me tell you something, she ain't any more Girone than I am. You know what her real name is?"

"No, I don't."

"Ricoglia." He spat the word, then wiped his mouth.

"Girone, my ass. You stay away from her, if you know what's good for you, hear me?"

"Yes, I do." I tried to look humble and stupid. He stared at me as if he couldn't quite make out what was wrong, then snorted and went back to his car.

As I walked down the hill I noticed that most of the people on the street wore dark clothing in old-fashioned styles; the women had long skirts and cloche hats. Several women I passed moved aside and then looked at me over their shoulders, and once or twice I saw them whispering together. My arriving seemed to have upset them, but why?

I found Tinker at the kitchen table, reading a book under the pendant light. "Where have you been?" she asked. "Have you eaten anything?"

"I didn't think of it. I suppose I ought to."

"No, that's okay. You're supposed to do these on an empty stomach." She took the plastic lid off a plate of brownies covered with some kind of whipped-cream topping. "It's got a little hash in it, and belladonna, and a bunch of good things. It'll fix whatever's wrong with you."

"Do you think so?"

"Believe it," she said firmly.

I sat down, took one of the brownies and nibbled. The topping really was whipped cream, and the brownie itself tasted like chocolate, but I detected an undertaste of something darker, more like molasses, and there seemed to be a certain amount of leaves and stems mixed in. I ate it to be polite, and saw that she was looking at me expectantly. "It's quite good," I said.

"Go on, have some more."

I took another one, but it was all I could do to get it down.

"More," she said.

"I couldn't, really. Thanks very much, though."

She came around the table and took another brownie from the plate. "Eat this." When I opened my mouth to object, she took my chin in one hand and popped the brownie in with the other. "Now *eat*," she said. Her face was set in severe lines, and she looked quite terrifying. Before I had half chewed the brownie, she seized my chin again and shoved in another one slithery over my tongue. The room seemed to be darkening, and my arms were paralyzed. She kept pushing in more and more brownies, stuffing me like a hare. We were huddled together in a dark well, where only her face shone; it hung over me like a kite, and I was nothing but a head, unable to speak or swallow fast enough to keep up with the boluses she was pushing in, bloating until I was purple and perfectly round.

Sometime after midnight

I dreamed that I was being presented by a very large robed alien creature to an even larger alien with a supercilious expression. We were standing in a brightly lit crystal throne room on another planet.

"This is the specimen," said the first creature. "What do you think of it?"

"It's not very large. How old are you, Specimen?"

"I'm sixty-four."

"Perhaps it has shrunk. Specimen, which parts of you are essential and which accidental?"

"I beg your pardon?"

"It doesn't understand you."

"No, I suppose not. Well, then, we must take it apart, no doubt. Can the legs come off first?"

I couldn't remember the rest. Then I dreamed of a brown darkness in which I could make out an empty hall-way with open doors on either side, a deeper darkness in the rooms. I knew that this image was somehow connected with the gate in the brown brick wall, and I had a feeling of helpless revulsion and horror.

Sometime after midnight, I had just come awake lis-tening to the wind under the eaves when I felt a sudden in-visible billow of cool air drop from the ceiling over my face. Next came the first premonitory tapping, then the all-encompassing voiceless shout.

When I was a kid listening to rain on that tin roof in the middle of the night, it would put me sound asleep again with a smile on my face, but now it seemed to be having the opposite effect. I felt comfortable and at ease but not at all drowsy. I turned on the light and found my robe hanging on a chair, and I put it on and went down the stair-way barefoot behind the curtain of falling rain. A yellow glow fanned out from the living room windows. I crossed the porch to look in. My father was sitting at the table, look-ing about the way he always did. He was smoking his pipe.

He peered up at me when I opened the door. "Couldn't sleep? Come in and sit down. Rain on the roof bother you?"

"No, I like it, but I woke up." I pulled out a chair and sat opposite him. It was a different table, and the room was smaller.

"Feeling okay?" he said.

"Sure."

"You know, we don't get a chance to talk much, even when you're here. You're usually out with your friends. Not that I blame you." He looked at his glass on the table, then picked it up and took a slow drink. "Other kids' fathers take them hunting and fishing, don't they," he said.

"I don't care about hunting and fishing."

He settled back in his chair. I saw that he was looking past me and rubbing his nose with the pipe bowl, the way he did when he was remembering something. "One time my father took me out in the woods and showed me how to make a willow whistle. You cut off a young willow shoot, about so long." He cupped the pipe in one hand and held his fingers four inches apart. "You cut one end on a slant, and you cut a notch near that end. Then you work your knife blade under the bark until you loosen it all the way around, and take it off in one piece. You cut a little slice lengthwise in the wood at the slanted end. You put the bark back on and blow. Moving the bark up and down changes the pitch."

"Could you show me how to do it?"

"Maybe. It has to be in the spring, or the bark isn't loose enough. I only saw it done once. I always wondered why he never took me out again."

After a moment he said, "Maybe he thought it was his duty to do it once. He and my mother showed me how to do cat's cradles, too, but I never learned. So much gets lost. That's why we read history." He shuffled the papers on the table. "I was just going over these maps, tracing the ley lines."

"What are ley lines?"

"They're lines of power, the network that holds things together. They're everywhere, but there's no better place to see them than this country." He pushed an atlas towards me; it was open to a United States map. "If you draw lines between towns, you'll notice there are a lot of places that are hubs in the network, most of them big cities—Atlanta, for instance, or Charleston. But there are a bunch of others that are hubs too, and yet you never heard of them." He picked up a pencil. "Look here at Ely, Nevada, or here at Oakley, Kansas. You ever hear of Oakley? No.

"Now, if you keep on looking, you notice you can connect up the dots with straight lines to make sea creatures. You don't think so? Okay." He handed me the pencil. "Start at Chicago and draw a line to Madison. Then La Crosse, Minneapolis, keep your lines straight, don't try to follow the highways. Watertown, Aberdeen, Pierre. Rapid City, Casper. Now north to Sheridan, Billings, Great Falls. Now south to Helena, Butte, Idaho Falls, Twin Falls. North again to Boise, Burns, Bend and Eugene. Now back the other way, from Eugene to Klamath Falls, Lakeview, Winnemucca, Ely—all roads lead to Ely—Salina, Green River, notice how many water names there are? then Gallup, Socorro, north to Albuquerque, Santa Fe, Raton, Pueblo— see it now?—and Denver, then Oakley, Great Bend,

Wichita, Kansas City, Hannibal where Mark Twain lived, Peoria, and Chicago again."

"Wow," I said.

"That's the big leviathan we're living on. Its eyes are in Dubuque and Davenport, its brain is in Sioux City, its heart is in North Platte, and its cloacae are in the Great Shit Lake." He laughed and I did too. After a minute he put his finger on the map and traced a route from west to east. "I'd like to go back sometime." He glanced up at me. "Not to go back to your mother. That's over. Just to make the trip again."

"I've done it a bunch of times."

"I know. Maybe that's the next best thing. You may not understand this till you're older, and I wouldn't tell you if I wasn't drunk, but when a man looks at his son, what he sees is the one who's going to take his place." He drained his glass and put it down with a click. "Rain's stopped. I'm going to bed."

"Guess I will too."

"See you in the morning."

I climbed the stairs and lay awake awhile thinking about what my father had said and how he looked when he said it, then fell asleep again. The next time I woke up it was early; the store was locked, and all I could see in there was stacks of labeled cartons. The house was locked, too, and I couldn't see anyone through the windows. I pissed in the bushes behind the store and went down to the beach.

The ocean looked colder than yesterday; the wind blowing through me was colder too, and I didn't want to take my shoes off or roll my trousers up. I set out walking the other way, up around the curve of the shore towards the lighthouse, crossing little watercourses one after another. Pebbles fanning out from the mouth of each one were sorted by sizes; near the trickle they were a bit less than the size of your fist, chalky white most of them, some streaked gray and yellow, each one different. It seemed wasteful to make so many different lumps of rock. Where the pebbles were dry they clattered underfoot like poker chips. Towards the water they were smaller and the smooth gray sand covered them, all but faint shiny curves like turtles hiding, and you wanted to wash them off because they might be water agates or moss agates, or anything.

An hour of easy walking brought me close to the foot of Lighthouse Rock. The lighthouse itself had been steadily receding as I got closer, and now I could only see the tip of its white upright column, looking for all the world like a spaceship ready for launch.

Ahead of me near the bluff, a man was picking his way out between the pieces of driftwood. I turned away to avoid him, but as I passed he raised his head and beckoned, and I saw that it was Roger.

He stood and waited for me with no expression on his face. "Come over here, we've got to talk," he said. Roger didn't look well. He had a shapeless old hat pulled down over his brow; he was unshaven, his shirt was half unbuttoned under a stained canvas trench coat, and he wasn't wearing a tie. He looked as if he'd been out in the rain all night.

"Roger, what are you doing here?" I said.

"I'm carrying a message. Do you know what you're getting into?"

"No, Roger, I don't."

"This Tinkerbell of yours is very bad news, Bill. She's out of reach now, but she'll stumble, and then she might bring you down with her, so watch out."

"I will, Roger."

"You think you know better, don't you?"

"No, not at all."

"You don't know anything. You don't even know that you've gotten me killed."

"What do you mean, Roger?"

"I mean I'm dead. So are you, or as good as, but I'm six feet down. How do you think that feels?"

"Roger, what can I say? You can't be serious."

"Oh, you don't think so? Put your hand on my chest."

I put my hand out; it went right in as if there was nothing there. When I pulled it out again, his chest sort of rippled like a pan of water.

"Now do you see? But you don't care, do you? Hell! I wish I'd never got mixed up with you." He gave me a last look, turned and walked into the bluff, there one minute and gone the next.

I stood awhile looking to see if he would come out again, but he didn't. There weren't any footprints in the dry sand.

Rather than walk back along the beach I climbed Yaquina Boulevard, meaning to make my way back through town, but when I got to the lighthouse parking lot at the top of the hill, I saw Tinker, in billowy white slacks and a black sweater, just getting out of the Cherokee with her armload of books.

"Thought I might find you here," she said with a smile. "You sleep okay?"

"Very well, thanks. How many of those brownies did you make me eat?"

She frowned. "I didn't *make* you eat any. You ate three and started to conk out. I had to help you up the stairs, do you remember that?"

"No."

"Well, I'll cook something that's good for your memory. Come on in with me, then I'll drive you home."

The lighthouse proper was behind a small white frame building with a red roof. The sign over the door said SEA-VIEW PUBLIC LIBRARY. Tinker left her books at the desk, where a smiling librarian took them, and we walked to the back of the room. "You ever been here before?" she asked me.

"No. How long has it been a library?"

"Oh, ages. Come on, the interesting stuff is this way."

The next room seemed to be the beginning of a picture gallery that spiraled up the inside of the lighthouse like a staircase shell. The pictures on the walls were in various media and styles, but they were all twentieth-century work by artists I did not know. One that struck my fancy was a colored woodcut of a leafless tree in a clearing. Dark gray strips of cloth hung limp from the branches. I thought it was quite powerful; the title was *Draped Death Tree*.

Near it was an oil painting called *At Feather Field*. In this one, half a dozen white-robed figures were standing in a field where the vegetation was represented by feathers of all sizes and various pastel colors. The figures were turned towards the rear of the field, but nothing was there for them to look at. A breeze was beginning to ripple the feathers at the right side of the canvas.

I saw Tinker watching me as we moved up the ramp. We came to a canvas in which a well-preserved group of oldsters stood crowded together on a set of bleachers as if waiting to have their picture taken. I liked the playful realism, and also I thought I recognized some of the faces. When I looked closer, I saw that they were all my old classmates, including Karen Woodland. The title was *Class Reunion, Yes.*

"When was this painted?" I asked. "Is it a local artist?" The name on the plaque, Rhonda Vassell, meant nothing to me.

Tinker shrugged in reply, and we walked on. Some of the other pictures were hardly more than visual jokes, for example an acrylic painting called *Erect Simian with Dog.* The simian was a bald young man dressed only in a belt and a necktie; the dog, a dachshund, was preceding him along a suburban street with a leash in its mouth. The leash was attached to the knot in the man's necktie. Then there was a painting of a man in Bermuda shorts addressing a ball teed up on the crest of a wave: the title was *Open Sea Golfer.* It made me smile; I wondered if the artist had been thinking of Marvell's "Where the remote Bermudas ride, In th' ocean's bosom unespied."

The paintings I had seen were varied in treatment and subject matter, but I noticed that they all had two things in common, the realistic treatment and the even, source-less light.

In another acrylic, the flattened bodies of toads lay on a background of autumn leaves as if seen from directly above. The toads looked like roadkill, or perhaps dried specimens; they were as flat as bow ties. Some were almost identical in color and shape, but when you looked closely, no two were exactly alike. This one was called *Unmated Toads*.

"What do you think?" Tinker asked.

"They're quite refreshing. Surely they're not all by local artists?"

"You haven't seen anything yet. Come on."

I followed her through a curtained doorway and found myself in total darkness. When the light came up, I was looking at a painting of a monster in a huge ornate frame. The frame was romantic or baroque, with a lot of gilt leaves and blossoms. The monster's head was human except for the grey horns that peeped out of its curly black hair. Its skin was waxy pale. It had a little black mustache, pointed like an Italian opera singer's, and a little goatee oiled into black ringlets. The body was that of a lion and had a rank circus smell, unless I was imagining that; the tail was a scorpion's. Every scale was distinct, and yet it looked flat and unconvincing, like a colored drawing in a book. I reached out to touch it.

"I wouldn't," said the monster.

I looked around for Tinker. My heart was thumping absurdly. She said to the monster, "Okay to take him through?"

The monster rolled its eyes at me, then closed them without speaking.

"Is it real?" I whispered to Tinker.

"No. Come on."

Next came a conventional oil painting in the style of Brueghel, but when I looked closely I saw that it represented a group of people gathered around a baby's head just emerging from the vagina. One of the men, a gap-toothed cretin, was grinning as he looked out of the frame; he had a wooden ladle in his hand, and now I saw that the crown of the baby's head had been broken like an eggshell, and there was nothing but darkness inside.

In the next alcove stood a life-size figure I recognized; it was the motel keeper who had told me about the word games. He had a dictionary on a table in front of him, but he did not move or speak, although a dove was perched on his head. Sawdust was leaking out of his broadcloth shirt at the shoulder; there was a small trickle of blood at the corner of his mouth. The dove fluttered its wings loudly a few times, then folded them again and sat still.

"Why are you showing me this?" I said to Tinker.

"Come on," she said, and took me by the arm. In the next alcove I saw my brother Tom standing, dressed as I had last seen him, so lifelike that I could not believe he was wax. I moved closer and touched his face; the mouth opened, and his familiar voice said, "Three black people. One of them, the one sitting across from me, was a man in his forties who had metal hooks instead of hands. He could hold a fork, but . . ."

After a moment I realized that he was repeating the

story he had told me in London. "Stop it!" I said. I grasped his shoulder, and his whole body rotated lightly and smoothly, as if it weighed nothing at all.

I saw that he was hollow in back, and that there was a box fixed to the middle of the shell, with a rod coming up out of it to move his hollow jaw. " . . . His wife put food on the fork for him, and she wiped his mouth . . ." I pushed him hard, and he fell over, repeating, "wiped his mouth, wiped his mouth, wiped his mouth . . ."

I was sobbing, for no reason that I could think of. I looked in my pockets for a tissue but couldn't find one, and wiped my eyes with my hands.

Tinker took my arm again and drew me on to the next exhibit. This was a long alcove in which large gray statues sat in stone chairs, too old to move, talking incomprehensibly to each other and rumbling with laughter like the grating of stone. I found myself saying, "Oh. Oh. Oh."

Next was a large mouth on a metal stand. The mouth opened and turned itself inside out, over and over. I closed my eyes. "No more."

Tinker led me through a final doorway into a circular lighted room. "That's the way things are," she said, and put a wad of tissues into my hand. I wiped my eyes, and saw that we were not in the top of the lighthouse, as I had expected, but under a vast transparent dome so clear that it was almost invisible. The stars overhead were brighter than I had ever seen them. In the middle of the dome two slabs of white plastic were afloat, like the halves of a crystal sandwich. I thought I heard theramin music in the distance.

Tinker passed her hand between the slabs, and the

stars jumped into a new configuration. Now one yellowish star was much brighter than all the others. "That's our sun," she told me. Her lisp made it sound like "fun." "See Venus, close to it on the right? Earth is on the bottom, far-ther down, and Mars is way up there on the left, that little red spark? It's hard to see. The other planets are too far out."

"Where's Mongo?"

"Get serious. There isn't any Mongo." She put her hand between the slabs again. This time we were looking at millions of star specks arranged into a spiral galaxy. "That's the Milky Way. Our sun is about halfway out from the center. You'd never find your way back if I left you here."

She turned and smiled. "Just kidding. Do you believe me?"

"Yes, Tinker."

"You're lying, but that's good. Try not to believe me too often." She put her hand between the slabs again. This time the sky was filled with galaxies and nebulas. Once more, and now the galaxies formed the shape of a ginger-bread man. An arrow-shaped sign appeared, pointing to the middle of his head: GROVERTOWN 23 BILLION LIGHT-YEARS.

"As below, so above," she said. "Do you understand that?"

"No."

She looked at me disapprovingly. "Bill, you're going to have to go through it just the same, no matter how stub-born you act. Are you ready?"

"No, I'm not. Ready for what?"

"Come on, I'll show you." She took my hand, and although I resisted, I seemed to tilt forward in spite of myself into a room whose sill was dropped a little, so that I staggered for a moment, and a woman in a white coat took my arm to steady me.

A man, also dressed in a white coat, came forward. We were in a circular high-ceilinged room with a smell of ozone in it. An iron hook dangled on a chain from the open skylight. On the wall behind an examination table I saw a large poster of the human nervous system in bright blue and crimson—brain, spinal cord and sprays of nerves filling the space of head, body and limbs, as if all the flesh had been dissected away or eaten by piranhas.

"Mr. Stout, I'm Dr. Gelb," said the man. "Stand over here, please."

"Morris Gelb?" I asked.

"We're not using first names," he said dryly. He pushed me against an upright screen that I recognized as an old-fashioned fluoroscope. "Put your head back."

He retired to a desk and the woman joined him there. I saw now that she was wearing a surgical mask. They bent together over a monitor. "Um-hm, there it is," said Gelb. He glanced up. "Turn your head to the right, Mr. Stout."

I put my cheek against the cold metal plate. "Are you the collector who bought Ms. Sanchez's cards?" I asked.

"Hold your head still. Yes, I collect cards," he said, still looking at the monitor. "It's a harmless hobby, or so I always imagined. Now turn your head to the left. Mm-hm."

"What do you think?" the woman asked in a low voice.

"The only way to be absolutely sure would be an exploratory or a post. As the case might be."

"Then will you cross him off?"

"We can't take the chance, Rosemary."

She muttered something, and he said irritably, "It doesn't matter *now*." He was rummaging in a drawer. "Mr. Stout, you're aware that you were hospitalized with a gunshot wound in Milan."

"Yes."

Gelb brought out a pen and made a note on a clipboard. "What you don't know is," he said, "that there was an accident on the operating table, late that night, or rather early the next morning. The wound to your head was more serious than they told you."

"Wait a minute, I'm not following. You say there was an accident?"

"Yes, and unfortunately this universe is falling apart as a consequence. You're hanging on to control fairly well, writing new scenarios as you go along, but of course that can't last forever." Gelb put the clipboard down and came out from behind the desk. "Step over here, Mr. Stout. Turn." He passed something around my waist, and the woman buckled it in front.

"Look," I said, "aren't you at least going to tell me what the hell you want?" I tried to move my arms, but they were constricted by the belt.

Gelb mumbled something, of which I caught the words, "All you're going to get." He threw a switch on the wall and I heard the whining of an electric motor as the chain descended from the skylight. When it was low enough to suit him, he carried the hook over behind me. The woman came closer and put one hand on my chest. "It will take just a moment," she said. The white mask sucked in and out as she spoke.

"Rosemary?"

She shook her head and turned away.

Gelb went back to the wall and threw the switch again. The motor whined, the chain tightened, and I was snatched into the air. "What are you doing?" I shouted.

The chain carried me up twisting and swaying through the open skylight, and I found myself on a railed circular roof under grey clouds. Traffic was moving slowly in the streets of the town below, and I could hear the distant swish of the tires. I could tell from the sound that the streets were damp. When I swung the other way I was looking out over the ocean. The air was salt and moist; a few tiny raindrops touched my face.

The chain that held me ran up to the tip of a gray-painted sort of crane apparatus and then down again to a gray drum. While I was looking at this, a trapdoor opened, and Gelb and the woman emerged. "All right, let's get it done," he said. "Wait a minute." He walked to the pipe rail and leaned across it.

Suddenly the woman ran towards him. His head began to turn, but she rammed her shoulder into his bum and he went over with a loud cry. His trousered legs waved upside down for an instant, then disappeared. After a moment I heard a distant echoing whack.

Into the silence I said, "Rosemary?" She did not reply, but walked back to the crane and began to work the levers.

I felt myself swinging helplessly across the roof until I was tilted out over the railing, then another inch and another, and now I was leaning head downwards looking at Seaview spread out to the horizon. I could see the stained concrete of the parking lot directly below. Near Tinker's Cherokee, the body of Dr. Gelb lay in a wide splash of red.

Tinker herself appeared in the edge of my vision. At first I thought she was really there, but then I saw that she was no bigger than a house cat. She sat on the pipe rail, then rose and stepped casually off into space. "Time to grow wings," she remarked. I saw that she had sprouted four gauzy wings, not separate like a dragonfly's but fused together in pairs like a wasp's. They vibrated prismatically in the sunlight, and there were dainty silver antennae on her forehead.

"I can't," I said.

"Then you'd better fall, hadn't you?"

Behind me, the woman's hands loosened the hook and gave me a vigorous shove; I would not have believed she was so strong. I soared out into the air like a diver, arms at my sides and legs extended, and rotated slowly head downwards while the concrete rose towards me like a shout.

The statue of a seated man

I closed my eyes and felt the blow, but I slipped on through the surface as smoothly as water. I sank deeper in the darkness, feeling rather like a peeled grape in a swimming pool, and at last I sensed that I was curving up in a long arc towards the surface again.

As my speed diminished, my legs drew up, bending at the knee, and when I opened my eyes I found myself seated comfortably in a chair, dry, alive, and quite calm, looking straight across a table at the statue of a seated man who was poised in the act of lifting a fork to his mouth.

The statue seemed to be made of grey pewter. To left and right of it were other statues, all posed like diners in a restaurant. The darkness beyond them was the funereal gray of wet cement, and I knew that I was deep underground, in some place where the sun never came. The room was silent except for a faint scratching noise at long intervals.

Everything on the tables was the same opaque grey, even the tablecloths, glasses and silverware. There were no shadows, and I couldn't tell where the light was coming from, unless it was radiating feebly from the pewter itself.

I screwed myself around in my seat to look behind me. Rows of tables and seated statues faded into the murk. I realized that I wasn't breathing, and I took a gulp of the dead air, but it didn't seem to do me much good.

All around me, the statues were frozen in fantastic attitudes, some thrusting forks into their mouths, some leaning together with arms around each other, some cupping their fingers at nose level, some with mouths wide open and eyes shut in silent laughter. All of them looked as if they had been cast in pewter at the exact instant when their faces registered some expression normally too fleeting to be seen.

At a long table behind me a family was sitting, all ages from grandparents down to a babe in arms. The grandfather, a bald little man, had his eyes half closed and his mouth pursed as if to spit. The grandmother's eyes were shut tight, her lip lifted straight across like an awning; farther along the table a young woman was watching with a leer of unbelievable lechery, and a young man had his finger in his nose. Behind them were two or three standing figures, leaning forward off balance, and I could make out another on the staircase to the left that led up to the mezzanine.

When I turned round and looked at the seated figure before me, I realized that it was tantalizingly familiar. It was a man with a bristly mustache, bending forward over the table with one hand on his tie and the other raising a fork. Everything was completely detailed, even his eyelashes and the herringbone weave of his jacket. His eyes were closed, his mouth half open and the tongue showing. I realized now that he bore a strong resemblance to Roger Wort, and this place might have been modeled after the restaurant where we had had dinner in Milan. For some obscure reason this realization terrified me, but I could not express my terror in any way.

The gray wall with its curious dado along the bottom was probably meant to be the plateglass window of the restaurant, pewter here like everything else; to the right was the closed entrance door and the display case, pewter too.

Roger still had not moved. His fork was halfway to his mouth, and now that I looked more closely I saw that a bit of food had dropped off the fork and was hanging in midair.

I thought there must be something holding it up, and I reached out and felt it all around. The thing was as solid and chill as a lump of glass, but as I went on handling it, it seemed to soften. Presently I could mold it between my fingers, and when I drew my hand back the lump came too. It had a pinkish color now, and looked to be corkscrew pasta in a shrimp sauce.

Obeying a frenzied impulse, I stuffed the gobbet into Roger's mouth, over his grey pewter tongue. The food kept dribbling out and I kept pushing it back in, until to my disgust I felt the mouth softening under my fingers. After I pulled my hand away the lips kept on working, and the pink tongue came out a little to lick up the sauce, which was dribbling down the statue's chin; then gradually everything congealed into pewter again, and Roger's fork was still halfway to his pewter mouth.

In a frenzy of disgust I wiped my fingers on the statue's face, into the hollow at the inside of its left eye and then over the closed eyelid itself. After a few moments I felt the eyelid begin to soften, and I forced myself to keep my fingers there until the lid rose and the eyeball moved. When I drew my hand back, the statue's insufferable blue left eye was glaring and blinking at me as if it alone were alive.

I sprang up and fled to the end of the row of tables, where the wall and the display case stopped me. I saw that the outside door was slightly ajar, and I wondered if I could bring it into real time as I had the shrimp pasta, and in that way manage to escape.

I ran my hands over the door again and again, especially around the margin and over the hinges, and eventually I thought I felt it yield a little when I tugged on the handle, but it always froze before it could actually move. Then I thought of the window: what if I could thaw a bit of it and break it out with my shoe before it hardened?

I rubbed the grey glass as if I were a child working at the frost on a window, and after a few minutes it turned transparent enough to see that statues were sitting outside at the sidewalk tables under the pewter trees, and beyond them pewter automobiles were frozen in the pewter street. There was nowhere to go.

Gasping for air, I ran around the tables. As soon as I got behind the row I could tell that there was something wrong with the seated figures. The diners didn't exist below the tabletops; they had no legs or feet, and their heads and torsos were empty vessels, all with the convex sides pointing towards the place where I had been seated a few minutes ago. Their faces were like the inside-out images in plaster molds, and when I moved past them their blank eyes seemed to follow me.

Those who had been looking in the other direction were worse: they had no faces at all, only the backs of heads turned outside in, like the burst heads of rubber dolls. I felt an electric prickle up my neck, because I knew I was seeing something unlawful, just as Gallagher had warned me I might: I was seeing the world as it truly was. The scraping sound came again.

I was closer to the stairway now, and I could see that a waiter halfway up was standing on one foot, twisted around very awkwardly to look behind him; he had evidently just dropped a large oval tray with some dishes and silverware, but it hadn't landed yet. Behind him there was a curious billowing in the air, as if it were in violent motion, although in fact it was perfectly still. When I squeezed up past the waiter, I saw another man above him at the head of the stairs. He had a gun in his hand, and after a moment I saw that it was Emilio da Lionghi.

When I retreated down the steps and looked again at the turbulent part of the air, I saw a tiny dark pellet hanging above the waiter's shoulder. There was a curious pattern, like the wake of a boat, going backward from it towards da Lionghi and his gun. I reached out and touched the bullet, but unlike anything else in the room it was intensely hot, and I jerked my hand away.

The faint scraping noise came again, and then again after only a short pause. It kept on at an increasing rate, and I thought I saw now that the waiter and the air around him were moving ever so slightly. I stumbled back down a step, as if I had lost my balance for a moment. Now I was moving backwards, and the figures around me were beginning to stir, groaning and creaking as they came back to life. When I got near the table I could see the empty chair where I was going to sit facing Roger, and where I would turn around just in time to receive the bullet in the most private part of my body.

I struggled to resist, but I felt as if I were trapped in the gravity of a giant planet. I sat in the chair and turned my head, which seemed to be in a vise. The whole room was vibrating now with a bass chord and the statues in it were jerking into motion a fraction of an inch at a time, flushing with color as they moved. At the top of the staircase I could make out the whiff of grayness where da Lionghi had fired his pistol. I looked for the bullet, and found it in the air a yard away, a tiny superheated pellet aimed at my eyes.

Then all the sounds screamed upward in pitch, and I heard the tray drop, a thick percussive sound that went on and on. A voice said, "Will he live?"

Sleep and dreams

I sometimes dream of horrible things, tortures too humiliating to speak to anyone about. What if I woke up someday and the dreams went on?

Years ago Myra read a book called *An Experiment with Time* and kept a dream diary, made me keep one too for a while. You were supposed to be able to remember the dreams better if you kept a notebook under your pillow and wrote them down immediately on waking. Then they were meant to make more sense, but mine didn't. In one of my dreams, I was riding with two people in a taxi. A half-eaten tamale sat on the jump seat in front of us. We were involved in some Mafia thing in New York, we were on our way to a ship at the docks, and this woman said to me, "Do you know what *Good Humor* means in Italian?"

"No," I said.

"Bad taste."

Sleep and dreams are two of the great mysteries. Do people who sell sleepwear sleep well, or do they lie awake dreaming about selling sleepwear? There used to be a shop in Chicago called Sweet Dreams. Did the women who bought their nightgowns there ever have nightmares? People deprived of sleep, and people in the last stages of alcoholic delirium, sometimes have hallucinations—waking dreams. Maybe we sleep just to keep our dreams safely inside. Sometimes I wish I could curl up and go to sleep the way I did when I was a child, deep and warm in the blankets, and just keep on dreamlessly sleeping forever.

There was another huge earth barrier near Corvallis, and I had to detour as far as Albany, then turn south on 99W. I couldn't get onto I-5, it was gridlocked in both directions by multiple wrecks.

Coming into Eugene from the west in cool sunshine, I happened to notice the motel I had stayed at before. I was driving Art Fleishman's old green Chevy again; the hood was dented, apparently by a collision that I had no memory of, and something had spilled and dried on the front seat. I was so confused that I parked in front of the open door of one of the rooms and went in, but when I opened the bureau I saw that all my things were in the drawers, and I had a sudden fear that I was about to meet myself. I rushed out and got in the car again, although I was exhausted, and drove to Klamath Falls, where I found a motel and dreamed that Tinker and I were standing at the top of Ocean Street looking at the barrier.

"It's your fault, you know," she said.

"Mine? How so?"

"It's all your idea, and it's coming apart. Other people can run around patching it up here and there, but nobody can put the whole thing together except you, and there's not much chance of that now."

"But what have I done wrong?" I asked. Her face turned towards me and grew larger, and I woke up. The room was shaking with what turned out to be a minor earthquake.

As I dressed I noticed that one of my fingernails, the middle one on the right hand, was acquiring a dull gray rim that looked like stainless steel. It was not at all uncomfortable, but it was very hard, and it occurred to me that it would be a problem when I had to cut my nails.

On the morning news, before I left the motel, I saw false bergs afloat in Lake Michigan. A Coast Guard cutter was steering through them to show that they were illusory, but the last time it did this it didn't come out the other side.

The talking head who explained all this had a somewhat retroussé nose, meaning that his nostrils were tilted up and prominently displayed as he faced the camera, and I found myself staring at these two round dark nose holes, wondering what their significance was for me, and losing track of the head's message whatever it was.

I tried to find other heads on different channels, but by that time it was futile; they all had nostrils aimed directly at the camera, and this seemed so bizarre to me that I could not concentrate on anything else. I did gather that craters were continuing to appear, in the eastern U.S. as well as the west, along with natural disasters of every kind. Towards the end of the week a swarthy man in uniform with a beret and a black mustache frequently appeared, but he had nostrils too.

Sometimes the television displayed a chart of the solar

system, with the Sun, Earth, and Mars prominently labeled, and between Earth and Mars another dot labeled MONGO. A polka-dotted arc showed still another object approaching Earth from Mongo, and this line was longer every time I saw the chart. In the evenings, and sometimes at night when I couldn't sleep, with Geppi's instrument I saw a little purplish disk rising over the western horizon.

The discarded newspapers I occasionally found were covered with exclamatory headlines: MONGOIDS LAND IN GOBI, COMET NEARS EARTH, etc. On the television news I saw phalanxes of flying drones filling the skies over Colorado and Nevada, and silvery streaks of "comet rain" descending on Michigan. The purple disk rising in the west was now much larger than the full moon, and sometimes in the evenings I could see that it was a purple face peeping over the horizon, like a boy looking over a fence into the next yard.

In the parking lot of a hotel in Winnemucca, Nevada, looking up on a misty evening, I saw one of the drones passing over, its lighthearted oven aflicker like a Chinese lantern.

In Ely, I noticed a scorpion on the sun-washed adobe wall of my motel. It looked like a little lobster carrying its tail over its head. I knew it was Ely because of the sign on the highway: ELY, BIGGEST LITTLE TOWN IN THE UNIVERSE.

In the middle of the night I woke up needing to piss. I had left the bathroom light on and the door open a crack for a night-light, as I always did, and I could see that there was something unlikely about the floor around the bed. When I looked more closely, I realized that the whole floor was gone; in its place were the tops of a number of white open pipes of various sizes. The pipes seemed to be randomly placed, and the gaps between them went down into darkness. There was a strong smell of sewage.

I didn't want to get out of bed, but my need was urgent, and I stepped down onto the nearest cluster of pipe ends; they hurt my bare feet, but I took another step and another, past a dark pile of luggage that hadn't been there before, and got safely into the bathroom at last. The soles of my feet were covered in the greasy arcs of the pipe ends I had stepped on. It was old dark sludge, and wouldn't wipe off.

When I was done pissing I left the door wide open for more light, and on the way back to bed I had a better look at the luggage that was piled in the middle of the room. It was grey leather, a matched set that looked like one that Jenny had once had; I noticed particularly an upright rectangular box of unusual size like the one she had carried hats in; it even had her initials, J.S., in silver letters in the corner. I got as close to it as I could, reached over and pressed the catches. They clicked open, the front of the box fell down and I was looking at a gelatinous purple-black human head, blind and swollen, much bigger than life. The lips moved slightly; they were gummed shut, and so were the eyes, but under the lids I could see the eyeballs turning towards me.

I picked up the front of the case and tried to close it, but the thing had bulged out of the box and the lid wouldn't shut. Where I touched the head accidentally with my fingers, it was ice-cold and sticky. In desperation I toppled the box over and pushed it scraping across the pipe tops to a gap wide enough to admit it. The box tilted and dropped silently, and a long time later I heard an echo.

In the morning I complained to the manager about the cloacal smell in the room. He said severely, "I'm sure you must be mistaken." There were dark rims all around my fingernails, but I didn't stay to argue with him.

Storm clouds made the sky almost as dark as night when I approached Green River in midafternoon, and I was driving into snow mixed with sleet that flew at me like the lights of a tunnel. The sense that I was a rolling egg came back to me more strongly than before; I was gathering mass like a spaceship traveling too close to the speed of light, and as I stared into the oncoming white stars they seemed to be leaving yellow tails in the darkness. The car radio was mumbling, "*. . . below-freezing temperatures tonight in the North Plains, with the mercury dropping as . . .*" Something made me look around, and I saw that the purple-black head was there, much larger now, filling the passenger seat. It lay on its side in the cup of upholstery, looking up at me out of the corners of its open jelly eyes.

My reaction was instant; I stamped on the brake as hard as I could and the car swerved off the road. The gelatin head hit the floor with a thump like a rotten pumpkin.

I got out, shaking all over, and staggered around to the passenger side, but the door would not open properly because of the way the car was tilted. I went back to the other side again. I thought the car would probably start, and I could drive it up onto the road and then see about the head, but I could not make myself get in and do it.

Headlights came towards me while I stood there freezing, and a large Greyhound bus drew to a stop behind the Chevy. The door opened and the driver called out through the snow, "You want a ride to Gallup?"

"I certainly do. Thank you!" I looked through the car window to make sure the head was still there before I opened the trunk to get my suitcase. I snatched it and left the trunk lid standing open. Grey pellets crunched under my feet as I ran down the road; I clambered up the steps into the breathing heat. "In fact, can I get a ticket to Boston?"

The driver was a frog-faced man about my age, with scant dark hair combed across the top of his head. "Go set down," he said. "Straighten it out later."

The interior of the bus was illuminated only by dim sidelights; in the greenish darkness I walked down the aisle until I found a window seat, and put my suitcase in the overhead rack. The door closed with a fart of compressed air, and I fell back into the seat before I was quite ready. I settled myself as best I could. The bus was warm, perhaps too warm, and there were strong odors of wet wool, oil, dust, sweat, and other things I couldn't identify.

Even the sidelights were turned off now. The tinted windows effectively shut out any view of the landscape to either side; I could see my fellow passengers only as silhouettes against the hurtling snow spattered by the headlights.

At Elgin a few passengers got off and another got on, a young man in a fishing jacket with many pockets. He came along the aisle, passing up several empty places in order to sit beside me. "You're Mr. Stout, aren't you?" He held some sort of metal instrument towards my face.

"Yes," I said, taken by surprise.

"What made you transition to this vehicle?"

I drew back slightly. "I don't know what you mean."

"Well, let me rephrase that. Do you feel more secure now in terms of wheelness?"

"Sorry, I'm not getting this at all. Who are you?"

"I'm a freelance quizzer from Albuquerque, Mr. Stout. Will you help me out? I need the money."

"Look, I'm tired and I don't think I'm up to it. I'm quite sure it's my fault."

"May I quote you on that?"

"Yes, sure."

"Thank you very much, sir. We've been talking to Wellington Stout, live on the omnibus between Green River Utah and Gallup New Mexico. This is Ed Teller for Reality One." He folded up his instrument, got up and backed away. At the next stop I saw him get off in a flurry of snow.

Late in the afternoon, the bus pulled into a little town and stopped in front of a hotel. The driver said through his microphone, "Folks, this is Mexican Hat, Utah. My relief driver isn't here, and I'm going to stop and have supper and get a night's rest. I'd advise you to do the same. There's enough rooms in the Peruvian Hotel right here or the Aurora Tourist Court across the road, and if you want to set up all night you can do it in the Peruvian lobby where it's warmer than this bus will be. Mexican Hat, all out."

In the lobby I asked him about my ticket, and he told

me we would "straighten it out" in Denver. "This isn't the regular route," he said. "Everything's screwed up account of the craters, so be patient." I thanked him profusely and went up to my room.

The bedstead was carved and painted with Mexican designs, and there was a pitcher on the dresser, although there was nothing in it but cobwebs. The room was large and airy, with two fans under the ceiling that were controlled by the light switch. As evening fell their cold breeze was unpleasant on my head, and I couldn't find any separate switch for them, so I turned off the lights and sat in the gloom looking at the red digital eyes in the black box and listening to the Western music it played.

After a time white scintillations of "comet rain" began dropping slowly through the ceiling and disappearing again into the floor. It was easy enough to dodge them. When one hit the back of my hand, I felt nothing, but later on I discovered that the spot was cold and numb. Luckily the shower stopped before I was ready for bed, but I had no sooner lain down than I discovered there was a dripping faucet in the bathroom. I got up and tried to turn it off, no luck, then I closed the bathroom door, but I could still hear it. Lying there listening to the drops fall into the stained porcelain bowl, I remembered a film I'd once seen of some highly magnified insect's ovipositor laying eggs. The image was spectral gray and white, in that funny lighting that such films have, as if everything were made of translucent gray plastic and yet horribly alive.

The business end of the ovipositor dipped and swelled, the egg came blipping out in a no-nonsense way, the aperture contracted, swelled again, dropped another egg. It was the tempo that was disturbing, the production-line briskness, nothing like the reverent "mystery of life" sort of films you see of human reproduction. Blip. Blip. Blip. Like drops of water into a bowl, and no more significant. I had remembered that film, because it had made me realize what people mean when they say that science is irreverent. Blip. What's the point?

Sometime before dawn I was awakened by a scratching sound that seemed to come from the closet. I got up and listened with my head at the door. For a while I heard nothing; then the sound came again, very faint, a creaking rather than a scratching noise. I thought of calling the desk, but at this time of night there was probably no one there, and besides, if someone came up and discovered a mouse, I would feel a perfect fool.

The worst part was that I really was afraid of encountering a mouse; I would almost rather it had been an assassin. I paced the floor a bit, then got my Swiss Army knife out of my trousers pocket, for reassurance more than anything else, and cautiously opened the closet door. There didn't seem to be anything there but my jacket and mac, and a few extra coat hangers. Then the sound came again, and I saw that there was another door at the back of the closet. I stepped in and opened this door too. I was ready to back out again in case there was anyone in the next room. It was empty, but the bedclothes were disordered, and now I saw that the front door was swinging back and forth with a creaking sound. Feeling relieved, I went to close it, and now I saw that I was looking out into a vast dark parking lot like the one where Geppi had given me the telescope. The more I looked out, the more it seemed to me that it was the same place; I could even see the Arby's across the road where I had met the drunken rancher.

Then I saw a movement behind a parked car, and heard a voice call, "Losted!"

I stepped out into the cold. "Geppi?"

Now his figure came towards me. "Forgive," he said plaintively. Too late, I saw that another figure was coming up behind him. It was Tom, in a blue blazer and string tie, with a cowboy hat on his head. "Let's go inside, for God's sake," he said, and brushed by me into the motel. I looked around for Geppi, but he was gone, and after a moment I followed Tom inside.

He was standing in the middle of the room holding an unlit cigar. "Welly, are you going to be a goddamn fool all your life? Do you know that the Spaeth people have been tracking you every damn inch of the way?"

"They can't, Tom. These aren't the shoes they put the strips in."

"Don't kid yourself. By now the locator strips are in your *feet*."

"My feet?"

"Don't you think they're smart enough? Don't you think they ever said to themselves, what if this guy takes off the goddamn shoes? Those strips make chemical impressions on your skin, right through your socks. The only way you could get rid of them would be to cut off your feet. Are you ready for that?"

"Tom, what are you so angry about?"

"Ah, you've screwed this whole thing up to where a saint couldn't untangle it. Have you got anything to drink?"

"No."

He was patting his pockets. "Well, have you got a match?"

"I think there are some in the other room." We went through the closet, and I handed him the matches from the ashtray on the end table. "What a dump," Tom said. He sat down in the armchair and began to light his cigar. "I wouldn't give a nickel for your chances if you don't get some advice," he remarked.

"Advice of what kind?"

"Christ, you're a blind man. For instance, walk around this room, as close to the walls as you can get. Go on, do it."

To humor him, I walked around the room. There was furniture against all the walls, and it was not possible to get very close to them except in one or two places. One of these was the corner between the bed and the bureau. I could have got right next to the wallpaper there, but something made me reluctant.

Tom said, "What did you feel in that corner?"

"Well, I didn't want to go in there."

"Right, and that's pretty obvious. There's a hole in that corner, you could lose a foot or a leg if you're not careful. Now try something a little trickier. Go into the bathroom and come out again."

I was interested now, and I did what he told me. When I came out, he said, "Again, a little slower."

I did it. "Slower still," he said. This time when I crossed the threshold coming out, a stab of vibration went through my body from head to toes, so unexpected that it made me cry out.

"All right, that wasn't pleasant, but it wasn't fatal. Some of them are."

"What was it?"

"They call it a blade. It comes from a higher energy level overhead, but it's too weak to hurt you unless you walk through it real slow. Which way is the head of your bed pointing?"

"I don't know. East, I think."

"East southeast." He handed me a chromed tube. "Here's a little compass. It won't do you much good right now, but the practice will come in handy later."

The black radio on the bureau cleared its throat and remarked:

—He's immurated and closurized, you know. Oyez, he's our man in-house, in-country, and in-continent.

—Ha, ha, he's a fissure of men!

—Lettuce go down and fecund their sanduages lest they become dogs like us.

I picked up the box and shook it until it stopped. "Why can't I get rid of this thing?" I asked.

"Don't you really know? Use Geppi's telescope."

I got the instrument out of the drawer and looked through it at the black box. Between it and my torso was a thin transparent tube. Little men in overalls were moving through it, almost too pale to see.

When I put the box down on the bed and tried to

touch the tube while looking through the lens, I could see
the tube moving away from my finger, but all I could feel
was a faint tingling sensation.

I looked up. "But what's the point?" I said.

"What do you think that gadget is?"

"Well, usually it seems to be a radio."

"No, it's an infernal machine. A planet buster—when
the time comes, it'll blow the Earth to bloody hell."

"But why? I mean, why is it attached to me?"

"You're going to find the right place for it. When you
do, boom."

"Tom, that can't happen. How can I stop it?"

"You could kill yourself, I guess. It wouldn't be easy,
but you could jump into molten lava or something."

"Would that keep the bomb from going off?"

"Probably, but you can't do it. You're controlled six
ways from Sunday. You may think you're a free agent, but
you're not. Do you want a clue? When things seem to be
more or less ordinary and normal, you can be pretty sure
they really are. When something crazy seems to be happening, you know they're controlling you for one of two reasons. Either they want you to do something you wouldn't
do in your right mind, or else something's going on you're
not supposed to notice. They own you, Welly, don't think
they don't. There's powers involved in this could squash
you like a bug on a fingernail."

"Why don't they, then?"

"You're a useful bug." He pointed to the black box.
"Like a flea pulling a thread in the flea circus."

"Tom, why are you telling me all this?"

"I haven't got any other choice. They want us both to squirm." He sighed and rubbed his cigar out in the ashtray. "You won't see me alive again, Welly." He walked into the closet and closed the door behind him. When I opened it to look, there was no one in there, and no door to the next room. Tom's cigar was still in the ashtray, but it had never been lit.

A salesman down on his luck

In the morning the driver rounded us all up in the coffee shop and we piled into the bus again. The sky was overcast, but there was no snow or hail, and we could see a little blue peeping out over the horizon to the south. The passengers were full of waffles and coffee, and their mood was cheerful.

At Kayenta an hour later, a middle-aged man puffed up the aisle with a heavy valise and sat beside me, arranging his overcoat around him; its pockets seemed to be so full that it was hard for him to sit comfortably. His jowls were unshaven; he looked like a salesman down on his luck. "Going far?" he asked.

"Boston."

"Oh, is that right? Nice town, nice town. I'm headed for Denver myself. Go there two, three times a year. Not by bus usually, but my car broke down."

"So did mine."

"That right? What's your line?"

"I'm in lingerie."

"Say, maybe we can do some business. Take a look at this." He pulled something out of his pocket and showed it to me: a wristwatch with a gray leather strap and a domed crystal, under which I could see green and red lines slowly revolving.

"What is it?" I asked.

"Galactic time. A year from now everybody will be using it. I'm getting five hundred smackers for these babies now, but next year you'll see them for thirty-nine ninety-five. That's all right, because the market is in the *billions*." He put the watch away and pulled out a silver device the size of a palmtop. It had a dark green monitor on which, when he pressed a button, I could see vague figures moving. "Galactic entertainment," he said. "Not ready for market yet, but the potential? Unlimited." He edged closer. "I can put you into a sweet little thing. These are being made in the largest off-sea lab in the Western Hemisphere, down in the Dominican Republic near Santo Domingo. You ever been there?"

"No."

"Perfect. Tropical climate, palm trees, not too many nigras. And cheap? They're begging for tourists. Hotel on the beach, seventy-five a night. Local rum ten bucks a liter, but it won't last. I'm buying real estate with every dime I can spare, it's a sin to pass it up. You want in for a thousand dollars?"

"No, can't afford it, I'm afraid."

He scowled and was quiet for a moment. "Well, you can afford this, anyway." He showed me an oblong brown slab with a label, REAR GOOD, and a picture of a shooting star. "Galactic candy, ten dollars. Try it, it's not bad."

I gave him the ten because I was sorry for him, and he instantly produced a can of soda in a silvery wrapper. "Something to wash it down with."

"How much?"

"Ten bucks."

I gave him the other two fives, taking care to let him see they were the last ones in my wallet, then closed my eyes and pretended to be asleep. When I felt that he was gone I looked at the soda can: it was labeled GALACTI COLA. I popped the lid and tried it, but it tasted like ink.

I took the black box out of my pocket and tried to get some music or news on it. There was a whisper of voices, too faint to make out the words, then a drift of melody, twanging guitars, almost equally faint. Then the box seemed to clear its throat and said, "Attention. Attention please. A message for Wellington Stout." It was a man's voice; the accent was vaguely Southern, perhaps Tennessean.

I glanced at my neighbor across the aisle, who was looking at me suspiciously under his canvas hat. "Did you hear that?" I asked.

"Sure."

"Did it say a message for Stout?"

"Yup." He turned away as if to dissociate himself from me.

Suddenly the box said, in Cicely's voice, "Uncle Bill?"

My heart was hammering at my throat. I said, "Cis?"

A pause, then, "Oh, Uncle Bill, we've been so worried! Where are you?"

"I'm on a bus. Cis, is this really you?" I glanced at my neighbor, but he was looking out the window and had one hand cupped over his ear.

"Tell me where you are, Uncle Bill, I want to see you."

"I think the next stop is Farmington." I turned towards my neighbor. "Is that right?"

"Right," he said in a muffled voice without turning around.

"Farmington? What state?"

"New Mexico. It's north of Albuquerque."

"Will you stay there, Uncle Bill? Please? Get off the bus and take a hotel room. I'll call later to see where you are. Will you do that? Say yes."

"All right, Cis. But where are you? How did you—"

"I can't talk now. I love you, Uncle Bill."

"I love you too." But the faint white-noise hiss from the box told me she was gone.

I got off at Farmington, too hurried to do anything about the ticket, or even to thank the driver, and went to the first hotel I saw. I didn't know what to expect, I took the largest suite they had. The living room was decorated in blue and white, and there were white gladioli in blue vases on the Louis Quinze tables. As soon as the door closed behind me, the radio burped in my pocket and said in Cis's voice, "Uncle Bill, where are you?"

"I'm in the Hotel Deluxe in Farmington, Cis. Where are you?"

"I'm on my way, Uncle Bill. Stay right where you are. Don't you dare move!"

"I won't move. I'll wait for you."

"Oh, I love you, Uncle Bill."

"I love you, Cis."

I unpacked and put the *karakuri* doll on the dresser.

There was a tap at the door. I opened it, and she was standing there, dressed in white. I held out my arms, but she made a warning gesture. "No hugs, Uncle Bill, not yet. Let me come in."

I backed away and she followed me into the room. She looked like a married woman. She sat in an armchair and I on the sofa. "I had to promise Roberto I wouldn't get any closer than this," she said.

"Is he here too?"

"No, Roberto is in Geneva. We're having a little prob- lem."

I felt a stab of painful joy. "You and Roberto?"

"I don't want to talk about that now. Uncle Bill, now listen, because I've got to lecture you severely. Do you know that you're a runaway?"

"I, a runaway? From what, may I ask?"

"From the Peabody Clinic in New York."

"I don't understand you. When was this?"

"October twenty-third."

"Cis, I wasn't *in* New York on the twenty-third. That was the day the meteor hit. They diverted my plane to Boston."

She looked at me sorrowfully. "That was one of the things you kept talking about. And being persecuted by dentists. Dr. Peabody wanted you to stay for more tests, but you walked out and nobody could find you. Uncle Bill, you've got to go back. You do know something's wrong, don't you?"

"Yes, something's wrong, but what is it? What are you saying, it's all in my head—"

"I don't mean that."

"Did you talk to this Dr. Peabody? I don't believe there is any such person, by the way."

"Yes, we talked for over an hour. He says you may not need surgery, just treatment and rest. Uncle Bill, listen to me, I came here in a chartered plane. It's at the airport now, ready to take us both to New York."

I hardly heard what she was saying, I was so absorbed in looking at her. "It's good to see you, Cis. You don't know. Look, maybe I'll go back tomorrow. Let's talk it over. Let's have dinner tonight, and a long talk tomorrow, and then we can make up our minds."

"I can't stay." She got up. "You've got to decide now, will you go back?"

"No, I can't do that, but stay and talk to me, Cis."

"I can't." She was at the door. She was pale and wan. She blew me a fairy kiss, and then she was gone.

After a moment I looked out, but of course the corridor was empty. I realized that I had gone about it all wrong, allowed myself to become too agitated. I might have talked to her more soothingly, persuaded her to stay overnight, or at least have dinner with me. It was possible, of course, that she had been subverted by the Dentists or the Spaeth People, it was even likely, but what did that matter if I could have had her dear company for another few hours?

When I turned around, I realized that I had forgotten to give her the *karakuri*. Its head was sorrowfully nodding, and I saw it roll back and forth, davening on the dresser top.

That night I dreamed of a huge boulder. It was almost perfectly round, channeled mossy green and brown underneath, smooth and sand-colored above. It was looming in the middle of a dry sunlit beach, but I knew it didn't belong there. I saw it tremble and sink just a little, and then a little more, and I knew that it would keep on sinking until it was completely covered, and after that it would go on sinking very slowly into the center of the earth, and nothing could ever stop it.

A bank of purple cloud

I bought a ticket, got back on the bus and settled in as if I had never left, although it was a different bus and a different driver. Almost immediately the sound and vibration of the engine, the swaying of the frame, the jerking and roaring when the driver changed gears, became familiar to me; I felt as if I had always been on the bus and that this was the normal mode of my life.

Early in the day I began to notice a buzzing sort of sensation in my body. At first I thought it was something the bus was doing, but it kept on when the bus stopped and we got out to stretch our legs. It was not unpleasant, but it was distracting. It felt like something that wasn't happening in my body but at a distance, something that I was receiving like a radio.

Towards noon the sky was clearing, but we could see ahead of us what looked like a distant bank of purple cloud. It grew thicker above the horizon until it became a wall that scimitared down to left and right, and kept on growing larger until it was grotesquely, impossibly huge. Even craning our necks to look out the windows, we could not see the top of it, and still it kept on growing.

After another hour or so the bus pulled into a makeshift-looking gas station in the desert. A large sign read LAST GAS FOR 250 MI. Most of the passengers followed the driver out, and stood gawking for a moment at the impossible wall whose top was now so high that we had to lean far back to see it; then they drifted off to the rest rooms.

The refreshment stand, which had an improvised look under red, white and blue bunting, offered ham-and-cheese sandwiches at one hundred dollars, candy bars and soft drinks forty dollars each. I asked for a glass of water and got it, but it cost me a dollar in quarters and dimes.

The driver was standing near the front of the bus, wiping out his hat brim in the sunshine. I asked him, "What is this about two hundred fifty miles?"

He looked at me curiously. "The crater," he said.

"Which crater?"

"The big one. It's two hundred miles across, five hundred if you go around."

"How high is the crater wall?"

He grinned, showing a blackened tooth. "Wait and see."

It took half an hour to fill the tank. The driver finally opened the door and swung aboard; the rest of us followed him into the bus, which now smelled principally of feet, and we pulled heavily out onto the highway.

"Folks," said the driver, "we are now approaching Big Crater. What you're going to hear is a recorded message for your information." He hung up his microphone, and after a moment the tape started, apparently in the middle.

"*. . . rrrater wall, rising more than sixty thousand feet from the desert floor, is the tallest object on earth, whether natural or man-made. It is twice as tall as Mount Everest in India, and encloses an area of approximately six hundred thirty square miles, more than half the size of Rhode Island, including the former cities of Albuquerque and Santa Fe. Army engineers, using sophisticated tunneling equipment, have constructed, urk.*" The tape stopped abruptly. The driver tried to start it again, but it only played a few bars of Dean Martin singing "Be My Love" and then stopped.

A tiny dot at the base of the wall slowly enlarged as we approached until it was the mouth of a cylindrical tunnel. We could see the broken and stitched surface of the wall itself, surrounded by scattered boulders, some bigger than houses. We glimpsed a sign going by: FALLING ROCK ZONE. The last half mile of the road was fenced on either side. In a lay-by a giant brown bulldozer was idling, and beyond it we caught sight of an even more gigantic crane.

The tunnel was formed of gleaming metal sections of a cylinder, or else was a continuous spiral, I could not tell which; it was illuminated only by a string of distant lights in the ceiling. Illuminated signs warned 40 MPH, and sentinels in Arctic uniform stood on the divider at intervals. Every now and then we passed some mechanism with a giant rotor whirring. The heating system in the bus could not contend with the intense cold of the tunnel; ice crystals began to form on the windows in graceful fernlike patterns like those I remembered from my childhood. After more than an hour we glimpsed daylight at the other end of the tunnel, and there was a spontaneous cheer from the passengers, but the cold did not abate.

From the tunnel mouth the highway ran straight ahead in shadow across a broad terrace on the inside of the crater wall. Beyond the edge of our terrace we could see other levels falling away into progressive blue distances. The wall above us slammed down ahead and curved around growing slenderer until it was so far away that it looked like a bank of purple cloud again.

Presently we came to the edge of the upper terrace, where the road dipped steeply for half a mile or so, then leveled out for several miles and dipped again. At the edge of each of these steep descents we could see far out over the crater basin. The center was wrapped in the haze of distance; it was surrounded by the concentric ovals of terraces, and I thought I could glimpse a plume of something dark arising from it. The cold grew more intense as we descended, and we had to keep rubbing the frost off the windows in order to see out. I thought that was odd, because it was my understanding that a few hundred feet below the surface the earth reached a constant temperature of about sixty degrees Fahrenheit.

After an hour or so we could see the plume more distinctly; it rose from a dark pit in the center of the crater, where there were huge constructions that I could not quite make out. No roads led to them, but I thought I could see pipelines connecting one with another, and there were things that might have been vehicles slowly moving between them, except that they were much too large. On the far side of the crater I could make out the threads of waterfalls in several places. It made me think of Edgar Rice Burroughs's peculiar novel *At the Earth's Core,* and the moment when Abner Perry's screw machine broke through a localized pun, the zona pellucida, into the warmth of another star.

The shadow of the wall behind and to our left crept slowly over the pit. Just at dusk we saw what appeared to be a bolide fly in from the northern horizon, spitting actinic sparks, and drop and disappear into the middle of the crater. It left a smile behind it, sketched across the violet sky.

Later, I was dozing or asleep when I was roused by the bus stopping. Forward in the headlights I could see some kind of barricade. The door clattered open and several armed frogs came up the aisle. Behind them I could see a struggle going on; the driver cried out hoarsely and then was silent.

The frogs seemed to be between four and five feet tall; they had no necks, and they walked like people wearing swim fins. They were pointing their weapons at the passengers, yanking some of them out into the aisle and passing them up to the open door. When they got nearer I could see that their bulging eyes had slit pupils like a snake's. Their faces were pale yellowish green under the brims of their floppy hats; their throat pouches bulged out and in. I started to get up when it was my turn, but one of them pushed me back. They cleaned out the rows behind me, and then a man came crouching down the aisle. He had something around his neck, and a frog behind him was holding the end of it. He looked up at me under his eyebrows and said, so quietly that I could barely hear him, "Is your name Wellington Stout?"

"Yes," I said, and then, because I was afraid, "What of it?"

The man looked down at a palmtop computer in his hand. He said, "When were you born?"

"January thirteen, nineteen thirty-five."

"Where?"

"Stroudsburg, Pennsylvania."

"Any brothers and sisters?"

"One brother. Tom."

"Is that Thomas?"

"Yes. How did you come to be working for these frogs?"

"I'll ask the questions." His voice and expression did not change. He looked at the palmtop. "You are to stay on the bus until further orders. If you try to get off the bus, you will be shot." He turned around and waited. The frog behind him looked at me over his bowed head; then it turned too and flopped off down the aisle. The man followed it, still crouching, and they went down the stairs. Only half a dozen passengers were left in the seats, mostly older folks. The driver was nowhere in sight.

Out the right-hand window I could see people lined up in front of a camp table, being moved along by armed frogs. As they reached the head of the line, they were made to bend forward, and a frog did something to their left ears. They all held their ears as if in pain as they moved on, but I caught a glimpse of several in a group who seemed to have something metallic attached to their earlobes, like the ID tags on the ears of hogs.

After a while the driver came up the stairs with a bloody mouth. He shut the door, sat down at the console and said into the microphone, "We'll be moving in just a minute." I saw the frogs in the headlights again; they seemed to be taking the barricade away. We waited another few minutes, then I saw a frog waving its arm, and the bus rolled forward.

For some time now

For some time now I had been aware that I was becoming partly mechanical; the front part of my torso was flesh, but most of my back under the skin was built up of cast-iron parts, rather heavy and clumsy, not lubricated terribly well; I could feel them grate when I moved. It was harder to guess about my legs and arms, but I was quite sure that parts of my skull were some kind of very thin alloy. Now the mass of my metal seemed to be exerting an influence all around me; I saw liquid glints from the walls and windows as the frame of the bus began to collapse into new forms. The bus was becoming much narrower, the passengers absorbed as the walls poured into them, and I could see that the driver had become part of the bulging bronze control board. I went forward and watched the process until it was complete, then sat down and took the wheel. Presently I myself merged into the control system of the bus, or else it was the other way around. Several times I passed vehicles going the other way; each of them was a cyborgian construct like myself, with beetle eyes under carapaces of steel.

In the early morning, after emerging from the far wall of the crater, I left the bus in a parking lot in Raton and walked around the town, not wanting to turn night into day, until deep dusk when I took a motel room and slept.

Later I discovered that I could turn into a bus again whenever I pleased. I was largely metal now, and I sometimes rolled myself into a sphere in order to hurtle with perfect smoothness down the channel of the highway. At such times I felt that everything outside myself was illusory, that I had somehow managed to swallow everything real and pack it into my spherical self, and this feeling gave me great satisfaction.

At night when I looked for a motel, I sometimes could not remember what shape I was. I imagined that I might say to the clerk, "I want a room for the night," and he might reply, "But you're a big ball." "That has nothing to do with it," I would say, and then the fantasy collapsed.

Crossing the plains I felt as if I were being tugged eastward by a narrowing noose, or as if I were riding down the smooth endless curve of some invisible geometry.

All through the Midwest the alternation of light and dark seemed random, as if the normal order had been suspended. For an hour or two we would have clear daylight, and then without any transition the sky would be dark and full of lightning bolts. East of Kansas City I passed on the highway the stubs of fallen skyscrapers sticking out of the earth like windowed javelins. There were fissures across the road, too many to count, and when I came to these I stopped and crouched until my metal parts coalesced into a winged shape. Then I ran, slowly at first, faster until my metal wings caught the air and I soared. Sometimes I did not come down but soared higher until the highway melted into the mist of the earth and I was rising above the storm clouds into the ranks of a flying metal armada. I found my place there and I was one of those winged torpedo shapes with their goggled eyes, hurtling steadily eastward all day long, but when sunset came I lost my power and had to descend.

In Hannibal the only motel room I could get had huge damp water stains down the walls. When I went to the bathroom, I found a strip over the toilet seat that read CULLIONS TO YOU. I put it with the others. I didn't quite know what cullions were, but I assumed it wasn't a compliment. I laid the strips out on the bed in order as I had found them.

LO GO GRI PHON
I NEVER KNOW WHEN YOU'RE KIDDING
YOU COME HERE OFTEN?
URANUS IS OUT
CULLIONS TO YOU

The first one had a puzzle in it, although the puzzle was so simple that the motel manager had unraveled it straight away. The next two seemed like very mild jokes, and the two after that were more like gratuitous insults. But if the first one was a puzzle, wasn't it likely that the rest were too? And if I wasn't getting them, the joke was on me?

I tried taking the first letters in order, then the last letters, forwards and backwards; nothing worked. The first two letters of each strip gave me LOIN YOUR CU, which looked mildly hopeful. Then I tried adding in the message on the card I had got at Diane Downey's—*Okra dokra, smart-ass.* Now the sequence read LOOK IN YOUR CU, which was almost too good but still didn't make any sense. I put the strips away again and went to bed.

In a motel near Fort Wayne that had a working television, I saw a phalanx of marching men and frogs. Suddenly there was a scattering of pink explosions among them. Then more and more. I thought at first that their heads were exploding; then I saw that the soldiers were leaping high into the air, turning as they fell into a shower of roses. When it was over, the field was heaped with blooms.

Coming up from the west into Potamos, I found that one of the piers of the bridge had been damaged in some accident, and only one side of the bridge was in use. The town itself looked sadly neglected. A large object, partly rock and partly rusted metal, had fallen onto the roof of the row of buildings that contained the pharmacy, and the whole block was cordoned off.

I drove down to Mary Street to look at my mother's house. It was vacant, the doors hanging open and all the windows broken. In the middle of the lawn I found a simple granite marker incised with the word REQUIESCAT. A yellow cat came across the lawn, stropped itself against the marker and looked up at me.

Driving out of town on the Matamoras road I saw a man in a brown suit in front of the hotel, looking down at something in the grass. I pulled off the highway and parked, because he looked vaguely familiar. Only when I got out of the car and it was too late did I recognize him as the school superintendent, old Marblenose.

"Come here, Stout," he said. "I want to show you something, since you think you're so smart."

"I don't think I'm smart, Mr. Mapleton."

"Don't talk to me. Look at this." He leaned down and grasped a bronze handle in the lawn, pulled, and raised a big rectangular section of turf. It must have been counterweighted, because it seemed to come up easily. Under it was a complex of greasy brown pipes, full of elbows, shunts, cutoffs and meters. Mapleton let me look and then lowered the section again; it blended into the lawn and disappeared. "That's what it's like everywhere," he said. "Now do you understand?"

"No."

"We're in a transition period between two domains," he said, "and they're using you to carry the necessary energy from one to the other." His face had changed; he looked patient and kindly. "You are actually the only waking indigine in the world at the moment; all the others are sleepwalking automatons. When you get to the other side of the transition, the new domain will be in place and the dormant population will be returned to live in it. It will all be different, of course."

"Different how?"

"I can't tell you. You'll take it for granted, though, and won't even remember that there was ever any other scheme of things."

"Will I remember all this?"

"Oh, no. That's understood, that you'll forget. It's necessary. We couldn't live if we remembered everything. Think what it would be like if you remembered all your pain. You wouldn't like that. It's better to forget. Now do you understand, Stout?"

"Yes, sir."

He smiled. "You're lying, but at least you're polite. Don't forget what I've told you." We shook hands, and he turned and walked back towards the hotel. I blinked when he was halfway there, and he was gone.

Up the Thames

North of the Massachusetts border, the interstates were tumbled cyclopean blocks of concrete. I was able to make some progress on secondary roads, crossing makeshift bridges across fissures and ravines. There was very little traffic, but I glimpsed men and women on horseback several times. Eventually even the dirt roads gave out, and I had to take to the air.

When I soared over the airport in Boston I saw that the runways were cracked and the towers toppled. Instead of landing there, I loaded myself onto a freighter in the harbor. It took me three days to cross, and I saw no other shipping. When I reached England, I cruised up the Thames to St. Saviour's Dock, and from there by a broken tube into the Underground, where I changed to an express coach.

The streets were gleaming with wet as I emerged from Waterloo, and I walked as fast as I could for fear the dampness might get into my metal components or interfere with my electronics.

I took a wrong turning somehow, and found myself walking past the block of flats where I knew Sylvia Plath had lived. The upper floor was lit up and transparent; a woman in the kitchen, evidently meant to be Plath, was kneeling before the open door of the cooker with a ring of tourists around her. Her clear voice floated down: she was reciting "Ariel." Then she leaned forward and put her head on the open door of the oven. The tourists watched in silence, then I heard them break into gentle applause behind me.

When I came to my building at last, I stopped a moment to look at that solid dusty-red block standing there as it always had, saying what it always said. Reassuring in a way, like the pavement and the lampposts, but enigmatic as the Sphinx. It wasn't the bricks and mortar I thought about, the workmen in their lime-dusted trousers, the vanished sun on the courtyard, but the whole lump of the

building itself saying its dumb sentence over again whatever it was, the same today as yesterday.

I let myself in and climbed the musty stairs. When I
got to my landing, I saw that there was a black wreath on
the door. A bad sign that. I slipped in. Everything inside
looked tidied up and there was a strong smell of furniture
polish. The table in the foyer was heaped with black-
bordered cards. In the sitting room, little crystal dishes of
nuts and candy had been set out on all the end tables.
There was a white satin ribbon around the telly for some
reason.

I dropped my suitcase and went down the hall to the
bathroom. A strip on the commode said FFUNNY, BIG GUY.
A hell of a way to welcome me home, and why the double
F? I tore the streamer off and pissed whilst looking at it, and
then went and sat down with it at the blue kitchen table.
I found a pencil and a scribbling block, and wrote down the
other messages as I remembered them.

LO go gri phon
OKra dokra, smart-ass
I Never know when you're kidding
YOu come here often?
URanus is out
CUllions to you

And the last one:

FFunny, big guy.

I sat very still for a moment, then leaned down and felt in my right trouser cuff. There was nothing in it but grey flug and a burnt cardboard match. Then the left one. It squirmed under my fingers suddenly, and I pinched up something that was as slippery as an insect. When I held it to the light, I saw that it was a little man, fully dressed but no bigger than an earwig; then I saw that the contorted face was Gallagher's. He was shouting something in a teakettle voice, but I could not make out the words.

I looked around wildly for something to put him in, and the only thing I saw was the Moulinex that I used as a coffee grinder. I stuffed him in there, holding him down with my thumb until I got the transparent lid on. Then I had him, because the lid locked with a half turn. I could watch him leap against it underneath, and hear the remote squeak of his voice.

My heart was racing. I hadn't had anything in mind except to prevent him getting away, but now I thought of all the ugly things that had happened to me since I first met Gallagher, and I shoved the prongs into the power point in the wall. I think he knew. He was down there, not leaping now, but standing on the blade and waving his arms crosswise: *No. No. No.* I put my thumb on the start button. I waited a moment to make sure I wanted to, then pressed it down just for a second, *rrt.*

I heard a crack and a crunch, and a brown smear splashed over the underside of the lid. I felt sick and hollow inside. I got up leaving the fouled Moulinex there on the table, and went into the bedroom, took my shoes off, and dropped on the bed.

After a few minutes I realized that my head was clearer and that my body wasn't full of metal anymore. Something that had been driving me and transforming me had gone, perhaps for good.

Waking

I may have dozed off, probably did, because when I came to myself again I was in darkness under a weight of perfumed wool and fur. I struggled up, and found that I had been buried by an avalanche of coats. I didn't know what time it was.

I heard voices and put my head out. The hall was crowded with people I didn't know, or barely knew: they were like the friends of friends one always sees at a party. They were holding glasses of wine, both red and white, and one strapping milk-fed lad had a stein of lager. None of them paid any attention to me. A plump woman in black with a fussy apron and cap came up the hall maneuvering a tray of empty glasses, and I saw that it was Mrs. Islip in unaccustomed uniform. She looked a bit subdued, and I thought for a moment I might speak to her, but she had her head down and didn't see me.

I got through to the sitting room and found it crowded too. Louis Hostetler was there having a serious talk to Hugh Rosenzweig; they were both holding whisky glasses. The liquor looked too dark to be White Horse, and the door of the liquor cabinet was open. I tapped Hostetler on the shoulder. "Excuse me, is that my Laphroaig?"

He gave me a cold stare. "You're not going to be a bore about it, are you? After all it is your wake." He turned back to Rosenzweig. "Now as for the West Country . . ."

There was a cut ham on the sideboard, and the remains of a plate of hors d'oeuvres. Empty glasses, soiled paper napkins, and rinds of sandwiches were everywhere. Glynis in a tea gown of black lace stood near the sideboard, munching a bit of ham. She had a glass of whisky too. Her eyes were bright, lipstick a bit smeared. "There you are, luv," she said. "You haven't seen Leonard, I suppose?"

I backed away, feeling a chill. In the corner behind the cold telly, sitting together in two straight chairs, were Tinker and an old woman with a paper sack of bread in her arms. Tinker was wearing a black sheath, black mesh stockings and black high-heeled pumps. Her hair was done up on top of her head, and she was rouged and powdered like a whore. She looked up and said, "Well, it took you long enough. This is Maria."

The old woman smiled up at me. She was sitting on the edge of her chair, dressed in a shapeless coat with one button, under which she seemed to be wearing layers of skirts in various dull colors. She showed me her loaves. "Le bacchette," she said.

"The baguettes."

Tinker said, "Yes, but it also means, like, wands. You understand? She dowses with them. She'll find us the way."

"The way to where?"

"To Milan. Are you ready or what? Come on." She stood up, and so did the old woman.

"Tinker, don't keep on saying 'Come on.' "

"Have I ever let you down yet?"

"You certainly have, you tossed me off a roof."

"Well, did it do you any harm? Come on."

They walked out, and I followed them sputtering. I was trying to argue with Tinker, but I couldn't catch her in the crush. She and the old woman were through the door to the landing, up the stairs, out onto the roof in a cold drizzle, and there I was without my shoes.

A sound made me turn, and I saw that Hostetler and Rosenzweig had followed me. Hostetler came up and began to fumble at my waist; I saw now that there was a thick cable coming out of my belly and trailing back down the stairs. "Might just help you out with this the rest of the way," he said. He turned something with a snap and removed the end of the cable. It seemed to have a wicked-looking drill at the end. "Hoist the slack, will you?" he said to Rosenzweig. Others were coming behind them, lining up on the roof and holding the cable in festoons like firemen. Glynis was there, waving cheerfully at me, and Lola Sanchez, and others I didn't know; it looked like the whole crowd.

The baguette lady had taken one of the loaves out of the sack and stuffed the other two into her pocket. With the one in her hand she turned left and right until the loaf dipped like a Concorde's nose.

"Link hands," said Tinker. The old woman was first, then Tink, then me, then Hostetler and all the rest. We marched to the edge of the roof, up onto the parapet; Tinker's grip was like iron and so was Hostetler's, I couldn't let go, and off into space we went one two three.

The wet roofs fell away and we were soaring north-easterly towards the Thames. When I looked back I could see a long line of people carrying the cable that trailed out westward. Where I lost it in the sunlit haze, there seemed to be a wrinkling in the landscape, probably an optical illusion, but it looked as if we were pulling the world behind us.

We passed Southwark Bridge in the misty distance; we were heading straight for London Bridge, but just before we got to it we circled the ruined spires of Southwark Cathedral, then shot off southeastwards, moving so fast that most of the raindrops missed us.

We crossed the Channel well south of Dover at the widest part of the Strait and flew over miles of angry gray water until we sighted the coast somewhere near Dieppe. Silvery rain followed us, and winds were whipping the tree-tops below. After miles of French countryside, lightning bolts the size of my wrist were striking all around us as we approached Paris. We circled Notre-Dame twice, then shot off southeast again. The rain slackened off, but the lightning never let up; the sky was sulfur and magenta, and there was a tingle of tension in the air.

Endless time went under us as we dangled like fish on a string, and then we descended on a long slant over open fields, an empty highway, then a big graveyard, and now I knew where we were. That was the Christian cemetery in Milan, with the little Jewish cemetery tucked onto it like a codpiece. Now we were crossing the Viale Certosa, and I still hadn't seen a single car or pedestrian. Even if it was Sunday, they couldn't all be at home.

Still descending, we passed over a little sports arena and a firing range, a cycle track just north of the Trade Fair, and now we were dropping into the Parco Sempione, landing all together on one of the winding paths west of the lake. "Take a breather!" called Hostetler in his officious way; the people behind him dropped the cable and stood rubbing their hands and chatting.

The baguette lady discarded her wand and took another from the sack in her pocket; I think it was a drier one. She waved it experimentally, shook her head, and discarded that one too.

"Why does she need a wand now?" I asked Tinker. "Don't we know where we are?"

"Sh. This has to be done right."

"Up load!" called Hostetler, and all the troops obediently picked up the cable again. The baguette lady set off walking and we all followed her, crossing lawns and gravel paths in a straight line. When we came to the lake the lady went around it, although the baguette tugged strongly. We went around the Castello Sforzesco, too, and then started working our way through a maze of little streets, leaving the trail at one and picking it up at the next. I lost my bearings again, but presently I saw where we were: it was the Corso Vittorio Emmanuele, the street that ran past the cathedral, and the Duomo was only a hundred yards away.

Yellow and white butterflies

A cloud of yellow and white butterflies was flittering over the street. They had black streaks under their wings, and long hairlike filaments trailing behind. They drifted northward and dwindled like living confetti. It was funny to see them here, where nothing else seemed to be alive but ourselves.

As we approached the Duomo, Tinker said, "Do you feel something strange, right about here?"

"Yes, I do. What is it?"

"In thirteen ninety-two a worker was killed by a falling slab of stone while he was stirring a trough full of mortar. They buried what was left of him, but they used the bloody mortar. It's in the fifth pier from the end on this side—along with some of his teeth. So they say."

The baguette lady was opening a side door. Tinker followed her in, and I followed Tinker. The long aisles were empty and dark, the ceiling lost in darkness, no light anywhere except a glimmer from the tall stained-glass windows. We walked down the center aisle, as noisy as pigs in a nave; our footsteps echoed down to the other end of the cathedral and back. And a blessing to George Paul Souva.

The two women began to mutter together, and I realized that theirs were two of the voices I had been hearing all this time; the third came from somewhere in the shadows, and sounded like Lola's or Rosemary's, or sometimes more like the cricket voice of the *karakuri*:

—He's as yellow as mecum.

—Give back the Ruhr, I say.

—Halimus thalamus. Ears is aspirations. Airs is alemet-tary canal. Hairs his ovolo. Now the abacus, the echinus, and the astragal in ordure. Capital!

Bitter blood was in our eyes and nostrils. At one end of the transept, we opened a varnished wooden door and descended a flight of steps. I could tell by the sound that only Hostetler and one or two others were following us; the rest had been left behind upstairs. When the lights blazed up, we were looking at red-bearded Saint Carlo Borromeo, laid out in his crystal coffin with a crown of gold on his head and an ivory mask on his face. In the eyeholes of the mask were two pearls the size of cocktail onions; other pearls were sewn to his robes and his falconer's gloves, along with sapphires, rubies, opals, and diamonds. One glove was draped over a sword and the other lay on an ivory sphere and cross. Over the breast of his robe was embroidered a black eagle on a red shield.

"Is he really in there?" I asked.

"His remains are; or his spoils," Tinker said. "Maria says it's the same word in Italian."

"Like the spoils of war? Are they mummified?"

"Desiccated."

Her lisp made it sound like "defecated," but I knew what she meant. "In other words, he's dried out? Do they have special drying rooms to do that?" I was babbling be-cause I didn't want to get on with it.

—Who's under the halter but the ostiary with his tink up? That was the old woman.

From the shadows: —*Tinc, tanc, tunc.*

"It was four hundred years ago," Tinker said. She went back to Hostetler for a minute, came forward again and put the end of the cable in my palm. "Press down. Right over his forehead."

The cable vibrated in my hand, without a sound, as if a dry electronic flood were running in it. I put the end on the crystal lid of the coffin, positioning it as well as I could. It was a little too much to the right, I thought.

"Go on. Do it."

I pressed down, and the cable seemed to buck a little, like a power tool biting into glass, although there still wasn't a sound. I held on and kept pressing down, and after a minute I could feel it break through. "Down," said Tinker.

I lowered the cable unwillingly until I saw the end of it hovering over the mask—over the forehead, right in the middle, where his third eye would be if he had one.

"Down. Don't be such a baby."

I lowered the thing again, feeding cable through the hole in the crystal lid, until I felt it bite like a dentist and saw it melting slowly through the mask, disappearing inch by inch into whatever moldy skull was under there.

After a moment I heard the sound change as it came out underneath. "That's enough. Good." Tinker reached down, got the end and carried it back to Hostetler. When she did that, I could hear the cable running through the casket with a dry rattling sound.

We climbed the stairs again, paying out cable behind us, and crossed the echoing transept to another wooden door behind one of the little side altars.

—Gimme the guy eye.

—It's the tooth!

—No, be like I am. (A tinkle of breaking glass.)

This time we went up an enclosed wooden stairway, and I could tell that the whole crowd was spiraling up behind us; their labored breathing echoed in the well. We stopped twice to rest before we got to the top, and then there was an angular stairway that took us up the side of the cathedral to the tilted slabs of roof under the sky.

That little pedestal

Up and down the roof life-size statues were standing in lines with inhuman patience, like circus performers on their pinnacles. One of the figures we passed was that of a young woman erect in a graceful posture on her spire, looking out over the lights and rooftops of Milan. Her face was a bit like Cicely's, and I wondered what she thought, standing there on that little pedestal in all weathers, night and day.

The main bulk of the Duomo was covered by an ordinary peaked roof like you'd find on a house, except that it was covered by massive stone slabs instead of tiles. But ahead of us the cathedral surged up into one last frozen leap of lacy stonework. That was the dome, encrusted with so many spires and arches that you couldn't see it, but it was there, and in the middle was the tallest spire of all, with the golden Madonna perched on top, a gold halberd in her hand and blinking violet neon in her halo.

Up the spire we went in a covered switchback stairway of stone, the troops grunting and cursing as they
humped the cable higher. When we got to the narrow part
of the spire we had to climb like Kong, fingers and toes in
the stone filigree. Tinker ahead of me had kicked off her
shoes, and that made me feel a little better about mine. I
noticed that as she rose she seemed to be growing steadily
taller, and so did the baguette lady below me.

A cold wind sprang up and thunder cracked; the
whole cathedral seemed to be swaying under us, but I
couldn't let Tinker and the old woman climb where I
wouldn't, and at last I was clinging to the halberd, looking
at the colossal golden face of the Madonna with her tight
mouth and blind cat's eyes too big for her head and set too
far apart. Her face with its flat nose was tilted a little, gazing out at nothing with an expression that might have
meant anguish, or just resignation. The heads of bolts pro-
truded from the bosom of her robe like buttons on a blazer,
and other bolts held a metal strap to her head to prevent
it falling off. And I was in my sock feet, clinging there
under the banging farina neon of the Virgin Mary's halo.

"How long has she been here?" I asked Tink.

"Since seventeen seventy-three." She was taller than
I was now, and her head was as big as a balloon. She handed
me the end of the cable.

"Why do I have to do everything?"

"Bill, there's nobody here but you."

Looking out over the lights and rooftops across the
Lombardy plain I could see other floating lines of people
with other cables, all converging on the Duomo. There

were other Wellingtons and Tinkers in those lines, and the horizon was wrinkling behind them as they pulled the world together, and that was as it should be. "Put it in," Tinker said.

Where I hung on the halberd, I was looking down at the blind golden roc egg of the Madonna's right eye. Distant lightnings flickered in it, and when I looked closer I saw veils of color; I felt that she was trying to tell me something. I leaned over desperately and pressed the drill to her forehead, felt it grind through the gold-painted metal.

Tinker had sprouted wings again, white eagle's wings this time, and she was hovering over the statue's head. "Up," she said, and after a moment I felt the whole spire rising, saw the cable go taut, and the great ball of the earth was wrinkling towards us. Then it wobbled and stopped. There was a crash like thunder, and all the lights of the city went out. A shocked silence fell.

"What's the matter?" I said.

Tinker dropped down and looked me in the face. "We couldn't get enough power. Now you've got to do it the other way."

"What other way is that?"

She reached out and touched me on the forehead. Her fingers were like a statue's, and they burned like ice.

"No," I said.

"It's the hardest thing you'll ever have to do," she said.

"I can't."

"It will hurt very much for a moment."

I turned the end of the cable towards me and looked

at it. The drill had big grinding teeth like a blind sea monster. I raised it a little to see if I could.

"Go on, I'll help you," she said. She put her big hands
on mine.

"I too," said the baguette lady, and I felt her hands
touching my feet.

I said, "Oh God," and jerked the drill up. It went in
cold and oily with a pain that was too large for my head.
Then I could feel my apple bollocks billowing the way I rose
into a stain of glass, and as I stepped across the ocean it was
cool and dark in the shade. Back there, Jenny was sitting
at a picnic table. She looked up, but I don't think she saw
me. Farther along, in another little alcove, Roger and Willie
Wort were playing cards. The pale things heaped on the
table beside them seemed to have fingernails. It was darker
now, but I saw Dave Hooper and Gloria Dunkel in our
alpine attic up in the trees.

Where the path forked, Tom was peeing under the
bridge into the brook in Potamos, and my mother was hanging a flowered cloth on the line. A child was running in
a field of daisies like little stars. Then it was full dark and
I was a boy again walking up the street in Potamos all
alone in the deep cold, past the oyster white pales of
the picket fences. Now I was climbing the hill.
Up there, past the darkness of the firs,
gently, almost apologetically,
the light was beginning.